HAPPY
ENDiNGS

HAPPY ENDINGS

Happy reading!

MINITA SANGHVI

Best,
Minita

HarperCollins *Publishers* India

First published in India by HarperCollins *Publishers* 2022
4th Floor, Tower A, Building No 10, DLF Cyber City,
DLF Phase II, Gurugram, Haryana – 122002
www.harpercollins.co.in

2 4 6 8 10 9 7 5 3 1

Copyright © Minita Sanghvi 2022

P-ISBN: 978-93-5629-027-3
E-ISBN: 978-93-5629-066-2

Typeset in 11/14 Adobe Caslon Pro at
Manipal Technologies Limited, Manipal

Printed and bound at
Thomson Press (India) Ltd

To my wife, Megan Di Maio, my favorite happy ending.

The Director

‑〃〜

MANY YEARS LATER, AFTER ALL WAS SAID AND DONE, Karan Raichand, the famous Bollywood producer and director, was once asked in an interview what his best creation was. He said that it was not a movie but a real-life story. 'You know, to be a success, every love story must have love *and* a story. Now this one, it had all the components of a Bollywood masala film before I even came into the picture. It was a story of *pehla pyaar* – first love. And because it was your typical Indian love story, it had all the ingredients – parents, drama, anger and betrayal.'

The journalist leaned forward. She was hooked. 'So what happened next?'

'I directed it, of course,' Karan said smugly as he leaned back in his chair and sipped his tea.

The journalist pleaded, 'Don't leave us hanging. Go on, tell us more.'

Karan smiled and began, 'The story starts at the airport. Where our protagonist is about to find out that I have changed the trajectory of her life.'

1

‘*THERE IS A CELEBRITY ON THE FLIGHT.*’ KRISH HEARD the whispers as she approached the boarding area. For a second, her heart skipped a beat. *She* couldn't be on this flight. Surely the gods wouldn't be that cruel to her, would they? Krish had read in the gossip columns that superstar Mahek Singh was shooting in New York with her boyfriend, Kabeer Agarwal, for Razia Akhtar's latest film. Surely she was still there. Surely she couldn't be on *this* flight.

Krish had been really looking forward to this flight. She had won the Big B English Fiction award for her book and they had paid for a first-class flight ticket to India for the award ceremony. *First class!* Krish had never flown first-class in her life. She had been so excited! But now she looked at her boarding pass and hesitated. Then she shook her head. *No. Not on this flight. It would be too much of a coincidence.*

Krish looked up to the heavens but found herself staring at the ceiling of Terminal 2 of the JFK airport. She said a small prayer anyway. *Please God … please.*

Just then, her phone rang.

'Hello Ma!' Krish said.

'Have you boarded?'

'No. Not yet. Just about to.' Krish looked at the line that had already formed around the boarding area, even though they hadn't opened the gates yet. 'Why are Indians always in such a hurry to board?' she wondered aloud. 'Do they think they're going to miss the flight? Or are they worried someone will take their seat?'

'Stop being mean, Krishna,' her mother admonished her over the phone. 'You're Indian too.'

'I'm not. I have an American passport to prove it.'

'You can be a citizen of any country you want, but your heart will always be Indian. It's your birthplace. It's where you grew up.'

It's where I got my heart broken.

The country was full of too many painful memories for her. Krish said nothing. Just then, the ground staff opened boarding for the first-class and business-class passengers. 'OK. They are calling first-class passengers now.'

'*Achha beta*. What do you want for dinner when you get home?'

'I don't know, Ma. Anything will do. Anything except …'

'*Baingan ka bharta*, I know.'

'Right.'

'How long, Krishi?' her mother asked.

'Someday. But that day is not today.' This was the same reply she had given her mother for the past ten years.

Her mother sighed, '*Theek hai*.'

Krish hung up the phone and started walking to the gate. 'Excuse me. Excuse me,' she said as she wove her way across people who were crowding the boarding area.

She'd almost made it to the podium when someone shoved her to the side. She stumbled. 'Heyyyy!' Krish exclaimed as she bent down to pick up her boarding pass.

As she straightened up, she saw, as if in slow motion, Mahek Singh being whisked into the flight by security. The same security that had pushed her out of the way. *Of course.*

Krish turned around and walked back, away from the boarding gate. Her heart was thumping in her chest. Her legs felt like jelly. She needed to sit. She was not ready to board. Not yet.

Alcohol. She needed some alcohol. She looked around for a restaurant or a pub, but so to close the boarding area, all she could see was a coffee shop. *Fine, this will have to do.* She sighed and started walking towards café. After taking an inordinately long time – it's hard to think when your brain is trying to work through anticipation, excitement, anger, resentment, and memories .... so many memories ... all at once – she said, 'Ummm ... I'll have an English breakfast tea.' The attendant at the counter nodded and started preparing her cup.

Soon, she was seated at a table, gingerly sipping her piping-hot tea. Deep breaths, Krish. Deep breaths. *You can do this.* She thought about calling Ma. What was the point? Ma would either get excited or worried. Probably both. She thought about calling her two best friends, Lauren and Chelsea. They would also get worried, and then angry. Probably both. Krish shook her head. Nope. None of those calls would be helpful right now. She needed someone calm and centred. Maybe she could call Allie. *That is the stupidest idea you could think of, Krish,* she told herself. *Call your current girlfriend to talk about your ex? That will win you bonus points for being a jerk* and *an idiot.* Krish sighed.

It's not like she hadn't imagined coming face to face with Mahek after all these years, but she'd never expected something like this. She couldn't do this. Not here, not now. And definitely not on a fourteen-hour flight to India. She looked at the hallway towards the exit. Maybe she could leave. Take another flight?

You're a sher ka bachcha, *Krishi. We face our problems,* Ma's voice called to her. Krish's shoulders slumped. She had to face it. Might as well do it now, right?

Krish saw the stream of passengers board as she took another sip of her tea. She sat there for a while, taking deep breaths, and waited for the last call. Just because she was going to face her demons, didn't mean she had to rush into it. Everyone had boarded. The flight staff was now checking the roster and shutting the boarding area. Krish got up and straightened her dark blue jeans and her new blue jacket; she slipped her brown leather satchel on her shoulder and walked up slowly to the podium. 'I'm here,' she said almost despondently.

'Hello, Ma'am.' The lady at the counter smiled cheerfully as she took her boarding pass.

She scanned her boarding pass and Krish slowly trudged up the narrow jet bridge. She let out a deep sigh and braced herself as she entered the plane. Mahek Singh was talking on the phone. 'Let's talk more about it. I'm not sure …' she said as she looked up and their eyes met. Mahek's eyes widened, her jaw dropped and her face blanched. Krish noticed that the person on the other side of the phone continued talking but Mahek was not listening any more. Her eyes followed Krish in disbelief, her mouth still open. *Ok. So she does remember me.* Krish had to admit Mahek's reaction gave her some satisfaction. Meanwhile, she could hear the faint voice of the person on the other side of the phone saying, 'Hello, hello. Are you there?' Mahek still didn't reply. Finally, she said, 'I have to go,' and hung up the phone.

Krish took in the lay of the land in first class. There were only four seats. And the two window seats were already taken, which meant Krish was next to Mahek. *Great!* She scowled as she headed over to her spot. The air hostess was out and offering her a champagne glass as she sat down in her luxurious, comfortableseat.

'Thank you.' Krish tried to sound nonchalant, but inside she was scrambling to understand how first class worked while trying to look cool about it. These seats looked different. What was this thing in the front? How did the seat recline? She didn't want Mahek to realize she was new to this. First class, that is. Not flying. She had flown plenty in the backwaters called the economy class. With their filthy toilets and cramped quarters. But this? This was nice. Krish went to tie her seat belt and realized Mahek was still staring at her.

The seats in first class were big but they were still next to each other. Which meant that Krish could smell her perfume. She smiled despite herself. *Still Opium.* Maybe Mahek saw that as an invite, and said hesitatingly, 'Hey, Ishq.'

Krish stiffened next to her. No one had called her Ishq. *Not since.*

'Hello.' She reached out her hand as if introducing herself to a stranger, 'Krish Mehra.'

Now Mahek stiffened at her response. She lowered her eyes. 'OK. Maybe I deserved that,' she said softly. So softly that only Krish could hear what she was saying. Krish didn't reply. Mahek was about to say something else when her phone rang again. Karan Raichand's name flashed on the screen. She grabbed it and instead of disconnecting the, she switched off her phone entirely and threw it in her purse. She turned to face Krish again, but Krish was now busy adjusting her seat and getting her blanket out.

'Really, Ishq … I mean … Krish. Are you going to ignore me for the next fourteen hours?'

'Fourteen hours is nothing compared to the ten years you've ignored me,' Krish said sharply. It was really more like a sharp whisper. The last thing Krish wanted was for Mahek to get ensnared in a scandal. Though why did she care? It wasn't like Mahek had cared whether she was alive or dead all these years.

'I … you know … I did what I thought was best for us,' Mahek explained meekly.

'You mean, best for *you*, right?' Krish practically spit out the words. She was done with this conversation.

Mahek gazed at her feet and bit her lip, saying nothing.

Krish said, under her breath, 'I thought so,' as she started scrolling her TV to choose a movie to watch.

'Fine,' said Mahek softly. 'Just tell me, how's Ma?'

Krish turned and glared at her. How dare she bring Krish's mother into this? But Mahek looked at her with her large hazel eyes, hopeful and sad. Why was she sad? She was the number one actress in Bollywood. She was the darling of India. She had a huge fan following on Twitter and Instagram. And awards. So many awards, including a National Award for her historical epic film. Everything she did was chronicled and fawned upon by millions of admirers.

Krish remembered some story of how Mahek Singh had worn a purple polka-dotted scarf from Fabindia and it had sold out in twenty-four hours at all their stores in all locations across the country. Her 'Mahi' didn't care about designer clothes or bags or watches. Mahek Singh, on the other hand, peddled all of those big brands.

'Please,' Mahek again asked softly. Still looking at Krish. Now pleading with her eyes.

Krish could never resist those big eyes. She sighed. 'She is well. The same, you know. Happy, fun Ma!'

'It's been so long since I've seen her. Or eaten the food she cooks, or felt her hugs. Her hugs were the best.' Mahek, tearing up a little, looked at Krish, as if remembering the fond memories. Krish nodded.

'I miss her,' said Mahek wistfully.

'I have a picture. Wait.' Krish got her phone out and went through her photos to find the one her mom had sent her yesterday. Krish showed her a photo of Ma in the garden of the row house Krish grew up in.

Mahek took the phone and saw Ma smiling next to her prized roses bushes in brown clay pots. Ma had always taken great pride in her garden. Mahek smiled a soft smile, and sighed. Almost unthinkingly, she swiped for more photos and came across Krish at the book signing of her bestselling book, *When Doves Die.*

'Congratulations on your book,' said Mahek as she returned the phone back to Krish. 'What did *The Times* call it? "A poignant love story that brings the best elements of Virginia Woolf's *Orlando* and Homer's *Odyssey* in a modern day telling of the quest to find the perfect love."'

Krish looked at her quizzically, 'You memorized that?'

'No. Just remember it.'

'Hmm ...' Krish said. 'I know what *The Times* thought about it. But what did *you* think about it?' Krish waited with bated breath. This was one review she cared about even more than the critics. And she had never imagined the person who had inspired the book would be sitting next to her.

'It was beautiful, Ishq. I … it felt very … real but also surreal.'

'Well, it is supposed to be,' Krish stated in a matter-of-fact way.

Mahek sensed Krish was ending their conversation again. She tried again. 'And your Booker nomination. Fingers crossed for you!'

'Yes, if it hadn't been for the Booker long list, it probably wouldn't have gotten much attention in India, right? Then suddenly overnight I started to get all these requests for interviews. And now, of course, the Big B Award.' Krish shrugged. 'Anyway, I'm not complaining. And neither is my bank account.'

'I bet Ma is proud.'

Krish's shoulders, which had been tightly coiled through this conversation, relaxed a little. 'Yes. She's so happy. I am glad I could do this.'

Mahi reached over to touch her hand. 'We are all very proud of you.'

Krish didn't recoil at the touch. And Mahi let it stay.

'Your mother must be just as proud. You've achieved her dream. Becoming the number one actress in India. Something she could never do.' Krish's eyes were cold and unfeeling as she mentioned Mahi's mom.

'Yes. She was.' Mahi didn't smile. Mahi removed her hand and placed it back on her lap. Mahi thought about her mother and their complicated past together. It was such a long time ago. But she remembered it, clear as day.

2

Back Then

MAHI'S MOTHER SUJATA HAD BEEN A SMALL-TIME heroine in movies and eventually became a character actor in television serials. Since Mahek's birth, she had been laden with her mother's unfulfilled dream. Mahek had been in dancing classes, acting classes, even finishing school for styling and make-up (not the Switzerland kind, more like the Juhu kind). But Mahi, her Mahi, just wanted to play. She loved making paper boats in the monsoons with Krish. She loved pretending to play *ghar-ghar* and *chor* police in the neighbourhood. Mahi was always the police, never the chor. And when she caught Krish, she'd tickle her till she cried. And then they'd start over. Till it got dark. And their moms called them home.

Mahi and Krish had been neighbours. Her earliest memories of them were playing when they were six years old. They were just Mahek and Krishi then. Krish came up with the nickname Mahi. And Mahi loved it so much that she insisted that her family call her Mahi from then on. They grew up on the same street but went to different schools. Mahi's mom had put her in an expensive private school where all the star kids went. Krish's mom couldn't afford such a luxury, so Krish went to the neighbouring convent school. But every evening they did their homework together at Krish's house. And then they'd run out and play. Well, except when Mahi had Bharatnatyam classes. Thankfully, the classes were only two streets away. And Krish and Mahi would walk together. Krish would read a book while Mahi learnt her dancing. Sometimes Mahi would catch Krish looking at her dancing with a sense of wonder and joy. They were only six, but the way Krish looked at her stayed the same even when Mahi turned sixteen. Only now, there was a hint of lust and longing to that sense of wonder and joy.

At sixteen, Mahi's body had the delicious beckoning of a perfectly ripe mango. Her body was slender yet curvy in all the right places. Mahi could feel Krish's eyes following along her curves sometimes, though she could tell that Krish tried her hardest to hide it. It would make Mahi's heart beat faster and give her goosebumps in places she was only now discovering in her body. Mahi didn't feel this way when boys at school flirted with her. Nor did she feel that way when sleazy directors and producers looked her up and made suggestive comments at those *filmi* parties her mom took her to. The lusty way they looked at her was different from the lust in Krish's eyes. Mahi remembered feeling surprised about the fact that there were different kinds of lust. Krish's lust was gentle, loving. Like she wanted Mahi's body and mind and heart and soul. And the others … they just wanted a piece of ass.

It came to a head one day around Valentine's Day. Mahi was sitting with her friends from school at a neighbourhoodmall.

Krish had come along to buy a book from the Big B book store at the mall. Now she sat nearby, her head in a book, while Mahi chatted with her friends from school.

'Did you hear Arnav is taking Radhika to see *Jodhaa Akbar* for Valentine's Day?'

'Oh really?!' several girls exclaimed at this information.

'Wow! That's nice!' Mahi said.

Radhika seemed to be glowing in the revelation as she headed over to the group. There was a lot of oohing and ahhing as she revealed details of the how, what and why of the plans. In a distance, the guys were chatting and looking at the girls. Arnav called out to Radhika – she quickly went over to where the boys were sitting, with the clickety-clack of her heels on the tiled floors. They all started talking rather animatedly.

'What do you think they are talking about?' Suhani asked the group.

'I bet they are talking about Mahek,' one of them quipped.

'Me?' Mahi looked surprised. She noticed Krish had stopped reading, her neck craned to hear news about Mahi.

'Yeah, I heard Imran wants to ask you out.'

'I heard Rishab wants to ask you out to the movie too.'

'What nonsense!' Mahi turned her face away. She was not interested in this attention.

'Are you really that surprised, Mahek? I bet you'll get the most roses on Rose Day tomorrow.'

'*Rose* Day?' Krish looked up from her book.

'Yes, it's Rose Day tomorrow. Radhika and I have a bet as to who gets the most roses. I put money on you,' Suhani stated with the know-it-all authority of a sixteen-year-old girl.

'Oh!' Krish feigned disinterest.

'What do you think, Krishi? Will it be Radhika or Mahek?'

Just then, Radhika came back to the group bearing news. 'Mahek, Imran wants to see if you will go see *Jodhaa Akbar* with him.' Krish stopped reading and put her book down, now completely immersed in the drama unfolding before her eyes.

'Wow! Imran Faiz! His father is so hot! I love his movies,' said Suhani, her eyes all dreamy.

The girls were so excited.

'What should I tell him?' Radhika asked, tapping her feet.

Krish's breath hitched as she waited for Mahi's reply.

Mahi looked uncomfortable. She hated all this attention.

'Please tell him, no thank you. My mom will not allow me to go with him.'

'Are you sure?' Radhika asked. She looked surprised.

Suhani stared at Mahi open-mouthed. 'Are you serious? Are you seriously going to say no to Imran Faiz? I bet if you ask your mom, even she would agree to this one.'

All the girls started talking over one and another, giving her tips to sneak out.

'Just tell your mom you're with us.'

'We can come get you and then you can go out with him.'

For a moment Mahi shut the cacophony of sounds and thought about it. She looked at Imran smiling at her in the distance. She saw Krish, trying not to look distraught as the various girls made a case for Mahi and Imran. Mahi imagined whom she would like to share her popcorn with at the movies, whom she would want to kiss in the dark auditorium. She closed her eyes. In that moment, she was in the dark auditorium, the soft chill of the air-conditioner on her body, the plush seats, the smell of popcorn. When she leaned over to kiss the person she was sharing her popcorn with, she imagined Krish's soft lips touching her tenderly and pulling her into a deep, passionate kiss. She smiled. *Yes, she was sure.*

'Listen! Stop, all of you! Radhika, I'm sure.' Here, Mahi's eyes met Krish's for just a second and then she turned to Radhika and added, 'Please tell him I'm flattered but the answer is no.'

The girls were all frenetic at this turn of events.

'What are you doing, Mahi?'

'This is crazy!'

'What if he takes Nidhi instead?'

'Tell him I'm available!' said Suhani boldly. Suddenly all the girls shifted focus and Suhani became the centre of the conversation.

'Are you serious?'

'This is crazy.'

The girls were having a great time with this new twist in the tale. Krish went back to reading but Mahi discerned a smile on her face that she tried to hide in the book.

∽

Later that evening, as they walked back to Krish's house from the mall, Krish was silent. Finally, she said, 'So Rose Day tomorrow, huh?'

'Is that what's bothering you?' Mahi stopped and turned to face Krish.

'Why would it bother me?' Krish shrugged and started walking again.

'You are uncharacteristically silent, no? I thought it was Imran asking me out.'

'Only an idiot would not ask you out.'

'That's what I think too!' Mahi giggled.

'So why did you say no to him?' Krish asked, dumbfounded.

Mahi grabbed Krish's wrist and looked her in the eye and said, 'Because I'm waiting for this idiot.'

Krish blushed a deep red.

'Mahi, Mahi!' Ma called out from the colony compound.

'Yes, Ma?' Mahi dropped Krish's wrists and ran towards Ma.

'*Arre beta*, your mom called. She is working late today. Your brother dropped off your clothes.' By now Krish had joined them and leaned down to hug Ma, who was sitting on a bench with the other aunties from the colony in the compound. '*Beta* Mahi,' Ma continued as she patted Krish's face gently. 'Why don't you leave a bunch of clothes at our house? That way you can stay over any time you want to.'

Mahi's eyes met Krish's and she said, 'A bunch of clothes? I want to bring all my clothes, so that I can stay with you both forever!'

Ma laughed. Krish blushed even more and looked away to hide her smile.

∽

The next morning when Mahi woke up, there was a single rose by her pillow. She looked around but no one was in the room. She could hear Krish outside, sitting with her mom as she did her morning puja. The flower was plucked from Ma's prized rose bushes. Krish must have begged Ma because she didn't usually let them cut her roses. Mahi picked it up tenderly and inhaled the sweet smell. She examined the rose. It was not long-stemmed but the thorns had been carefully removed so it wouldn't hurt. It was a simple gesture, but it touched Mahi's heart. She felt so complete when she was here – she didn't have to be this way or that, no one had expectations of what she would do with her life. Ma and Krish just loved her for who she was. Mahi wore the rose behind her ear with her school uniform as she came out for breakfast.

Krish saw the flower and smiled slowly, but then looked away quickly, just in case the emotions at her face said too much.

Too late, grinned Mahi as she sat down on the breakfast table.

'What are you wearing?' Ma asked, looking amused.

'You don't like it? I thought it looked great,' Mahi smiled. She got out her copy of *Romeo and Juliet* and was about to put the rose in it when Krish cried out loudly, 'Stop! What are you doing?'

'What? What happened?' Mahi looked up, confused.

'Not in that! That's a tragedy! They both die. Here,' Krish quickly pulled another of Mahi's book out of her school bag and handed it to her.

'*Pride and Prejudice*?'

'It has a happy ending. Don't you want a happy ending to your love story?' Krish looked at Mahi meaningfully. *Ahh, finally*, thought Mahi.

Mahi was about to reply when Ma came into the room, '*Chalo*, girls. Off you go. Mahi, your car is here. Krishi, your bus will be here soon. Have a good day at school!'

And Krish was out the door. Mahi's moment was gone!

≍

Later that day, Krish texted Mahi.

> Krish: Who won the bet?
> Krish: Did you get the most roses?
> Mahi: No, Radhika got the most.
> Mahi: But I got the one I wanted. From the one I wanted.
> Krish: Oh.

A few moments passed. Krish said nothing more. Mahi typed back.

> Mahi: Guess what? Suhani is going for the Valentine's Day movie with Imran.
> Krish. Oh, are you jealous?
> Mahi: Yes.
> Krish: Really?
> Mahi: Yes. I want to see Aishwarya Rai and Hrithik Roshan too :)
> Krish: LOL.

∞

Later that evening, 'Ma, Krish said, let's do something fun this weekend. I feel like we haven't hung out together in so long!'

'That's a good idea. What do you want to do?' Ma asked.

'I don't know. What can we do?' Krish's eyes moved to the paper on the coffee table strategically opened to the full-page ad of *Jodhaa Akbar* that she had placed earlier.

'Hmm.' Ma's eyes followed Krish's and landed on the ad. 'Oh … do you want to go for this movie?'

'That's a great idea, Ma! I know how much you love Aishwarya Rai. We should buy the tickets.' Krish pounced on the idea like white on rice.

'OK.' Ma opened her phone to book tickets.

'Ummm … Ma, didn't you want to ask Sujata Aunty? I thought you guys had made a plan to go for a movie soon?' Krish tried to act casual.

'Oh, that's a nice idea. I'll call her and see if she wants to join us.'

∾

'Mahi *beta*, do you want to go for *Jodhaa Akbar* tomorrow?' Her mom called to her, still holding the phone.

'Noooo …' Mahi shouted from across the house. She came out of the bedroom, putting her long hair in a bun as she saw her mom on the phone and asked, 'Why?'

'Krishi and her mother have made a plan. They were asking if we wanted to join them,' her mom explained as she returned to the phone and continued talking. '*Achha*, so Mahi is not coming. But I will join you … I don't know … Mahi said she doesn't want to come. Maybe she is going out with her friends?'

Shit, shit, shit. Mahi needed to get into this plan. She knew this was Krish trying to take her to *Jodhaa Akbar* for Valentine's Day. Oh, why had she answered so hastily? How could she get back in? 'Mummy, mummy, mummy!'

Sujata looked at her, irritated. 'Now what?'

'Actually, I just remembered the test I was studying for is not untill next week. Let's do it. Let's go see the film. It will be fun! We haven't gone out in a long time.'

'Now she's saying she'll come. These kids, I tell you.'

~

At the movie theatre, Krish and Mahi sat next to each other and the two moms chatted away about their lives and work and relatives.

'Is this your idea of a Valentine's Day date? With our *moms*?' Mahi asked as she reached over for more popcorn.

'Huh? Better than your idea, which was me, by myself, with *both* our moms. You weren't even going to come.'

'You could have texted and told me your mom was going to call my mom. Anyway, where's my gift?' Mahi turned to face Krish.

'What gift?' Krish looked confused.

'For Valentine's Day,' Mahi said coquettishly.

'Why should I get you a gift for Valentine's Day?' Krish raised her eyebrows. Her lips curved upwards in a sly smile. She was feeling rather brave!

'Umm … I thought …' Mahi looked surprised. 'I mean … don't you?' Could she say the words? What if it wasn't true? Did she get her signals wrong? Was it just friendship? Panic hit Mahi. Then she looked Krish in the eye and saw the same wonder and joy she had seen all her life. Nope. There is no way she could be wrong. Not about this person sitting next to her.

'Tell me you do!' Mahi whispered fiercely as her mom sat down next to her as the theatre lights dimmed.

In the darkness, Krish's little finger reached for Mahi's. Startled by the touch, Mahi turned to Krish. Krish smiled and whispered, 'I do.' In the blackness of the theatre, Mahi's smile lit up her world.

While they bantered about love without saying it aloud, Mahi waited for Krish to make a move. *Say it out loud. Do something.* But nothing was forthcoming. Maybe Krish was too shy, too scared to try anything. After months of this, Mahi resolved that she would have to do something about it.

≈

'What are we watching tonight?' Mahi asked. She had stayed over since her mom, Sujata, was working late again. Ma got some popcorn and joined them on the couch. Krish was sitting by Mahi's feet on the floor with a book. She picked up the remote and started flicking through channels.

'*Arre, Rang De Basanti* is playing on TV. You want to watch? Orrrrr get ready for this ...'

'Let me guess ... another Govinda film?' Ma grinned.

'Yes. *Saajan Chale Sasural!*' Krish exclaimed happily.

'Why do you like these films? They are so ...' Mahi made a face.

'Are they too downmarket for you?' Krish asked, grinning at Mahi turning up her nose at Govinda films.

'How you can read *Madame Bovary* and watch *Saajan Chale Sasural* at the same time is beyond me,' Mahi marvelled.

'One is classy and one is massy!' Krish smiled easily.

'You two keep arguing and we won't end up watching anything. Give me the remote,' said Ma and started channel-surfing. '*Arre* look, *Chori Chori* is playing.'

Mahi and Krish looked at each other with accusatory eyes. Now they were done for. Nargis and Raj Kapoor movies were a big hit with Ma. No way were they going to get to watch anything else. Krish sighed and picked up her book again.

Mahi didn't particularly mind black-and-white movies. She loved the chemistry between Raj Kapoor and Nargis. Speaking of chemistry … she looked at Krish, who was absorbed in her book. A few minutes later, Mahi said, 'I'm cold.'

'Come here. I'll share my blanket,' said Krish innocently, unaware of Mahi's resolve.

Mahi moved in next to Krish, who was sitting cross-legged on the carpet. She fidgeted around trying to get comfortable. 'Krishi, stop hogging the blanket!' And saying so, she picked up Krish's arm and put it around her shoulder, so she could snuggle in next to Krish. Krish went very quiet. The way Mahi had dropped her hand, it was right on her waist. Her T-shirt had ridden up from the fidgeting and Krish's hand was on Mahi's bare skin. Krish should have said something or moved it, but she was unable to. She couldn't bring herself to move her hand away from Mahi's soft skin. Krish was glad Ma couldn't see her face right now.

Krish tried to read the sentence in her book but her mind was short-circuiting from the heat rising in her body. Mahi's proximity and her warm skin were playing havoc on her mind and body. Her face was flushed. Without really realizing she was doing it, Krish was softly stroking Mahi's skin. Mahi smiled slyly and snuggled in closer, her hand landing on Krish's thighs. She stroked it gently. It felt so good. Krish wasn't sure if Mahi was aware of what she was doing. And the effect it was having on her. Krish wondered if she should move or say something, but was paralysed, enjoying all the sensations coursing through her body. They sat there for a while, caressing each other under the blanket. Then Mahi moved her hand higher, closer to the source of heat emanating from Krish's body. Krish's breath hitched.

She put her book away. And feigned a yawn. 'I think I am tired. I am heading to bed.' Saying so, Krish got up. This was getting out of hand and Krish didn't want to take undue advantage of Mahi.

Her mom looked at the time. '*Chalo*, I should go to bed too. I have to go to the temple early tomorrow morning.' Ma looked at Mahi. 'Mahi beta, you're staying tomorrow? I'll prepare *poha*. Krishi, you heat it up in the morning, OK?'

'OK, Ma.' Krish and Mahi smiled. Mahi got up. By the time she folded the blanket and put it back on the couch, Krish had brushed her teeth, changed her clothes and was ready for bed. Krish slept on a mattress on the floor and gave her bed to Mahi.

Krish had picked up her book again. Mahi brushed her teeth and then joined Krish on her mattress on the floor. She leaned in. Her fingers traced designs on Krish's arms, humming softly from the melodious song from *Chori Chori*,

Kyun aag si laga ke, gumsum hai chandni.
Sone bhi nahi deta, mausam ka ye ishaara.

Her ministrations made the fine hairs on Krish's arm stand up. Krish gave up. There was no way she could get any reading done tonight. Quietly, she put her book away. She turned off the lights and they sat next to each other, their bodies touching lightly. They often stayed up late into the night talking. Tonight Mahi was telling Krish about her mom's new hand for her to join the movie industry. How her brothers were bossing her around. 'I hate being home nowadays. I can't wait to come see you every day.' Mahi reached for Krish's palm and intertwined her fingers through Krish's. Krish swallowed quietly. Mahi could feel the heat from her body, the electricity running from her fingers all the way to the core of her body. Mahi looked around the room, thanking the heavens for the privacy of Krish's own space. It was a three-bedroom row house, and Mahi estimated that Ma would be fast asleep in her room by now.

Mahi said suddenly, 'Krishi, close your eyes.'

'Huh?' Krish looked a little startled. Like she was thinking of something else. Mahi probably could guess what.

'Close your eyes,' Mahi said boldly.

'Why?' Krish looked at her, surprised.

'Because...' Mahi grinned. Yes, this was it. This felt right. She'd been thinking about this for a while now.

'Ummm ... OK.' Krish closed her eyes, wondering what was going on.

'Are they closed?' Mahi asked, giggling. Feeling nervous herself, Mahi had butterflies fluttering around inside her body. Her body quivered in anticipation.

'Yes.'

'Promise?' asked Mahi, now feeling a bit scared. *Would everything change forever?*

'Promise.' Krish said solemnly. Something about Krish's face and the complete trust and faith she had in Mahi made Mahi's heart melt. *OK. This is it.* Mahi thought to herself. It was time to be bold. Time to tell Krish what she had been feeling in her mind and body for the past several months – years. How does one figure out the beginning of a love story with your childhood best friend? There is no beginning. Maybe one of those times when they were playing in the

rain? Or those times when she and Krish went cycling around
the colony? Or the time Krish had fallen off the bicycle and
injured her knee and had cried out, 'Mahi, help!' Krish had
needed three stitches. Mahi touched the scar from the stitches
on Krish's knees.

Krish felt her touch. 'What's going on?' Krish said, opening
one eye.

'No, no, no. Close your eyes,' said Mahi, admonishing her.

Krish closed her eyes again and smiled softly.

Mahi looked at her face and said tenderly, 'You're beautiful.
I love you.' Before Krish could open her eyes at that revelation,
Mahi leaned forward and kissed her on the lips.

Krish's eyes flew open. But Mahi reached for the back
of her head and pulled her back into the kiss. Krish closed
her eyes and gave in, sighing deeply. It was soft. And tender.
But Mahi could feel the passion bubbling. They were gently
exploring each other's lips, mouths. Krish was almost reverent
about kissing Mahi.

'Are you sure about this?' Krish asked as she tore away
for a second. 'I mean, you're my dream. You've always been
my dream. But I didn't think we could be together, *like that.*'
Krish looked down again.

Mahi lifted her chin and their eyes met. 'There was only
you. There will always be only you. I promise.'

'But...'

'I have a new name for you.'

'What is it?'

'Ishq. You're my Ishq.'

Krish grinned. 'I like it. Promise me. I'll always be your
Ishq.'

'Promise.' She pulled Krish closer and said, 'Now ... Kiss
me again.'

They came up for air the next morning.

Now

Krish looked at Mahi now on the airplane, lost in her thoughts, smiling away. 'A penny for your thoughts?' she asked, looking at Mahi inquiringly. Part of her wondered if she should pick on that scab. Mahi had hurt her so much.

'I was remembering the origins of Ishq.' Mahi smiled shyly, as if still feeling that first kiss on her lips.

Krish's fingers moved towards her own lips as the memory flooded her senses. For a minute they didn't say anything, but just revelled in that beautiful memory. Till Krish broke Mahi's trance, as she said, 'Promises are cheap, aren't they?'

'How does that Raj Kapoor song go?' Krish added. 'Ahh, yes …

Jaane kaha gaye woh din,
Kehte the teri raah me,
Nazaro ko hum bichaayenge@…

But this time Mahi was not going to take it. She sang the next line from the song from *Mera Naam Joker*.

Jaane kahi bhi tum raho,
Chahenge tumko umr bhar,
Tumko na bhool payenge.

'Fucking promises,' Krish said, looking into Mahi's defiant eyes. 'I bet you tell your boyfriend all these things too, right?'

'Ishq, please. Leave him out of it.'

'Leave him out of it? Why, Mahi? Why should I leave him out of it? You chose him over me, no? I wonder, Mahi, does he make you come like I used to?'

'Ishq, please.' She looked around, wondering if anyone had heard anything. The others seemed fast asleep and Mahi knew Krish was whispering, but still. She turned and faced Krish, who was still not done lashing out. Mahi sat quietly through this tirade, tears welling up.

'Do you scratch his back like you used to scratch mine? Do you nibble his ears and whisper promises to him? Have you thought of your kids' names? Or are you going to recycle ours?'

'Fuck this,' said Krish. 'I don't need this.' She buzzed for the air hostess. 'Do you have any seat in business class? I'd like to change seats.'

'I'm sorry, Ma'am. We're a full flight.'

'Of course,' said Krish, visibly irritated.

Mahi had hidden her face so the air hostess wouldn't see her tears. As the air hostess left, Krish sighed. She knew her words had cut Mahi. Krish could see the hurt on her face. Hurting Mahi felt good. But seeing Mahi hurt felt terrible. Watching Mahi in tears moved something inside her. Her rage receded rapidly as regret and remorse took over. This was so puzzling. Krish had dreamt of this moment for years but hadn't expected it to happen. And now that Mahi was here, next to her, she felt confused. There was rage, so much rage, but also something else. A softness that Krish was not expecting. No matter how much she thought she hated Mahi, their emotional connection hadn't been severed. She turned to face Mahi and all that she had done.

'Shit. I'm sorry. I know I hurt you. But I can't seem to help it. I am so angry with you. I am so angry about all those years we spent together. And everything you meant to me. And every dream I saw with you. And then you left me. You promised you'd join me in the US and we'd be together and then you just disappeared on me. And became Mahek Singh, Karan Raichand's new heroine.'

'What would I have done in the US? Who was going to pay for my college? You know I wasn't smart like you to get a scholarship. Be practical, Ishq. I did what I thought made the most sense at that time. I had to get you away from my family. You don't know what they were planning ...' Mahi shuddered at the thought.

'We would have managed,' Krish said, grasping at straws. She hadn't thought through this stuff. She had just lived with Mahi's betrayal, stroked it like a pet, and carried it along with her in her heart. Not thinking about Mahi's perspective.

'Look, you're successful. I'm successful. We both got what we wanted from our lives,' Mahi said, trying to move on.

'I wanted *you*.' Krish was unable to let it go.

'I did too. But life doesn't always turn out that way, does it?' Mahi said wistfully. 'And now look at where we've reached.'

Krish scoffed. 'Only I didn't have to suck cock to get where I got.'

'Krishna Mehra.' Mahi's eyes were blazing fire. 'Take that back, NOW!' Mahi's whole body shook with rage.

Krish knew immediately that she had gone too far. Why couldn't she stop herself? She'd been dying to say that, to hurt Mahi for choosing to live a lie. Krish shut her eyes. 'Sorry,' she whispered.

And then she turned and put her blanket over her head. And went to sleep.

The airplane breakfast was had in silence. Krish heard Mahi's phone chime and saw her typing away quickly and furiously. Mahi was escorted out first. Mahi turned to look at Krish one last time as she exited the plane. Krish, refusing to look at her, busied herself with her satchel, as if looking for a pen to write on the immigration form. Mahi sighed and left the plane.

3

KRISH GOT OUT OF THE AIRPLANE JUST AS DEJECTEDLY AS she had got on. Mahi was long gone by then. Yes, she had finally come face to face with Mahi and confronted her. Ten years of pent-up rage and sorrow had burst out, and yet Krish felt empty inside. She didn't feel like she had found justice. Hurting Mahi only ended up hurting her.

With all these thoughts running through her head, Krish almost missed the driver waiting for her outside the airport holding up a sign with her name on it.

'Oh, OK, that's unusual,' she thought to herself. She was used to getting a taxi and heading home.

'*Bhaisaab, apko kisne bheja?*' asked Krish as she got comfortable in the car, wondering who had arranged a taxi for her.

'*Maloom nahi.* My company got a phone call and they asked me to pick you up from the airport and drop you home,' the driver said as he navigated the traffic, heading to Andheri. Krish wondered who had sent her the car but the thought soon left her as she readied herself to see her mom. She hadn't been home since the pandemic and now, after three years, she was returning home a hero. Her book had been nominated for a Booker. It had been on the New York Times Bestselling list for several weeks and had gotten rave reviews. Her agents and publishers were talking to some Hollywood studio about movie rights. In the past, when she had come home, she had either been a poor, struggling grad student or a struggling writer working as an adjunct faculty, but now she was coming home a full-fledged, successful writer. And now Ma could stand proud by her side. Krish shook her head. Ma had always been proud of her. Her face broke into a big smile at the thought of Ma!

'Ma!!!' Krish called out to her mom as she got out of the car. She was waiting outside their row house. The same row house she had grown up in. At that point it had been on the outskirts of town. And then the town had grown around it. Now their house in Andheri was smack dab in the centre of the city. It was a prime location and the property had appreciated by over 300 per cent. Her mom, over recent phone conversations, had been hinting at selling the place. Krish wondered if her mom was having financial issues. Her mom was a CA and they had always been comfortable even after Krish's father's death. Krish knew that her mother didn't make enough to pay for Krish's undergrad education in the US but enough to pay for her deposit on a house rental or for her to visit India from time to time. Finally, Krish was home on her own dime (or rather, Big B Bookstore's dime).

Krish held her mother in an expansive embrace and they swayed from side to side, excited to see each other. 'Ma, I missed you so much. I love you.' When Krish was done hugging her mom, she was quickly pulled into other embraces from neighbourhood aunties who had come to greet her too. Krish looked like a deer in the headlights as these aunties started fawning over her.

'Arre, beta, congratulations!'

'We always knew you would do something big.'

'You've made a name for yourself, beta. Our colony is so proud of you.'

Krish hadn't seen these aunties in years and now suddenly they were all clicking selfies with her.

Krish looked at her mother—her expression was part amusement and part pride. Krish stood up taller when she saw the pride in her mother's eyes. Soon, the aunties left and Krish and her mother went inside.

'Phew! What was that?' Krish asked as she put her bag down.

'Everyone is just happy for you, beta.'

'Yeah, sure. They only care about it because now I'm in the papers. No one cared about me all those years ago. Then they were happy to call me names.'

'Krish, let go of the past. You're successful today, *na*?' said her mother from the kitchen while getting the food ready as Krish moved her laptop bag and her suitcase into her room.

'Go take a quick bath and come for lunch. I've got the geyser running for the past half an hour, so your water should be hot,' her mom added as she started making rotis.

'You know, Ma, I don't feel so dirty. Maybe it was because I was flying first-class!'

Her mom smiled.

'Can you believe it, Ma? But, you know, after flying first-class it's going to be hard to go back to economy.'

'I hope you never have to,' her mom said. Krish hugged her mom's shoulders as she continued cooking, and kissed her on the cheek. 'I love you, Ma.'

'*Achha*, now go, get ready quickly,' Ma put her *aata-wala* hand on Krish just like she used to when Krish was a little kid. Krish smiled.

'I'll be right back,' she said, rushing off to the bathroom. Krish looked around at her room and bathroom. The drapes, the bed sheets—nothing had changed. Sometimes it reminded her of all those nights she had spent with Mahi … Anyway, she was not going to think about her. She was here with Ma. Her wonderful, amazing Ma. Krish's father had died in a car accident when she was about eight years old. Mahi had stayed over at their house for a whole month, holding her when she cried. Darn it, no matter how hard she tried, Mahi kept creeping into her thoughts. Why was this so hard? This is why she hated coming to India. Everything reminded her of Mahi.

Krish decided she was going to focus on Ma. She wasn't sure what she had done to deserve such a wonderful, patient mother. Ma was the most loving person she had known and so ahead of her time.

About eleven years ago

Krish had been nervous about coming out to her mother. She had known as soon as Mahi had kissed her that all those feelings in her mind and body she had felt since she was three years old were real. She had known it in her heart. She had known she was different—but not really a good different, like when she could read when she was just four. This was not like the kind of different her mother would brag about to her friends. But it wasn't a bad different either. She had seen images in the *Kama Sutra* that involved only women. She and her friends had giggled at the temple walls on their school trips. But she was different from her friends. They couldn't stop talking about boys. But Krish only imagined kissing girls—imagined Mahi's hands

on her body. And that day, after kissing Mahi, she could finally name it. She was a lesbian. She tried saying the word in her head. It always seemed like a cuss word. She had tried rolling it around on her tongue. Lesbian … lessss … bian … lesbian … like Jodie Foster or Martina Navratilova. Or that lawyer from *Sex and the City*. She had seen the wedding pictures of Ellen DeGeneres and that actor from *Ally McBeal*. Things were cool now. Or not such a big deal. The world was changing. Maybe Ma would understand, she had thought. After all, Ma had never asked her to grow her hair or wear skirts. But what if she didn't? Krish had shuddered.

Krish had tried talking to her mother several times but had always chickened out in the end. Somehow it had never seemed like the right time. One evening, Ma was oiling Krish's hair, as Krish sat cross-legged at Ma's feet.

Hesitatingly she said, 'Ma …'

'Hmm…'

'Ma, do you love me?'

Krish got a light thwack in response. 'What kind of stupid question is that?'

'I mean … will you always love me?' Krish asked quietly.

'Yes, of course. That's what being a mother is about. Someday, when you have children, you'll understand too. No matter how old they are, no matter how smart they think they are …' Ma turned Krish's face towards her. 'I will always love you.' Krish could see the pride in Ma's eyes.

'What if I …'

'What is it, beta? What's troubling you?'

'Ma ... I ... I don't want to get married.'

'It's OK, beta. You don't have to get married right away. Go to America, study, get settled ... then someday maybe you will meet a nice boy and want to get married ... No one is rushing you, don't worry about what your Mami says.'

'What if I never want to get married?'

'How do you know that now? You're only seventeen. Things change, priorities change.'

'I meant ... what if I am ...' Krish just couldn't get the words out. Everything would change if she did. What if her mom stopped loving her or disowned her or never spoke to her again?

Ma's voice was gentle. 'What is it, beta? What's on your mind? I promised your father I'd love you for the both of us. You can tell me anything.'

'Ma, what if I am a lesbian ...'

Ma stilled. 'A lesbian?' There was no judgement or disgust in her voice (Krish was watching for both). It was more a confirmation. Like she was taking it in.

'Like you don't like men?' she asked.

'No. That I like women,' Krish said softly, a tiny smile escaping her.

'How do you know? You're only seventeen. It's different having crushes. It's different when you get married.'

'Ma, would you believe me if I told you I've known since I was three years old? Or maybe even before that. I just know it. I don't feel any attraction for boys, unlike all the girls in my school. I like Kareena Kapoor and Kajol, not Shah Rukh Khan. I just ... have always liked women. A lot.'

'But what about marriage? What about children … ?' Ma fell silent. She looked like she was turning it around in her head as she spoke. Krish waited, wondering what was coming next. She hated the idea of disappointing her mother. Her mother was

her whole world.

After a few gut-wrenching minutes, Ma finally said, 'Beta Krishi, I will always love you. You know that, right?'

Krish nodded.

'But this … beta, your life is not going to be easy. Are you sure this is what you want?'

'It's not what I want, Ma. It's who I am. Do you still love me?' Krish's voice quivered. Did her mom still love her after knowing her deep, dark secret?

'Of course I love you. No matter what happens, never doubt that.' Ma gently thwacked Krish and went back to massaging her hair with oil.

Krish had tears in her eyes.

Now

Krish wiped her eyes as she looked in the mirror. She knew Ma would always love her. Now all this recognition for her book made her feel like she was able to thank Ma for everything. After a long bucket bath with piping-hot water, Krish came out in a T-shirt and shorts. 'Come, beta,' her mom beckoned her to the dining table. Her mom had made tindli and dal. There was also raita with onions and cucumber, Krish's favourite. There was a stack of rotis being kept warm in a casserole.

Krish sat next to her Ma and quietly put a gift-wrapped box on the table.

'Arre, what is this?'

'It's a gift for my wonderful mother ... Allie helped me pick it out. I hope you like it.'

Her mom opened the gift and saw a beautiful Longines watch.

'Do you like it?'

'I love it, beta. But you didn't need to.' Ma gently touched Krish's face. Then her eyes went back to the watch in her hand. As she put it on, she said, 'It looks expensive.'

Krish was filled with so much pride as she saw Ma put on the watch.

'How does it look?' Ma asked, raising her hand to show her daughter the watch.

'It looks great, Ma,' Krish said, smiling. They sat down at the dining table but as Krish started putting food on her plate, she noticed something.

'Ma, something is missing.' Krish looked at her mother and then at her plate, trying to figure out what.

'I know. It's the achaar. Wait, I'll get it.' Her mom got up with the slight huff of old age and went into the kitchen to get mango pickle. Krish noticed that her mother looked a bit more frail than she remembered from last time.

'Thank you, Ma,' Krish said as her mom put fresh mango pickle on her plate. 'Ummm ... this tastes great. Yumm, Ma.'

Her mother smiled at her as Krish happily ate roti after roti.

Over lunch, Ma asked, 'How was your flight?'

'It was great.' Then Krish hesitated. 'It was also odd. You won't believe whom I found sitting next to me in first class.'

Her mother looked at her, waiting in anticipation of this revelation.

'Mahi. Ma, can you believe it, after all these years, I met her on a plane ... for a fourteen-hour flight. I mean, I couldn't even escape the situation. Just my luck!' Krish sighed unhappily.

'You weren't happy to see her?' Ma looked at Krish in surprise.

'Happy? I hate her, Ma. I hate her. She left me. We were supposed to be together forever and, instead, she pushed me off to the US and became an actress, with that jerk Kabeer as her boyfriend.'

'She didn't push you off to the US. You were dying to go there. You had been planning that since you were fifteen.'

'Yes, but she was supposed to join me,' Krish protested.

'I know, beta. But you knew what was happening in her house. And what her mother had planned. That poor girl had no choice,' Ma reasoned.

'How can you take her side?' asked Krish angrily, pushing her plate away.

'Krishi, beta, you are my child. I'll always be on your side. But that doesn't mean I am blind to the reality or the past. I know you were hurt. But that was ten years ago. You have to forgive her. You know she didn't have a choice.'

'She promised me I'd be her Ishq forever.' Tears welled up in Krish's eyes.

'And maybe she meant all of it.'

'But she didn't, Ma. She didn't pick me. She picked Kabeer. She picked her family, her career. I was nowhere in her life!' Krish practically spit the words out. Why wasn't Ma getting it?

'Why are you so angry, Krish? Your life has been fine. You're successful. You're in a relationship. You're happy, aren't you?' Ma looked at Krish, her eyes boring into Krish's soul.

Could Krish honestly say she was happy? 'Of course I am happy. But it's no thanks to Mahi,' Krish said, not making eye contact with her mother.

'Are you sure you're happy? When you came home, you were upset with those neighbourhood aunties—now you're upset with Mahi. What's going on?'

'I don't know, Ma.' Krish paused, trying to get a pulse on her thoughts. 'Seeing Mahi after all those years … it just reminded me of my past. One that I don't want to remember.'

'Mahi was your first love. I get that. You were hers too. She lost you just as much as you lost her. You had your righteous anger; she had nothing but a pushy mom and a lot of guilt. You need to give her a break, beta.'

Krish said nothing. She had never thought about it that way. Ma was right. Mahi had lost just as much. But then anger bubbled back to the surface when she thought about Kabeer, Mahi's boyfriend. I bet he was happy to soothe all that pain away, thought Krish grumpily.

'Maybe I need to rest,' said Krish as she got up and decided to retire to her room. She found her phone, plugged in her headphones and turned on the music. A mournful love ballad poured through the speakers. Krish settled in.

4

On the Other Side of Town

━╱╲━

'**D**ID YOU PLAN THIS?' MAHEK ASKED AS SHE PUT DOWN her Prada bag on the large conference room table and accosted her best friend, Karan Raichand. She knew where Karan would be, so she had come straight to the conference room—Karan's favourite spot in his office. Karan was not only a director and producer but also had a big film-production company. He had a large office and a large desk but it was so cluttered that he would often sit in the conference room.

'What?' Karan didn't bother looking up. He just continued scrolling through the Instagram accounts he was checking out on his phone.

'You know what!' Mahek said irritably. Mahi and Karan were not only best friends but also had a very successful partnership. Why was Karan pushing her buttons? Mahek was in no mood today. She wanted answers. He looked up and their eyes met. She knew he knew what she was talking about. And he knew she knew what he had done ... or, rather, conspired to do.

'Do you think I can direct people in real life? That's a lot of power I must have over people. Especially someone I haven't even met,' Karan said, smirking.

'So you know whom I'm talking about.'

'Kabeer may have told me,' he said casually, and moved to looking at the budget papers on the large glass table.

'So it just happens that we want the rights to this particular story to adapt into a screenplay?' Mahek asked, glaring at him. He looked at her, raising his eyebrows in characteristic Karan Raichand fashion.

'Akash may have mentioned something … ' Akash was Karan's assistant and practically managed his whole life.

'Fine,' he finally said, giving up. 'It's an award-winning story. It has been on *The Times* Bestselling list for the past twenty weeks. It fits well with the arc of our upcoming films. Have you read it?'

'Obviously,' said Mahek, now feeling awkward about this conversation, not sure how much she wanted to get into this. They hadn't spoken about Krish in such a long time. Karan was her closest friend and confidante but it had been a while. She had been so busy with her life, the life of Mahek Singh the superstar, that maybe she had forgotten why she had become Mahek Singh in the first place.

'Obviously,' Karan smirked. 'Since it's written about you.'

Mahi scowled at him.

'Don't you think you're perfect for the part of Meher? I mean, even the name sounds like yours.'

'A lesbian love story?' Mahi asked Karan.

'Why not? Everyone else is,' said Karan. 'It's about time the Raichand banner dipped its toes into all this lesbian love too.' He smirked.

'I'm still confused. Why not just talk to her agent or publisher?'

'Ah. That's the million-dollar question. See, my darling, the publishers are already in talks with a Hollywood studio. We needed to get an inside edge.'

'So let me get this right - you called me back from the US mid-shoot to present the Big B Book Award so I could talk to Ishq ... Krish—who, by the way, hates me—about talking to her publishers to move away from a Hollywood studio and convince them to sell you the rights of her book? So I could play the character that is based on me?'

'The character is based on the idea of you, no? I mean, they do get a happy ending in the book, unlike your sad little love story.'

It was a throwaway comment but Mahi choked on the sorrow that had welled up inside her. 'Karan, really?' Why was everyone hell-bent on hurting her today? She looked vulnerable and hurt. Karan looked up and saw her struggling. He quickly tried to placate her.

'Mahi, I was just kidding. Look, you're the number 1 actress in our stable. Of course the role is yours. I mean, it was literally written for you. Besides, you've been playing the same-old-same-old for a bit. This will shake things up, add some spice to your repertoire. We can market it in the US too. Maybe you'll catch the fancy of some Hollywood producer.'

'Hmm ... what makes you think she'll give it to me?' Mahi asked.

'Whom else will she give it to?' Karan grinned. 'If you want Nirali or Mia to try, I bet they are just dying to experiment with a lesbian ... you know those girls. They'd do anything for that part. Besides, I think Mia might even swing that way.

Don't you get a closet lesbian vibe from her? I feel like I've definitely seen her checking you out.'

'Shut up, Karan. You know I'll do it.' No way Mahi was going to let those little nymphs get near Krish.

Karan smiled smugly.

'I am assuming Shalini Baweja was on board with the idea. Why wouldn't she be?' It was the perfect event to launch her takeover of the bookstore chain. Shalini Baweja had a production studio and media agency with strong ties to the Raichand banner. A media mogul, she had recently taken over a dying newspaper, a failing bookstore chain and a radio channel in a major media deal. She had been re-tooling the bookstore chain, and this would be a major launch event. Oddly enough, all the chips were falling in place. Or Karan was just that good at making the wind sway his way, thought Mahi. He was directing even when it was not a movie.

'I'm not promising anything,' said Mahi as she picked up her bag.

'Don't worry, I'll be your wingman,' Karan said, smiling.

5

-⁀⁄⁙⁀-

It was a beautiful, star-studded Mumbai night. Shalini Baweja had many Bollywood investors in her media deal. Stars who had gotten smart and got accountants and financial planners and wanted to diversify their investments. They knew her, trusted her. And so, when it was time to launch the Big B bookstores, she knew whom to call. Karan had been all too happy to support her launch. In fact, he'd even offered Mahek Singh to give away the awards.

'Won't this be a bit … below her status now?' Shalini wondered.

'Of course not, darling. You know how much she wants to support female writers. And Krish Mehra was her childhood friend. I heard she won the Fiction award, right? In fact, I can have Ruchi handle Krish's logistics. I bet Mahi would love to catch up with Krish on the flight.'

Shalini knew there was more to the story, but didn't press. With Mahek Singh and Karan Raichand attached to her event, she knew it would become an A-lister. And she was right. When people found out that Karan Raichand and Mahek Singh were going to be present, everyone showed up. Young actors, older actors, character actors, anyone who wanted half a chance in Bollywood. That brought out a whole bunch of other folks—young entrepreneurs and old business families. Before the CEO of Big B could blink, the awards had become a must-attend event. The CEO was aware that meant many PR teams working on promoting their client's presence at the event, and since her media channels had exclusive rights to the awards, it would mean a big boost to her business.

'We need a good hashtag for the event,' Shalini told her marketing and PR team. 'Something all these popular folks can put on their Instagram photos and videos. Something that will promote our sales across platforms. God knows we need some.'

~~

Krish and her mom got ready for the award reception. Krish was wearing a blue suit, freshly pressed, with a white shirt and a blue-and-yellow tie, brown belt and brown shoes. The outfit, along with her short cropped hair, made it pretty clear who she was. She wasn't hiding it. She had no reason to. Krish was grateful that her mom loved her for who she was, and was proud to walk by her side. Her mother was wearing a pale green Ritu Kumar salwar kameez and her new Longines watch. Krish noticed her walk was a bit slower and that she was getting out of breath a lot faster. As they were about to enter the hall, Ma stopped Krish and said, 'Krishi, I am so proud of you. I wish your father was here to see it. I miss him a lot today.'

'Aww, Ma. I wish he was here too. But honestly, I did all this for you. He was my father but you are my hero!'

Her mom sighed happily. 'God bless you, beta.' They stood for a moment together.

'Alright Ma … ready?' Krish gave her arm to her mother. 'Ready,' said Ma as she slid her arm through Krish's, proud to walk in with her daughter, the award-winning lesbian author.

Flashlights went off and a couple of reporters tried to talk to Krish. Most weren't that interested but the few that were clicking their pictures excited Krish and her mom. They were just about to walk away from the area when there was a hullaballoo—a firework of flashlights started going off, blinding Krish. She heard her mother cry, 'Mahi!'

Before Krish could react, Mahi was hugging Ma. 'Ma! How are you? I missed you so much, Ma. I miss your hugs. I miss our conversations.'

'I miss you too, beta. Come see me sometime. Now Krish is also home. We can make pakodas and tea, and talk about old times.' Ma gently reached to touch Mahi's face. Mahi took her palm and cradled it against her face.

Krish stood there silently, overcome with emotion seeing Mahi with Ma. How she missed those wonderful days. Why was Mahi back in her life again? Was the universe sending her a signal? Krish wondered. Was it time to let go of all the hurt, the pain, the longing?

Mahi turned to Ma and said softly, 'Pakodas are fine. But you know what I really want when I come?'

Ma's face crinkled into a big smile. 'Don't worry, I'll make that too. Just pick a date.'

She reached over to Ma and said, 'I'll definitely come soon.'

Her secretary, Ruchi, stood behind her, alert and typing away on the phone, taking in all the details.

'Can we have a picture, Mahek Madam?' asked one of the reporters.

'Of course.'

Mahek Singh smiled for the cameras. Krish realized in that moment that Mahek's smile was different from Mahi's smile. She couldn't explain it but it was like Mahi was inhabiting another skin.

Krish and her mother started to move away, but Mahi stopped them. She turned to the reporters and said, 'Everyone, you should be taking her picture, not mine. She's the winner tonight.'

Mahi posed with Ma, who stood between her and Krish, holding both their hands. The reporters obliged.

Then Ma quietly slipped away and Krish was about to too, when the reporters suggested another photo with just Krish and Mahi in the frame. Krish demurred. But as she started to walk away, Mahi reached out and grabbed her arm. 'Come on, Ishq,' she whispered softly. '*Ek photo toh banta hai.*'

Krish turned around and smiled. That instant a camera went off, capturing the smile Krish was giving Mahi and the way Mahi was looking at Krish. They both knew right away that they wanted a copy of that photo. As they posed, Krish put her arm around Mahi's waist, thinking why the hell not. She might as well, since Kabeer was nowhere to be seen. She smelt her perfume. Of course, Opium again. She found herself leaning in. What surprised Krish was that was Mahi didn't pull away. Rather, she relaxed against Krish's touch, as if this was how it was always meant to be. Like they were here together—not just as two successful individuals but as a couple.

Krish whispered, 'Will you get me a copy of that photo too?'

Mahi smiled at how seamless their communication still was. Krish hadn't felt the need to explain which photo and had assumed Mahi would be getting it too. Oh, how much Mahi missed this. 'Yes, of course,' she whispered back.

And then they parted ways as Mahi continued posing for photos until she walked in and started mingling with the guests.

'Hey, Mahek, loved your picture on Insta today,' said Mia.

'That's quite a compliment coming from the queen of Instagram!' Mahek said, smiling. There was a whole generation of younger heroines chomping at the bits for bigger, meatier roles. Many were quite brilliant. Unfortunately, Mia was not one of them. But that didn't mean she was useless.

Some were brilliant at acting, some at self-promotion. Mahek saw value in both.

'I heard TRW is making a remake of Mahabharata. Is it true?' asked Nirali, joining in. Nirali was one of the younger actors who did have potential.

'That's what I heard too. Is it true you've been tapped for the role of Draupadi, Mahek?' Mia and Nirali both turned to look at Mahek. Mahek looked at the two young, beautiful and ambitious actors in front of her. Acting with other actors was always tricky and Mahek had learnt to be discerning in an industry where fortunes changed faster than clothes in an item number. 'I've heard that rumour since I joined the industry.'

'Yes, but I've heard that this time it's actually happening.'

Mahek shrugged. 'I'm sure it will be grand.' She excused herself and moved on.

Her mind was far away. Actually not too far away. The object of her desires was very much in the room. Leaning in to Krish's touch had Mahi craving for more. She had to find a way to be alone with her away from the media glare. Mahi called Ruchi, her most capable secretary, and whispered something in her ear.

Then Mahi pulled herself together and got into work mode. Guests were still arriving. Mahi had come relatively early so she could chat with Krish. But now she was avoiding contact. Mahi was sure she wouldn't be able to stop touching Krish, and she couldn't do that in public without raising a lot of eyebrows and several months of gossip.

Instead, Mahek went over to talk to an oil tycoon who had just begun investing in movies.

'Ah, Mahek. How are you? You look so beautiful in that sari. Maybe Kabeer wouldn't mind if you went home with me tonight.'

Yuck, thought Mahek, but her face belied the emotion. Instead, she replied provocatively, 'I don't need Kabeer's approval but you might want your wife's before you make such propositions.' Before he could say anything, Mahek's eyes, which were searching for the signal she got from Ruchi, lit up. She excused herself quickly and walked away.

In the hallway, standing outside the green room, Mahi paused. Pull yourself together, she told herself. Don't be too obvious. She took a deep breath and opened the door.

Krish had her hands in her pocket as she stood at the far end of the room. As Mahi opened the door, Krish had an inquiring look on her face that was also tender. And Mahi's resolve went to hell. She found herself running towards Krish and, to her surprise, Krish actually opened her arms and let her in. They embraced like two kids in love. It was almost like a scene from the love stories they had grown up watching. Like Shah Rukh Khan opening his arms for Kajol to run into them.

They stood like that for a few seconds. Neither wanting to break contact. Neither wanting to move. Mahi could hear Krish breathing harder. Krish could feel Mahi's body's against her and it made her lean in closer. Mahi slipped her hand inside Krish's jacket towards her waist, hugging her tighter. Krish's hands went lower to Mahi's waist, pulling her closer. Their bodies fit so well together. Like they were meant to be. Mahi moaned softly. This emboldened Krish, whose hand went further down. Krish was no longer that shy teenager. Her body was vibrating with desire. Mahi was trembling in anticipation from her touch. She looked into Krish's eyes with a deep longing. Krish gazed back with a gentle warmth, and Mahi's lips opened in response. Krish's eyes moved south to Mahi's majestic lips, inviting her in. She leaned in closer but just then a soft knock on the door broke their contact.

They both sprang apart and moved away from each other. The knock came again and Mahi said, 'Yes.' Her secretary Ruchi opened the door. 'Sorry, Mahi, but Karan just walked in and is asking for you.'

'Of course,' said Mahi. 'You go ahead, we'll come soon.' And with that Ruchi shut the door.

'I have to go,' said Mahi, straightening her sari.

'What's happening?' Krish asked. 'I was told you wanted to see me privately and then you suddenly ran into my arms. What's going on?'

'I need to talk to you about something but I have to go now.'

'Come on, Mahi. Just tell me what's going on?'

'Can we please talk later?'

'What the hell, Mahi!' said Krish, now looking miffed.

'I promise we will talk soon, OK?' She looked back as she walked towards the door, smiled and shut it after her.

∽

Krish came out of the room and moved to the reception area. She was feeling so many emotions that she thought she would burst. She was conflicted about seeing Mahi. She felt anger about the past but her body was still buzzing from Mahi's touch. And she was puzzled about Mahi's behaviour. Krish couldn't figure out what was happening between her and Mahi. Could this mean they could or would get back together? There was no knowing what the future held. She shook it off, trying to focus on the present moment. It was her moment of triumph. She wanted to enjoy it. She looked around and saw people milling around. Like all typical parties, this one was running fashionably late. There was a band playing soft jazz music. Her mom was enjoying some of the hors d'oeuvres and chatting with another winner's mother. Krish smiled. She looked around at the cacophony of colours of fashionable evening wear and the sounds of people mingling, and realized she knew no one.

Just then Shalini Baweja walked over. 'Hello, Krish, we spoke on the phone.'

Shalini had beautiful brown hair that cascaded down her shoulders, and her green-brown eyes sparkled with intelligence and curiosity. She looked resplendent in a white sari that sparkled just like her eyes. Krish noted the elegant and modern-day *mangal sutra* that was the signifier of married women in India.

Krish smiled. 'Ah, yes. Nice to meet you too, Shalini.' Krish shook her hand.

'Can I say how much I loved your book? I am so glad our judges selected your book. I was really rooting for you.'

'Thank you.' Krish blushed. She was still learning how to take compliments about her success.

'I hope your flight back home was comfortable.'

'It was. Thank you so much.' Krish looked at Shalini and confessed, 'It was my first time flying first-class. I can't thank your generosity enough for that luxury.'

'We didn't do that. Karan Raichand's team handled all your travel arrangements.'

'Oh!' Krish said, confused. 'That's odd. I wonder why.'

'Do you, really? There is a lot of buzz around your book. And I thought you were friends with Mahek Singh and ...' Shalini looked around as if she was about to reveal a trade secret.

Just then Karan Raichand approached them. 'Hey Shalini, great event!'

'Speak of the devil.' Shalini smiled as she kissed Karan on his cheeks.

'You look luminescent in this white zari sari.'

'Aww, thanks, Karan,' Shalini said, blushing. 'Have you met our latest fiction award winner, Krish Mehra? I was just telling her about how you handled all her travel arrangements so she could catch up with Mahek on the plane.'

Mahi, who had just joined them in the conversation, blanched when she heard Shalini.

'Hello, Krish. Nice to finally meet you,' Karan said with a slight smirk.

Krish very firmly gave Karan just her hand, unwilling to initiate any cheek-kissing. Karan noted her steely-eyed look and shook her hand. Shalini turned to Mahek, and said, 'I heard from Karan that you knew each other since you both were little kids, is that right?'

'Yes, they were in school together,' said Karan.

'Actually we were not in the same school,' Krish gently corrected Karan with a smile. 'Mahi was in school with Imran Faiz. I went to a local convent school.'

'Oh, Imran Faiz was your classmate! Wait, he's here tonight too!' Shalini addressed Mahek, her eyes now searching for him. 'Imran, Imran …' she called out.

Imran, who was an actor just like his father had been, was standing nearby and joined them with his wife. 'Hey, Shalini, great turnout!' he said as they air-kissed.

'Suhani? Whoa! Long time no see!' Krish smiled at her.

Suhani hugged Krish warmly! 'Krishi! Wow, look at you!' Suhani took a moment to appraise Krish. 'You look so dapper, Krishi … Right, Mahek?'

Mahek nodded and smiled weakly.

'And I loved your book! *Would you live a thousand lifetimes to find that one perfect love!* Wow! What a book!' Suhani quoted the book's punchline as she turned back to face Krish. Which made Krish wonder if she had actually read it.

'It is definitely a good book!' Karan agreed.

'So you all knew each other as kids?' Shalini looked at the scene unfolding in front of her.

'Mahi … I mean Mahek … and I were neighbours. Suhani, Imran and Mahek all went to school together,' Krish explained.

'But Krishi and Mahek were inseparable, since they were little kids. So we all hung out together,' Suhani added.

'Aww. How cute! It all makes sense. I was wondering why Mahek Singh would want to give away the awards today. But if it's her best friend … that makes total sense.'

Krish gave a slight cough and looked at Mahi pointedly, 'Oh, really?!'

Mahi was miffed at Krish's slight. But the others didn't particularly catch on. Except Shalini. But before she could ask any more questions, Shalini caught sight of the chief minister and his family walking in through the door. 'Oh, I have to run,' she said and hurried off to greet them. Suhani and Imran also found other friends and excused themselves.

Krish stood there awkwardly with Karan and Mahi. 'Shalini just told me you guys paid for my first-class ticket. I didn't know that earlier. Thank you.' Krish eyed him sceptically. She was still trying to make sense of Karan.

Amused and unfazed, Karan replied, 'Yes, we wanted to make sure your return home was comfortable. Right, Mahi?'

Mahek nodded but didn't meet Krish's eyes. Krish said nothing, so Karan continued, 'We're hoping we can talk to you about your book rights. We'd love to make a movie.'

'I don't handle any of that. You should talk to my agents.' Krish put her hands in her pockets. How had she walked into this?

'We did but they're already in talks with a Hollywood studio,' Karan explained.

'Well, I'm not sure what I can do.' Krish looked for an exit strategy to this conversation.

Karan put his hand on her shoulder and tried to stop her. 'We think you should explain to them that you have something better here. That our studio can give you something that no one else can … I think Mahi would be perfect for the role, don't you?' Karan smirked again.

The wheels that had been turning in Krish's head finally connected the dots. But the final picture made her furious. 'Is that why you pimped out Mahi for the occasion? I mean, Mahi on my flight sitting next to me was not a coincidence if your office was making all the bookings, right? Mahi giving away the award tonight. None of it is a coincidence, right?'

She turned to face Mahi and said, 'All that fake concern for Ma and that hug right now—it was all just for a movie part?' Now Krish knew why Mahi was back in her life. It had nothing to do with Krish and their puppy love. It was all about a movie role. Krish's eyes narrowed; her nostrils flared. There was anger, hurt, resentment, disgust and cynicism written all over her face.

'I didn't know about our flight, Krish. I was just as surprised as you are now. And you know that,' Mahi replied honestly.

'I did. But then, you know you're such a good actress. Sometimes I forget.' Krish was like a wounded tiger, ready to lash out.

'I am not sure you're thinking this through rationally, Krish. We're ready to make you a very competitive offer,' Karan interjected.

Krish knew she should be happy that her book was getting such a tremendous response. But that buzz she had been feeling had turned into burning wrath for the betrayal she felt. It was like Mahi was betraying her all over again.

Just then someone called out to Karan. 'Excuse me, darlings, but duty calls. I think Mahi can take it from here. Right, Mahi?'

Mahi and Krish stood facing each other. Krish still had her hands in her pockets, and stood there glaring at Mahi, her eyes smouldering with rage. 'All these years I meant nothing to you, and now you want to get in touch with me because you want film rights to my book? Is that all I am to you – your next big role? I can't believe how I cried for you – you are not worth it. You never cared about me, did you? Was I just there to scratch an itch? And now I'm just a means to an end. You are nothing but an opportunistic bitch.'

'Krish, it's not like that.' Mahi looked miserable. 'Listen, can we please talk about this when you've cooled off?'

'How about we talk … never?'

'Grow up, Krish.' And Mahi walked away, smiling at the others who happened to loo at her, as if nothing had happened. As if their two hearts hadn't broken a little bit more tonight.

≈

Mahi was furious. Her secretary, Ruchi, had got her a glass of wine and as she sipped it, she started thinking. Karan must have conspired for her to spend fourteen hours in close proximity with Krish. Was he being sadistic or did he really mean something by it? Did Kabeer know? What did he think about it? She had to talk to Kabeer about it soon. What would he say? Before she could ponder further, her mind moved on to the next thought and rested on her irritation with Krish. Things between them were going from bad to worse. This is not what she wanted.

Mahi had imagined life with her Krish someday. After she had finished her reign as India's number one actress, she had imagined meeting Krish in a bookstore in New York City and getting back together and living happily ever after. Never in her wildest dreams had she imagined this much anger and resentment between them. What had happened to her beautiful, darling Ishq? She had always been so optimistic. She had briefly seen that Ishq tonight when taking photos or when they had held each other in the green room, when she had looked at her in that moment with wonder and joy and lust and longing. Like she used to. Maybe it was too late. Maybe they couldn't find their way back to each other. That thought hurt Mahi deep within her heart.

'Hey, Mahek darling! How are you? Loved your new action movie trailer. You look smashing as an inspector. Have you met my nephew, Aryan? He is just back from Boston. He wants to get into movies,' chirped Mrs Mehta, a Mumbai socialite in her glittering diamonds as she smiled at Mahi.

Mahek Singh pushed away her thoughts, gulped down the last of the wine and got back to work, smiling at Mrs Mehta and Aryan. 'Oh, hello darling!' She air-kissed Mrs Mehta and then turned to her nephew. 'So, Aryan, what did you study in Boston?'

6

᠆ᢣ᠆

SOON THE AWARD CEREMONY BEGAN AND KRISH FOUND herself sitting behind the politician's family, many of whom congratulated her on her book. The seventeen-year-old teen who gushed about the book was probably the only one who had read it, Krish mused. She could see it really meant something to the girl and was surprised when she took out her copy and asked Krish to sign it. The book looked well worn already. Krish turned the pages to find the young girl's markings on specific sentences, including her own thoughts. Krish smiled, remembering she used to do the same as a kid. In fact, she still did.

'Do you like writing?' Krish asked her.

'I do. I hope to go to Columbia next year.'

'If you want to send me some of your writing, I'd be happy to read it,' Krish offered.

The girl looked like she had just been told she had won the Nobel Prize and the Oscar both at once. Her eyes widened. 'You would?! Ohhhhmygawd! That would be beyond awesome! Mom, did you hear that?'

She shook her mother's shoulder. 'She said she'd read some of my writing!' She practically jumped in enthusiasm. Her mom smiled benignly at Krish and mouthed, 'Thank you.'

'No problem,' said Krish, grinning.

Krish signed her book and gave the girl her new email address. Krish's agent had set her up with a professional work address to share with her fans. Krish was glad she had a great team behind her as she navigated all the fame and fans that came with her success.

As Krish sat down, Ma smiled at her. 'This is the Krishi I remember.' Krish noticed that Mahi was sitting next to Ma and was also smiling at her. Krish took a deep breath. Why was she always so angry? Did she need to see a therapist again to resolve the Mahi issue in her life? Why did Mahi bring out this teenage angst in her? Krish decided to start being more of an adult.

'Mahi, I am sorry for calling you an opportunistic bitch.' Ma looked at Krish sternly. 'Krishi! How could you?'

'I know. I am sorry. I just reacted badly earlier.'

'At what?'

'Karan Raichand wants to buy the rights to Krishi's book for a movie,' explained Mahi.

Ma's face lit up. 'Really, Krishi? Isn't that good news? Why were you upset? That is such a compliment. What a great idea!' Ma gushed.

Krish was surprised at her mother's reaction. She had never seen her that excited about anything. 'It's complicated, Ma. We can talk about it later,' said Krish, trying to dismiss the idea.

'It's a big deal, Krishi. This is huge. Mahi, will you be playing Meher?' Ma asked as she turned to face Mahi.

Her Mahi smiled and nodded. 'If we get the rights.'

'Krishi, can you imagine? Isn't this your dream come true?' Ma said excitedly.

'Ma, we'll talk about it later, OK?' Krish still wondered what had gotten her mother so excited about the movie deal. It was a side of her Krish hadn't seen before.

Ma was now excitedly talking to Mahi. Krish focused her attention on the stage as Shalini Baweja walked on to it and introduced herself and the awards. She explained the categories—Fiction, Non-Fiction, Business and Management, Biography, Health and Fitness, and Children's Literature. She also spoke about the jury and the process for picking the winners.

'Now I'd like to invite the gorgeous and talented Mahek Singh to the stage to give our inaugural Big B awards.'

Mahek got up and walked up to the stage. She wore a sleeveless, strappy blouse and a turquoise sari with purple embroidery, and beautiful diamond earrings and three-inch heels. Her long, black, shiny hair hung elegantly down her gorgeous back. She carried a Bottega Veneta clutch. While her diamond earrings were huge, Krish noticed that her neck was open and inviting. No jewellery there. Oh, the things Krish would have done to her, if only … Krish smiled. It made her crazy—she felt so many duelling emotions when it came to Mahi. The constant attraction, the memories, good and bad, that kept bubbling to the surface, leading to anger and resentment when she saw her. This cacophony of emotions made no sense to her and Krish had no idea what to do with it. She shifted uncomfortably in her seat.

On stage, Mahek announced the winners, starting with the Children's Literature category, working her way up to English Fiction.

'When I read *When Doves Die*, I cried, I laughed, I smiled and, most importantly, I learnt something about the world and myself. Good fiction helps us see the world in a different way. Great fiction helps us see how we are different in our world. I am honoured to present the inaugural Big B Book English Fiction Award to this year's winner and my childhood friend ... Krishna Mehra.'

Krish hugged Ma, got up from the seat and straightened herself. She felt all eyes on her and feeling about six feet tall, walked up to the stage. Mahi leaned over to kiss Krish on her cheeks, and Krish's hand instinctively reached for her waist.

'So proud of you, Ishq,' Mahi whispered in her ear. Mahi graciously moved aside to give Krish the microphone for her speech.

'Thank you, Mahi. Wow ... I feel like I've imagined this moment for so many years, where I get an award for my work ... but nothing really compares to this moment.' She surveyed the crowd.

'All right, I'd like to thank the Big B Book Award judges and jury for this honour. We live in precarious times—where judgement is swift, ideology is heavy on emotion and not always rational, and anonymous assaults via social media are relentless. In such times, to choose my book for this award is truly a bold decision and one I am very thankful for. It gives me hope for a newer, better tomorrow, that is more loving and tolerant. Where everyone deserves a happy ending, no matter who they are and whom they love.

'I would like to thank the people who have made this journey possible—my editor and publisher, my publicist, the faculty at the University in New York, where I teach, and my best friends Chelsea, Lauren and, of course, Allie. And, finally, I want to thank my mother, my Ma. She has been my lifelong champion and my hero. And last but not the least, I'd like to say love freely, love deeply, live honestly. Thank you.'

There was a big round of applause at Krish's speech. Krish's eyes searched for only one response. She looked at Mahi. She was smiling as she clapped but her eyes were not smiling. Was she thinking about what Krish had just said?

Lots of people came up to Krish and said how much they loved her speech, how proud they were of her, how she had inspired them with her life. Mostly, it made Krish wonder: How can one be proud of a complete stranger?

Shalini Baweja went excitedly to her team. 'I found it! I found the perfect hashtag! #HappyEnding. Every photo we have, every tweet—make sure we have that hashtag. And make sure you tag Mahek Singh.'

Shalini's team got busy and, unbeknownst to Krish, a photo of Mahi hugging her with the award went online with the hashtag #HappyEnding.

≈

As the evening started winding down, Krish and Ma decided to leave. Krish was jubilant and wished her friends were there so they could go party. She didn't particularly want to leave but Ma was getting tired. Besides, it's not like she had any friends there.

Right about then, Suhani and Imran came to say goodbye. 'Don't be a stranger,' said Suhani as she and Imran left. After they left, Mahi came to say goodbye to Ma. As Mahi and Ma coordinated their plans, Karan Raichand, never one to leave a deal unfinished, came to talk to Krish.

'That was a great speech, Krish,' he said sincerely.

'Thank you,' Krish replied. 'And I'd like to thank you for all the work you've been doing in India. Sometimes I feel like a traitor. It's easy to be out in another country, where I have certain rights. I feel guilty that I am not in India, making change happen—one family, one troll at a time.'

Karan laughed. 'Yes, trolls take their toll. Which is why I think your book as a film will be an important touchstone in Indian cinema.'

Krish couldn't help but grin as she saw the business side of Karan coming into action. This behaviour should have felt irritating, but it mostly felt like home. India was surging at breakneck speed, people were rising quickly, making deals, finding novel opportunities and they were not shy about '*dhanda*' and money. Ma was right—it was a huge compliment to her book that the Raichand Film Company was interested in buying the rights to her book.

Before Krish could answer, Ma, holding Mahi's hand, asked Karan, 'Beta, will Mahi play Meher's role?'

'Of course, Aunty. If we get the rights, Mahi gets the first right of refusal. Honestly, I can't think of anyone better than Mahi to play Meher, amiright?' Karan smirked again.

Mahi and Krish looked at each other.

Krish sighed. She could handle Mahi and Karan, but not her mother. That was probably a losing battle. 'I'll think about it. I'll talk to my agent and get back to you.'

'Sounds good. We'll be in touch,' said Karan, reaching over to kiss Krish on her cheek. Krish stepped back and offered her hand again. Karan's looked at her, amusement writ large on his face, but along with it something else—as if wondering what Krish's tough façade was all about. It was almost a challenge.

Krish sighed and led Ma out. Mahi said softly, 'There is a car waiting for you two.'

Krish looked at her quizzically. 'No. We came by Uber.' Then she realized that it was not a question. Mahi had arranged for a car to take them home. More pieces were falling into place for Krish. 'So you had arranged that car back at the airport?'

Mahi blushed. 'I figured you might need a ride home. When we landed, I asked Ruchi to arrange one.'

'Even after I was so nasty to you?'

'Old habits.' Mahi gently touched Krish's face, smiled and walked away.

~~

Later that night, Mahi and Karan sat in her house drinking red wine from Napa Valley.

'So?'

'I am trying to make sense of your ex-girlfriend. She is not what I had expected.'

'What do you mean?' Mahi leaned back on the couch. She was in shorts, without any make-up. Karan was her closest friend and they often hung out late into the night.

'Why does she not like hugging or kissing people? And she doesn't trust anyone. She seems very angry. I think you broke her, Mahi.'

'I had no idea ... But now you understand why I said I doubt she will give me the rights. She's so full of wrath. I never imagined that after all these years we'd meet each other, and ...'

' … And it would be like you were never apart. Her rage is so visceral. Like you broke up with her yesterday, not ten years back.'

'I know, right!'

'But you know that means she's clearly not over you, right?'

'Are you serious?!'

'Oh, if she was over you, she wouldn't be so angry. And her anger wouldn't be so raw. Poor thing. And the fact that you're in a relationship with the most handsome man in India doesn't make it any easier, I guess.'

'Nope. I guess not. I just don't want her to hate me.'

'I know … I am sorry. After all you've been through, I had no idea it would turn out like this when you guys met.'

'Me neither, Karan!' Mahi sighed.

She wanted to fix this, but had no idea how. 'You had promised me a happy ending. But I don't see it as a possibility now.'

They were silent for a few minutes.

'Mahi, maybe you should talk to her. She's only seen your public persona these past ten years. She doesn't know how you've struggled. She doesn't know about your loss. You need to talk to her, babe!'

Mahi's phone buzzed.

7

―ﾉﾉ\~

KRISH AND MA PICKED UP A BUNCH OF COPIES OF Baweja's newspaper the next day. The award event had got exclusive coverage in their newspaper and Ma wanted a few copies, especially since there was a picture of Krish receiving the award from Mahi. And while Krish outwardly complained about Ma making such a big fuss, she got a few copies for herself too. Especially when she saw the hashtag #HappyEnding with all the pictures. If her mother noticed the longing in Krish's eyes every time she saw pictures of her with Mahi, she didn't say anything.

Krish's social media was blowing up and she could barely keep up. Suhani and Imran had posted pictures of them with Krish, Mahek and Karan. Shalini Baweja had posted a picture of her with Krish, Mahek and Karan. Krish looked at the various pictures of her on various news and entertainment websites and blogs. Most places used the same story and the same pictures provided by Baweja Media, but some places had carried picture of Mahi giving Krish the award. Most of all media sources applauded Krish's speech and raved about the book.

'A much-needed love story for our times,' said one.

'Amen to a more loving, more tolerant India,' said another.

Many old friends from Krish's school and Mahi's were contacting her, congratulating her and wanting to make plans. Her doorbell kept ringing all day as aunties came by to say congratulations. Her website had got a whole bunch of visits and some trolls too. The same was true for social media. It was largely positive but there were a whole bunch of hateful comments, such as 'Lesbians just need a good fuck' and 'She should die in hell'. Ma teared up when she read some, so Krish quickly closed all social media apps for the day.

Overall, Krish was feeling good. Even the trolls didn't bother her much—they just made her aware that she was now troll-worthy. She smiled to herself. She had finally arrived. All those years as she saw Mahi go from strength to strength, she felt like a castaway, like a piece of garbage. And now that Mahi was photographed with her, Krish was finally worth her place in Mahi's life. Only, there was no place. They had lost their chance. And they had moved on. Mahi was with Kabeer and Krish was with Allie.

Allie! Shoot! Krish had forgotten to message her since she had reached India. *I'll FaceTime her tonight.* She made a mental note. Who had known Mahi would crash her life like this?

Lauren and Chelsea messaged on their group chat.

'WTF, Krish? How ironic that Mahek Singh gave you your award.'

'And did you see the hashtag?! OMG!'

'I know, it was pretty crazy. Thankfully it's over,' Krish replied ruefully, glad her friends couldn't see her face.

'Did she remember you?'

'Did you guys talk?'

'Yeah, a bit. She was saying something to the effect that we should let go of the past, and look how successful we both are in our present.'

Krish felt terrible bending the truth, but she really couldn't explain her conflicting feelings over chat. It needed a much longer conversation, with a lot of alcohol.

'Whoa! That bitch! Can you believe her nerve?' wrote Lauren.

'What did you say?' asked Chelsea.

'I told her I didn't need to suck cock to get to my success.'

'Whoaaaaaa!!!!!!!!! KRISH!!!!!' Chelsea wrote back in capital letters.

'Did you really say that?' Lauren inquired.

'MAD REPSECT, BRAH!' Chelsea continued.

'You bet your ass I did,' Krish replied to Lauren.

'Wow! I still can't believe the irony. Hashtag! Suck on that!' Chelsea again.

Krish nodded but didn't smile.

Later that evening, Krish, who had been buried in her laptop all day, finally looked up and said, 'All right, Ma, what's for dinner? I am so hungry.'

She was hanging out in her shorts and sleeveless tank top with her laptop and phone open, as it kept vibrating with notifications. The bell rang and before Krish could get up to open the door, Ma was rushing to open it.

'Who is it, Ma?' Krish asked distractedly.

She heard someone say, 'Just stay here. I'll call when I need you.' And then a person walked in in an old, loose T-shirt and jeans, sunglasses and a cap, carrying a travel bag.

'Who is it, Ma?' Krish asked again. She got up from the couch when she got no answer. Then, all of a sudden, she heard Mahi's laugh. Ma and Mahi had made a plan to meet today? Ma had not mentioned it. What the heck!

Krish quickly put her stuff away and tried to look more put together with her shorts and T-shirt.

'Hey, Ish … I mean … Krish,' said Mahi as she took off her cap and sunglasses. Her smile was gorgeous. As hard as Krish tried, she couldn't stop her heart from racing. So much for all that tough talk with Lauren and Chelsea.

≫

Mahi reached around her old, loose T-shirt to remove it and saw Krish's eyes widen. But when she took it off to reveal a beautiful top that was elegant yet fit in all the right places, she saw Krish blush a deep red. Krish looked away quickly, hoping no one had seen the emotions writ large on her face. Too late. She saw Mahi grinning. She was happy to see Krish's eyes still filled with the same lust and longing, though the wonder and joy were a lot dimmer than they used to be. Mahi knew she was to blame for this. But her life had not been a bed of roses. If only Krish knew …

Ma came over to appreciate Mahi's outfit. 'Arre waah! You look so beautiful, Mahi. I can't believe this girl, who used to do her homework every day on this table with Krishi, is now India's biggest superstar.'

Mahi smiled, blushing. 'I'm still the same Mahi.' She hugged Ma.

'Same Mahi? Only with a security detail now,' Krish sniggered.

Mahi smacked Krish lightly. 'Be nice, Ishq. It's been so long. Let it be like old times. Just for tonight.'

'All right. Fine. What's for dinner, Ma?' Krish asked.

'Baingan ka bharta.' Ma cried out from the kitchen. 'But we haven't made that since … '

'Yes. And you had said you can't eat it without her. But guess who is sitting next to you?' Ma was smiling broadly.

Mahi thought she would burst with happiness. Oh, how much she had missed this house.

'Did you seriously not eat baingan ka bharta for the past ten years?' Mahi asked Krish incredulously.

'It was our favourite food. We always ate it together. It felt odd having it without you. I tried once. It tasted like tears.' Mahi smacked Krish again, but this time more lovingly.

They looked at each other. No words were necessary. There were so many emotions to feel; words didn't seem useful in that moment.

Just then Mahi's phone rang. Krish saw Kabeer's name flash on the screen. Mahi declined the call and texted him. Krish looked away. The spell was broken.

Krish got up and went to the kitchen. Ma was humming.

'You look happy!' Krish was happy to see her mother so happy. Ma was different around Mahi. Krish wondered what it was about Mahi that created this magic.

Ma looked at Krish and said, 'I am happy. You two are back home. What else do I need?'

At that moment, Mahi came into the kitchen too. 'Ma, can I help?'

'Arre beta, we're almost ready. Krishi, play some music.'

Krish got her phone out and played one of Mahi's songs from her new film. 'See, I keep up.' Krish smiled. Mahi returned it.

'It's a good song. You know, catchy,' Krish said and hummed along.

'Thanks.' Mahi wasn't sure why, but it made her glad to know Krish liked her work.

'Do you like it?' Krish queried.

'What? The song?'

'You know, acting, being a brand ambassador, being Mahek Singh the superstar.'

'It has its perks. And there are lots of them. But most of the time it's work. Like any other job.'

'Hmm.'

This almost felt normal, Krish thought.

'You know, oddly enough, I get it. People often have a warped notion of creativity—for writers but also artists of all sorts. But it really is just work. I mean, don't get me wrong, I enjoy my work—a lot. But I wake up, I go to my desk and I write. And then in the evening I have dinner and I read. And that's that.'

'You make it sound so unglamorous.'

Krish laughed. 'Yes, our locations are not as exotic as yours. We are not gyrating on fancy beaches or shopping in Paris. Not to mention you guys make the big bucks.'

≳

As they talked about her work, Mahi reflected on how normal this felt. For a moment earlier, Mahi wasn't sure if she had made the right decision by coming over that day. But Ma had been so insistent. Now Mahi eased into the evening. Talking to Krish had always been so easy. Mahi's eyes wandered to Krish's arms. Krish was wearing a yellow tank top with denim shorts. Mahi noticed that Krish's arms had definition and strong muscles. And her legs were ... gosh ... her legs were so hot. That was the only word that came to Mahi's mind. Krish had clearly started working out. Mahi felt the heat building in her body. Whew! Mahi got up, feeling Krish's eyes on her. She was about to turn to see if Krish's eyes were on her ass as she walked but resisted the urge. Of course they were. Who in India could resist her ass?

She went into the kitchen, tying her long hair up in a pony as she asked Ma, 'Can I help?'

'No. We're done. Can you please take that rice to the table?'

By now Krish had come into the kitchen too. 'Krish, beta, fill the glasses with water. Beta Mahi, will you have something to drink? I got Diet Coke for you.'

Mahi laughed. 'No, Ma. Water is fine. Just because I'm in the ad doesn't mean I drink it all the time.'

Krish laughed too, and took a water bottle to fill the glasses. The table set for three brought back a flood of memories.

Mahi was nine years old. When Ma asked her what she wanted for her birthday, she answered, 'I want baingan ka bharta.' Ma had laughed so hard. 'Of course, beta, I'll make it for you. But what do you want as a gift?'

'I want baingan ka bharta,' Mahi repeated, not sure why Ma had not understood.

'All right. Baingan ka bharta it is.'

And since then, baingan ka bharta had been Mahi's dish in their house. Ma made it every time Mahi came to stay over. Which was often when they lived next door. But after her brothers got married, their family moved farther away. They bought two flats next to each other farther away. Mahi wasn't close to her brothers, whom she found bossy and overbearing. And she hated her mother's ambitiousness. It was like her family only saw her as a meal ticket. But Krish and her mother saw her and loved her for all that she was. Mahi always felt more at home with Ishq. And when their relationship changed, it felt even more so.

Mahi was a hundred per cent sure that Ma would have loved her dearly as a daughter-in-law. And that they would have been happy together. But as Krish used to say, 'wishes-horses-beggars-ride', which was the shortened version of the saying, 'If wishes were horses, beggars would ride.' Mahi smiled wryly.

'Mahi … Mahi,' Ma was calling her name.

'Sorry, I was a little lost in memories.' Mahi smiled. 'Ma, the food is delicious. It tastes just the same as all those years ago.'

'Yes, Ma. It's so yummy! Oh, I've missed this so much,' said Krish enthusiastically, taking more on her plate.

'I've missed you both. The house feels so wonderful with both of you in it again. Let's do this again while Krish is in town,' said Ma, looking at Mahi.

'Ma, Mahi is busier than I am. She's probably got shoots planned out months in advance,' Krish reasoned.

'Yes, but she can make time for us, no?' Ma looked at Mahi, almost pleading with her eyes.

'I will. I am travelling and my plans are up in the air right now, but I'll stay in touch,' Mahi promised.

'Yes, and add Krishi to the WhatsApp chat too. We can make a group,' Ma suggested as she took another bite.

'Wait, what? We have a Whatsapp group now?' Krish chuckled and looked at Mahi in amazement. Mahi felt the same way. If someone had told her a week ago that she would be here with Ishq—her Ishq—and Ma, eating baingan ka bharta, she would have told them they were dreaming. But here she was. She had to thank Karan for this miracle.

'So tell me, what's new at your end?' Ma asked.

'Not much. I am working on two movies. One is an action movie and I am playing an inspector, so I have some really cool action shots. I've been taking some martial arts lessons.'

'Really?' Krish looked interested.

'You know, Krishi is a third-degree black belt,' Ma said proudly.

'Really?' This time Mahi looked at Krish in surprise and admiration. That explained the toned muscles.

'Yes,' Krish said, suddenly becoming more interested in the bharta.

'So you can teach me some moves?' Mahi asked suggestively.

'Don't you guys have trainers and all?' Krish deflected.

'We do, but my trainer just got pregnant and is on bed rest,' Mahi stated.

'I'm sure there are thousands of people willing to take that spot.' Krish didn't want to get involved in this. This felt like a trap, somehow.

'Fine, if you don't want to do it, just say so,' Mahi huffed.

Ma stepped in. 'Krish ...' she reprimanded.

'Of course, I'll be happy to teach you anything,' Krish said, sighing.

'I don't want your charity, thanks,' Mahi said petulantly. Krish used to love her *nakhra*s, and also loved *manao*ing Mahi. To be fair, Mahi used to love manaoing Ishq's nakhra back then too.

'Mahi, stop taking so much *bhaav*. You know I'll do it, na?'

Mahi giggled. She enjoyed being manoed by Krish. 'Great. I'll tell Ruchi to find a spot in my schedule.' Mahi took out her phone and texted Ruchi.

After they were done with dinner, Krish and Mahi cleaned up the table. Ma went into the kitchen.

'Is Ma's health OK?' Mahi asked, concerned. 'She looks weaker ... older.'

'She is older, weaker. I have been meaning to talk to her about her health but you know things have been crazy these past few days. Maybe check her medicines and visit her doctor. I've been asking her to move to the US for years now. But she says she is happy here. I don't know how to take care of her from there.' Krish looked worried.

Mahi reached out and held her hand.

'She doesn't tell me anything. She keeps insisting that everything is OK,' Krish continued.

Mahi wanted to take Krish in her arms and make everything better. Mahi touched Krish's face gently. 'It's OK. I can help.'

Ma came out of the kitchen with three bowls filled with rabri and gulab jamun.

'I know you young people are always on diet, but today I'm not listening to anything,' Ma warned them as she placed the tray on the coffee table.

Mahi clutched her stomach. 'Oh my god. My trainer is going to kill me tomorrow.'

'No, she won't. She's pregnant, remember?' Krish grinned. 'I bet she's dealing with her own cravings.'

'That's my martial arts trainer. I have a regular trainer too.'

'Oh, fancy.' Krish laughed and smacked Mahi's leg. 'Now eat.'

'Can I just share from you? Come on, Ishq. Won't you share with me? Like old times?' Mahi looked at Krish with her big brown eyes. One thing that Mahi knew was that few people could resist her charms. And definitely not the person sitting across from her in this room.

'Of course you can. Come here. *Nautanki*,' said Krish as she picked up a rabri–gulab jamun bowl and settled by Ma's foot on the floor.

Mahi laughed. Krish used to call her 'Nautanki' all the time when they were younger. She got up and sat down cross-legged next to Krish, resting her head on Krish's shoulder. As Krish fed her little bites of rabri and gulab jamun, Mahi realized she hadn't laughed and felt so at ease in years. Krish gave her the last bite, as always. And then Krish reached for the second bowl and they started the process all over again. Of course, Mahi knew she could have eaten the whole bowl herself. But this … this was so much better. They sat like that for a bit and then Ma got up and said, 'Krishi, beta. Can you please go get some paan for all three of us?'

Krish protested at the idea of walking three galis at night to get paan, but Ma and Mahi just reminded Krish of her black belt and assured her that they had complete faith in her abilities to get paan. Krish felt like it was some sort of a plan to get her out of the house but couldn't refuse Ma and Mahi. So she heaved a sigh of resignation, got up and made a production of getting ready to make the trek.

About half an hour later she was back with paan.

'I'm back,' Krish called, carrying several small packages. 'Ma, here is your Calcutta saada paan. Mahi, here is yours and mine. The same order, as always,' Krish said, smiling.

Earlier that day when she had seen Mahi walk through that door, she was not sure how the evening would go, but this was so much like old times. It was like slipping into an old T-shirt. It was warm and friendly and snug.

After they had had their paans, Mahi said, 'You know, I am really missing my second half of the Maghai. I didn't realize we were sharing it. Otherwise I would have told you to get two.' Maghai paans were smaller and often came in pairs. Krish and Mahi had split the pair so they had each had one half.

'Won't your trainer object to all this gulab jamun, rabri, and now paan? Eat one half. That's enough for you.'

Krish, who was back to sitting by Ma's feet and next to Mahi, got two thwacks—one on her back from Ma and another on her arm from Mahi.

'Don't tell her what she should or should not eat.'

'Exactly,' Mahi added, giving Krish an I-told-you-so smile. Krish remembered how Mahi and Ma would often team up and admonish Krish for some boorish behaviour or another. She unwrapped another paan package and as she handed it to Mahi, said, 'I knew you'd complain.'

Mahi squealed in delight and thwacked Krish again.

8

AFTER A FEW MINUTES, MA SAID, 'ALL RIGHT, I AM TIRED. I am heading to bed. You girls can hang out for as long as you like. Mahi, if you like, you can stay over. I got the maid to make an extra bed in Krishi's room. Just in case. But if you want, Krishi can sleep out here and you can sleep in her room.'

Krish and Mahi blushed furiously. 'Umm … I … I …' was the best Mahi could manage.

'It's OK. We get it. You don't have to stay here. There is no issue. You have your driver outside, right?' Krish spoke up.

'Umm …'

Ma looked at the two girls, who looked at each other. Krish looked befuddled and Mahi was blushing. 'You girls figure it out. I am heading to bed,' said Ma. She went into her room and shut the door.

Krish and Mahi said nothing for a few minutes. They just stared at each other. It felt so much like old times. Usually they were all over each other by now. Krish sat back down and decided to sit on her hands to physically restrain herself. Just in case.

'Umm … I didn't know about her making the bed in my room. I would have told her not to,' said Krish.

'Since when did we use the other bed anyway?' Mahi grinned.

Krish grinned back. Mahi's smile, their easy camaraderie, spending all this time together like old times—it was dangerous for Krish's resolve. Yes, hands were definitely staying under her thighs.

'Shall we?' Mahi asked, getting up and started to walk.

'Umm …' Krish wasn't sure this was a good idea.

Before Krish could really object, Mahi had walked into her room. She looked around. It looked almost like no time had passed. Even the bedsheets looked the same. Mahi remembered their first time right there on that single bed.

Back then

She had been making out with Ishq every day since their first kiss. They had fondled each other but clothes had stayed on. It had been two weeks. As much as Mahi loved Krish kissing her, exploring her mouth with her tongue, kissing her on that sweet spot on her neck or behind her ears, she wanted more. So much more. She also knew Krish would not dare do anything without Mahi giving her explicit permission, because what the world did not see, that Mahi did, was as butch as Krish looked on the outside, she was just that soft and gentle on the inside. So Mahi knew the reins were very much in her hand.

And today, Mahi decided, was the day. She was tired of being a virgin. Her mother had given her dialogue after dialogue about guarding herself. About being careful. But Mahi was in love and, gosh, she wanted Krish inside her. Just the thought of Krish removing her panties and touching her, entering her, sent Mahi's body into overdrive. So, that evening, as soon as Ma retired for the day, Mahi took Krish by the hand and led her to bed. They switched off the lights, leaving just a bed lamp on, as usual. Mahi pushed Krish down on the bed and straddled her. Mahi still remembered the shock and excitement on Krish's face as Mahi removed her shirt and her bra, letting it fall like she had seen in English movies. Krish had touched her breasts reverently at first but soon hormones had taken over. She looked up at Mahi, who was still straddling her as Krish took her nipple into her mouth. Krish closed her eyes, enjoying the nipple grow bigger, firmer, in her mouth. A moan escaped Krish's mouth, and Mahi, seeing Krish's reaction and feeling her tongue on her tender breast, went into high gear from all the sensations happening to her body. She held Krish's head close to her breasts, enjoying these new sensations. She got up quickly, removing her panties and, lifting up her skirt, guided Krish's hand.

'I need you. I need you so bad,' Mahi whimpered.

Krish almost died in shock. 'What? Are you crazy?' she whispered as she drew her hand away.

'Then stop touching me,' Mahi said sharply. Krish, who still had one hand on her nipple, rubbing it gently, looked sad about the idea of giving up her new and very beloved possession but was unsure about what to do next. She looked at Mahi, confused. Mahi took her hand again and this time guided it firmly towards her wetness. Krish felt the soft curls and touched Mahi's wetness.

'Yes,' said Mahi, encouraging Krish's exploration. Krish kissed Mahi's neck and ears, and whispered, 'Is it OK if I go down, so I can see you better?'

'Yes ... please.'

Krish slid down and started her exploration of Mahi's femaleness. She looked at her clitoris in awe, seeing it slick with Mahi's juices, erect and enlarged, waiting to be touched, licked, sucked. Krish couldn't help but heed its call. She took her clit into her mouth. Softly and tentatively she licked it. Mahi went crazy as Krish continued licking her. She pushed against Krish's face, rubbing her face in her mound, bucking her hips.

'I need you inside me, Ishq.'

Krish's own body was pushing her over the edge. She quickly removed her jeans and underwear. She needed Mahi as much as Mahi needed her. Krish pushed her finger inside Mahi's body. Soft, warm tenderness enveloped her finger, drawing it further in. As if speaking a new language, Krish could hear what it needed. She put another finger in. And the wetness embraced it. Soon Krish was pushing inside in an unspoken rhythm. Mahi had her eyes closed and bucked from side to side as Krish draped her body, her two fingers deep inside Mahi, their bodies moving in unison.

'I love you,' said Krish.

'Umm ... ummm ... ohh ... this feels so good,' Mahi cried softly. 'Oh yeah ... deeper. Oh yes ... yes ...' Mahi was in the throes of passion, her body moving with crazy abandon, so close to the edge. And then suddenly she felt her body and mind explode. 'Ahhhhhhhhhhhhh,' she grunted, unable to keep her cries quiet. Mahi felt like she had died and gone to heaven. When she opened her eyes, Krish was looking at her in wonder and joy, her eyes smiling at what she had just witnessed. No, what she had just accomplished. Mahi felt so much love in that moment. She put her hand behind Krish's head and pulled her closer. 'I love you so much. I always will. You are my heart, my Ishq.'

After a few minutes, Mahi got on top of Krish. 'My turn now,' she said as she started moving down on Krish's body, her eyes amused, looking at Krish's, which were as wide as a deer caught in the headlights. Neither of them slept a wink that night.

Now

Mahi turned red as those memories came flooding back, filling up her senses, awakening her body to a need, a place deep inside her soul that only Krish could touch.

'Umm … not to be rude or anything, but what's going on? You made this plan with Ma to come to dinner. And what, stay the night?' asked Krish apprehensively. Her hands were deep inside her pockets. Just in case. They had so much history in this room. And Krish was only human.

Mahi turned around. Krish was looking at her puzzled, still a deer in the headlights. Why was she in her bedroom? Their bedroom, Mahi thought.

'Ma asked me to stay the night. I couldn't refuse.'

'Wait, what? You, Mahek Singh, are seriously staying the night here? At our house?'

Just then a FaceTime call pinged on Krish's phone.

'Shit,' said Krish as she went to answer it. All of this was spinning out of control and now Allie was calling as Mahi was standing in her room. Their room.

'Hey, hey, hey!' Krish quickly angled the phone so that Allie couldn't see Mahi.

'Hi, sweetheart … Oh, I miss you so much,' said Allie.

Krish smiled anxiously.

'Where have you been, baby? I haven't heard from you. Is everything OK?' Allie cooed.

'You know, things have been kinda crazy busy here,' Krish chuckled nervously as she ran her hand through her short black hair. A nervous tic. Mahi narrowed her eyes.

Who was this?

'By the way, congratulations. I saw all the coverage, and your Facebook is a hot mess full of tags from everywhere around the world. You're famous, my Jaan. Famous!'

Mahi was about to leave the room but turned around when she heard the word. Wait, had she just called her Ishq—her Ishq—'Jaan'? Krish looked nervously at Mahi. She could see the anger building on Mahi's face. Oh, this was such terrible timing for her two worlds to collide.

'Uh, Allie, sweetheart. I can't really talk right now. I have some guests over. I'll call you later, OK? Promise.'

'Krishiiiii … baby,' Allie protested from across the world. 'Call me soon. Oh, and Chelsea and Lauren say hi. Bye, Jaan.'

Krish disconnected the call. She looked at Mahi, who was standing there, her face a deep red, and chuckled nervously.

'You want to explain?' Mahi crossed her arms.

'I don't have to explain anything to you,' Krish said defensively, crossing her arms too and standing as far away from Mahi as possible.

'Krish,' Mahi growled. Oh, yes, Krish remembered that growl well. It often led to fantastic make-up sex, but first … first came the big blow-up. Here goes.

'Allie is my girlfriend. We've been dating for the past six months.'

'And you couldn't tell me this on our fourteen-hour flight from hell? Or at the award ceremony?'

'I thanked Allie … in my speech … at the ceremony.'

'As a friend, if I recall correctly.' Mahi's eyes narrowed again.

'Well, I … anyway, why do you care?'

'What do you mean by "why do you care"?'

'What I mean is that you have no right to come back into my life, in our house, in our room, and pretend like we are together again. You have no right to ask me about who I am dating or for how long, or what I feel about them.'

Mahi bit her lip and said nothing.

'Besides, you have a boyfriend, remember? So don't pretend to be angry when you see someone loving me when you have clearly moved on. Just because you discarded me as garbage doesn't mean someone else can't see value in me. I am lovable. Do you hear me, Mahi? I AM LOVABLE! Allie, she sees me. She loves me.' Krish had a meltdown. She held her head in her hands and started sobbing. Her deep fears and hurt were unravelling in front of Mahi. Mahi saw for the first time the scars she had caused deep within Krish's psyche.

She reached over and held Krish's head against her breast. 'Come, babe. Come here. Shhh … stop crying. It's OK … it's OK,' Mahi said softly as she tried to soothe Krish.

But the tears were flowing freely. And so was the rage.

'Mahi … you ruined me and my life. I felt so alone. I spent so many years doubting myself, wondering what I had done wrong. But I wasn't wrong. Loving you wasn't wrong. You were wrong for leaving me. You were a coward. You are still a coward. I hate you, Mahi. I hate you.'

9

~⁄|\~

WHEN KRISH OPENED HER EYES, IT WAS MORNING. HER eyes felt swollen and crusty from all the tears that had dried up . What had happened last night? Had Krish fallen asleep while crying? She looked around for Mahi. She was nowhere to be found. Krish stilled herself to hear the sounds from outside her room. But it was just her mom, singing a bhajan softly as she did her morning puja. She couldn't hear Mahi's voice or any other sound indicating another person's presence in the living room. Oddly, Krish felt a sense of loss. Like something had been taken away from her. She washed her face and brushed her teeth hurriedly and stepped out of her room to look for Mahi. Just in case. But she was right. It was just her mom. Krish looked disappointed, but before her mom could say anything, the doorbell rang. Krish ran to the door, her face hopeful, but it wasn't Mahi. It was a delivery boy carrying a large bouquet of white roses. He gave her the roses and a package that had come along with it. In it was a letter from Mahi. Krish tore open the package. It contained a photo frame with the photo of the two of them looking at each other at the award ceremony when Mahi had told Krish, '*Ek photo toh banta hai',* and Krish had turned around and smiled at her. Krish looked suave in the blue suit and Mahi stunning in the turquoise sari. Their outfits looked coordinated and the love in their eyes would be obvious to anyone who looked at the photo.

There was an envelope. Krish opened it to find a letter, which read:

Dearest Ishq,

I am so sorry for all the hurt I have caused you. Please believe me, it was the last thing I wanted. Since I've known love, I've loved you. I still do. But I understand if you don't love me any more. And I understand now why you don't love me.

Last night I realized I was being selfish for coming back into your life. You have moved on, and you're right, so have I. But yesterday, for a moment, when I was at your house with Ma and you, and we were having baingan ka bharta like old times, I forgot I was Mahek Singh and just felt like Mahi. It has been years since I felt that sense of comfort, that feeling of being home. And I want to thank you and Ma for that. And perhaps in that feeling of nostalgia, maybe I reacted badly to the idea of you having a girlfriend. Of course you have a girlfriend. Who wouldn't find you lovable! You were always lovable.

You are right about one thing. I was a coward for leaving you. But I promise you this, I really didn't think I had any other choice. I made the best of the

*circumstances given to me. Perhaps you don't agree or
understand, but there was no malice in my decision.*

I love you.
Yours always,
Mahi.

Krish read the note and read it again. She shook her head
in complete disbelief. By this time, Ma had finished her puja
and had walked over to her.

'Oh, what a beautiful photo,' she said as she picked up the
photo frame that Krish had forgotten about already. 'I'll keep
this here.' And she picked it up and put it in her living room
on the shelf with their family photos. The shelf had a photo
of Ma and Pa on their wedding day, one with Krish as a baby
with them, and one of a grown Krish and Ma with the Statue
of Liberty in the backdrop. And now of Krish and Mahi.

'Ma, are you sure?' Krish asked.

'Of course I am sure,' Ma answered. She looked at Krish,
noticing her tear-crusted eyes. Disappointment was writ large
on Krish's face.

'What happened?'

Krish said nothing—she just handed the letter to her
mother and went into her bedroom and closed the door. She
came out later that afternoon, but they didn't talk about it.

≫

The next few days went by quickly. Krish had a few interviews
lined up with some newspapers, magazines and literary blogs.
For one very prominent newspaper, Krish sat down for an

interview with the representative, her boss, a stenographer and two assistants or interns—Krish couldn't figure out what their designations were—but wondered if it had anything to do with her being a lesbian. Did the woman taking the interview not feel safe with her?

'So, Krish Mehra, we are very pleased to have you here today.'

'Thanks. I'm happy to be here too.' Krish gave a broad smile.

'Congrats on the Big B Book award and your longlist for the Booker Prize.'

'Thank you.'

'How do you feel?' The reporter flicked her hair.

'I feel honoured. It is always nice to see one's work appreciated. Especially since mine is not very ... mainstream.'

'Can you tell us a little about your process?'

'My process? I have an MFA in creative writing. I read every day. I write every day. In many ways, it's a job like any other. I go to work—every day. I'm just lucky that my work makes me happy.'

Krish could feel the interviewer getting irritated with her. She wasn't giving her any juicy titbits. No good sound bites.

'Your story ...'

'Yes?'

'It's a love story.'

'You can say so.'

'Between two girls, Rehan and Meher, in search of perfect love,' the interviewer clarified, signs of irritation apparent on her face now. Like Krish was not getting what she was alluding to.

'Yes.'

'And you're an out lesbian. So is this book autobiographical?'

Krish hesitated. The interviewer sensed it and pounced.

'I mean ... are *you* Rehan?' she asked.

'Am *I* Rehan? I am each of the characters. I made them. They exist in a world I created. I crafted each one of them. So I'm Rehan, sure. But I'm also Meher. I'm also Rajiv and Priya and Varun. Aham Brahmasami. They are all me and I am part of all of them.'

'I see. So not autobiographical?'

'Well, I think we write what we know. So far at least I do. So yes, it is based on my experiences. And in that sense autobiographical.'

The reporter was just not getting the juice in the story. Her boss was getting antsy. Krish could see him, shifting around. The interns could see the train wreck and busied themselves with something else. The reporter threw in one last Hail Mary.

'So you haven't loved and lost like Rehan?'

'I have. I think love stories work best when the writer has felt pain. Unbearable, unfathomable, deep pain, like you're sinking to the bottom of the ocean. Only then do you understand the value of hope, right?'

The reporter was beat. Krish had taken every question and turned it into an answer about her craft. There was just no gossip to be had. The interview was terminated shortly after. Krish read the interview a few days later in the newspaper with a photo of her and Mahi posing at the award ceremony, along with an image of her book. She imagined, for a moment, Mahi reading the paper. Did Mahi, who knew the truth about many of the characters' origin stories, laugh at Krish's deflection? Had she also felt the unbearable, unfathomable, deep pain when they were apart? Krish wondered, knowing she would probably never know.

Mahi read the interview. She had loved the book and was happy to see it doing so well. Krish's story used magical realism and their own love story to weave a beautiful, compelling narrative that had moved millions across the world. It was still on the New York Times bestseller list. Mahi was happy for Krish and sad for both of them.

She was sitting on her bed reading the news on her phone. Mahi loved her bedroom—it was her private domain. She snuggled into the soft, warm sheets as she read about Krish talking about her book, her craft. As Krish had imagined, that one line stood out: 'Unbearable, unfathomable, deep pain, like you're sinking to the bottom of the ocean.' It was as if Krish had said that for her. Little did Krish know or understand the vast sea of loneliness that had been Mahi's life. The unbearable pain that had made her want to kill herself. Krish had her righteous anger, but Mahi couldn't even share her grief with anyone. Everyone thinks they know stars if they follow them on Instagram. But Mahi knew the truth and her deep wells of sadness were hers and hers alone. She shared that part of her life only with Kabeer and Karan. But Ma had discerned it at their dinner the other day. Ma, whose capacity to love always amazed Mahi, had understood her grief.

Her phone rang. But she wasn't ready for the rest of the world yet. No, she decided to stay in bed a little longer. This was cosy. She burrowed into her blanket as she continued to scroll through her phone to look at the photo of Krish and her smiling at each other at the Big B Book Awards. She loved how Krish was looking at her. She remembered how often Krish used to look at her like that when they were younger. Mahi had learnt from Krish and Ma what it was love unconditionally. They had loved her for who she was and not who she was going to be. Those were such wonderful happy days. These past ten years had probably been the most fulfilling of her career and also the most empty. People were often jealous of her success. Mahi would give this up in a heartbeat if that meant she could go back and change the past. She sighed.

Mahi knew now that she had hurt Krish irreparably. She had wanted to make things up with Ma and Krish over dinner. She knew Ma had wanted that too, but clearly Krish didn't want it. Mahi knew that Krish felt that Mahi had abandoned her, but that wasn't true. If only she knew.

10

‐∕∣∖‐

MAHI HAD CRIED, BEGGED, BAWLED, PLEADED AND grovelled in front of her mother and brothers. 'Please, Mummy. Please. I need Krish. I can't live without her. I beg you. Please.'

All she wanted to do was go to Krish. They wouldn't let her leave the house. Every day Mahi stared at the walls of her room. She had no phone. They wouldn't let her talk on the phone. They dropped her to school and picked her up. They monitored her e-mail and her postal mail. They had imprisoned her.

Mahi had heard her brothers talking to her friends, asking them to report any sort of issues at school. They had spoken to the principal and the teachers. They had painted Krish as a crazy, obsessed, unhinged stalker. While they never mentioned that she was a lesbian, they had hinted at it. Now everyone looked at Mahi oddly in school. She remembered their eyes, them shaking their heads as they whispered behind her back.

Mahi begged her friends to let her use their phone. But they were worried about the teachers, the principal and her brothers. Heck, even the peons didn't help her. Mahi had become a ghost in a shell. She cried. Every night her brothers warned her that if she kept this up, they would just stop her from going to school. One day, a peon took pity on her and gave her his phone. She quickly texted Krish. 'I'm being held prisoner. Can't talk. I love you.'

Krish came right over to her school to talk to her. Mahi saw Krish being thrown out of her school compound by her principal. People were hurling abuses at her. The security guards was roughing her up. Something broke in Mahi that day. She didn't care what was happening to her, but she didn't want Krish to suffer her fate.

She knew that if she talked to Krish, she'd say that they should run away. And that was all Mahi wanted to do. But she was scared. Scared her brothers would find her and kill them both. These things happened. Mahi had read news stories of lesbians and gays being murdered all over the country. She wasn't going to let that happen to Krish. Mahi wasn't worried about her own life. She had decided to kill herself. She knew she didn't want to live without Krish.

At home, Mahi went on a hunger strike. She refused to have dinner that night. Her mother had slapped her across the face, something she had never done in her whole life. Mahi looked at her mother, stunned, her cheeks stinging from the slap. She knew how much her mother valued her face and her flawless beauty.

'Mummy, please. I can't live without Krish. Please, Mummy.'

'And then what? Who is going to give you a role in their movie? Who will hire a lesbian?'

'I can get a job, Mummy. I will pay you my whole salary. Whatever you want.'

'A job? Salary? Are you serious? I've worked my whole life to give you the chance to become the number one heroine in India. Acting lessons, dance lessons, your fancy school … what was all that for? And you want a lowly job? Who is going to give you work? You haven't even finished college.'

Mahi begged, 'Please, Mummy. Please.'

'Listen, Mahi. Give it a few months. You will soon forget her. Imagine the life in store for you. Imagine everyone in India will know your name. They will sing your songs. Don't you want the world to love you?'

Later that night, Mahi had heard her mother talk to her brothers. 'I don't know how long we can keep this up. We need to find a solution to this Krishna problem.'

'I'll go fix that lesbo right now.'

'Don't be stupid. I don't want this to become a police issue.'

'But, Mummy, it is a criminal act. We can contact the police,' the other brother offered.

'You're such a duffer. They will ask who the other girl is. I can't risk such a stain on Mahi's career.'

'So then what should we do?' the older brother asked.

'Listen, just go threaten Krishna and her mother. And find out when she is heading to New York.'

∼

If it hadn't been for Karan, her mother would have started peddling her to directors and producers using any means possible. *Any means possible.* Mahi shuddered at the thought.

At one of those *filmi* parties that her mother forced her to attend, Karan came into her life like a knight in shining armour. He was gay and understood what it meant to be gay in India. Karan understood her like no other. He had truly saved her. The night Karan met Mahi, she had been planning to kill herself. It was the same night that Krish had left for the US. Mahi knew Krish had probably waited for her at the airport. But she had had no way of communicating with her. No way of running away. So she had decided to end it all. She hadn't told anyone. Whom could she tell, anyway? Maybe he saw it in her eyes. He pulled her aside to talk to her.

'Aunty, do you mind if I take Mahi out for a drink?' Karan asked her mother so sweetly, they felt compelled to say yes. How could they refuse Karan Raichand, the big director and producer? He was the kingpin of Bollywood.

At the bar, he ordered two glasses of wine and said, 'Talk, young lady.' Mahi hadn't been without her mother and brothers in forever. She felt like she could finally breathe for the first time in months. 'Can I please borrow your phone? I need to make a phone call,' were the first words out of her mouth.

She looked at her watch. Maybe she could still catch Krish. She dialled the number and waited. But the phone was switched off. Krish had left.

'Shit.' She had hoped to talk to Krish one last time before she killed herself. She felt so alone in that moment. So helpless.

'What happened? What's going on?' Karan asked.

Mahi started crying, and once she started she found that she couldn't stop. She sobbed and sobbed and told him the whole story. Karan would have asked her what most gay people get asked: 'Are you sure it's not a phase?' But something in her eyes told him that was useless. It was not a phase. Mahi was a lesbian as much as Karan was gay.

'Look, I can help. But right now Krish can't be part of your life. It's a crime in India. You will get into trouble. She can go to jail. You know your mother will do that in a heartbeat. You said she is on her way to New York, right?'

Mahi nodded, tears streaming down her face.

'Let her go study. And then maybe once you've made enough money, you can join her.'

In a world where she was all alone and without hope, Karan's idea came like a ray of light. It wasn't much but it would do for now. Mahi clung to it. Once she made enough money, she could join her. It marked a turning point in Mahi's life. Now her focus became work. She gave her everything to it.

He signed her up for his upcoming movie.

'Mahi, the movie won't start until next month but we are sending you to a body and exercise camp for a few weeks. It will get you away from your mother.'

'Yes, please.'

Mahi started working in earnest.

≈

'Are you excited?' her mother asked.

Mahi looked up from the book she was reading, *An Actor Prepares*.

'Your *mahurat* is tomorrow. I'm so excited for you, beta. This is a dream come true. Have you decided what you're wearing?'

'*Your* dream come true,' Mahi said in her head.

'Yes, the production team has finalized all of it,' she said out loud and went back to her book.

'Maybe I should come with you to these meetings. You need my help. I have lots of experience dealing with these people,' Sujata offered.

Mahi put down her book. She and Karan had talked about handling this. 'Mummy, I explained this earlier. Karan doesn't like it. Do you trust him?'

'Of course, beta. I know you're safe with Karan. But still … I'm your mother. I want the best for you. You need someone looking out for you.'

Mahi sneered. *You want the best for me? Are you sure?* Mahi silently challenged her. The venom in Mahi's eyes left her mother speechless. Mahi just got up and went into her room.

≈

Her mother tried to put these thoughts away the next day as she got ready for her daughter's mahurat. It was going to be one of the best days of Sujata's life. Sujata, her two sons and their wives got dressed and came out.

'Where is Mahi?'

'She left early morning,' the servant replied.

'Today? What work does she have today?' Sujata wondered.

≈

Mahi was with Karan lounging in plush chairs and sipping champagne. They were getting a manicure together.

'It's the mahurat of your film today.'

'Yes?' Karan arched his eyebrow, with the your-point-being expression.

'Well, how come you're not handling all the calls and last-minute preparations?'

'Because I have Akash.'

'Akash? Your personal assistant?'

'Yes. The key to a successful career is a great personal assistant.'

'Hmm … that's good to know.'

'Are you excited?'

'Honestly? I don't mean to sound ungrateful—because I truly am grateful—but Karan, I just miss her. I keep thinking about reaching out to her. But I'm scared my family will find out. I just found out that her mother had come to visit mine and it didn't end well. Krish is safe in New York City but I'm worried that if I contact her, they'll take out my anger on Ma.'

'Mahi, darling, listen. You have to choose between Mahi and Mahek. You need success to become independent and you can't be successful without fully committing to Mahek. In some crazy way, you have to kill Mahi and become Mahek. And once you've become a star, you can give Mahi her happy ending.'

Mahi nodded. From that day on, Mahi forgot all about her previous life and focused on becoming the superstar Mahek Singh. Of course it had turned out to be quite profitable for both Mahek and Karan. Mahi was talented and strategic. As soon as she got her second paycheque, she moved out of her mother's house. By her fourth movie, she had bought her own house. Her movies did well and she quickly earned spots with famous directors. She moved from the actress dancing around her heroes to meatier roles that showed off her acting chops. Mahi worked hard for every role. Directors often talked about how they had never worked with an actor who worked harder than Mahek Singh.

When her brothers had children, she visited them in the hospital with her lawyer. The brothers and their families had to sign non-disclosure agreements and terminate all relations with Mahi. In return, Mahi made a fixed deposit of Rs 10 crore for each child. They glared at her, but thought about the money and signed it. She never saw them again.

It was justice, no doubt. But it left Mahi all alone in the world.

11

~/|\~

FOR KRISH, EVENTUALLY, THE FUSS OF THE AWARDS DIED down and what had been a deluge of calls and e-mails become a manageable trickle. After her blow-up with Mahi, Krish hadn't bothered calling the agent to discuss the Raichand Group offer. No, Krish was done with all that. She decided to focus on her writing and let her agent handle the movie rights.

Her agent had set up a few talks at writing groups and communities—some had serious aspiring writers and some had housewives with a lot of spare time and some inclination. Krish didn't mind. Ideas were democratic—they could come from anyone. Honing that art was critical and if her talk inspired someone to take their writing more seriously, or see it in a different light, she was happy about it. She was surprised at how well they paid and liked talking about writing as a craft to young, aspiring writers.

Life went on. Ma and Krish spent a couple of weeks of the summer together. Krish tried to forget the brief interlude in which Mahi had come into her life again. All she had were the photographs from those days. She often found herself looking at them. One day Krish got a call—she was being offered a yearlong free membership to the Soho Club, the hip new spot for artists and writers and everyone in the field of art. Krish would have said no, as she did to every other such offer she got, but she hesitated with this one. Hadn't she read somewhere that Mahi worked out at this club sometimes?

'All right,' she said. 'Sign me up.'

'Yes, of course, ma'am. When would you like to tour the premises?'

'How about today? I'm not doing anything interesting.'

Krish and Ma went for a tour of the place. The membership was expensive but Krish figured she would be back in the US in a few months and could cancel it then. When Krish saw the place, she actually liked the working spaces they had made that could be collaborative, but she could also be completely isolated. Krish had been finding it difficult to get any reading or writing done at home, with the constant interruption from aunties, delivery boys and *doodh* and *bhaji walas*.

'This is nice for work. What do you think, Ma?'

'It's very fancy.'

'But free, na?' Krish winked at Ma. Ma rolled her eyes.

'I like the exercise room they have downstairs. I can book it and do my taekwondo there in peace, with no interruption and no outside company. I like that idea.' Krish nodded, thinking how hard it had been for her to do her forms or her kicks at Ma's house or in the community compound.

The person in charge was explaining that in return for the year's free membership, they would use her name and photograph in their promotional material and that she had to be seen working at the club at least twelve times in the year. Krish shrugged. She put the manager in touch with her agent and once they had sorted everything out, he sent her the documents to sign at her house. Within a few days she became a member of the Soho Club. She was there almost every day. She worked out in the mornings and went home, where she showered, had food with Ma and then headed back to write in one of those isolated cubicles. Sometimes people came to chat with her. She was always polite but indifferent. The only person she did respond to was the seventeen-year-old girl, Anaya, whose book she had signed at the award ceremony. Anaya and Krish corresponded regularly now. Anaya had sent some of her writing to Krish, who had then offered some constructive criticism on it. Some days Anaya came to the Soho Club and worked on her writing with Krish. The two of them would sit next to each other and type away. One day as they sat drinking chocolate milkshakes, after putting in a good evening's work, Krish sighed. Anaya reminded her of herself at seventeen. Without the butch lesbian vibe.

'Do you want some chips?' asked Anaya, motioning at the waiter.

'Like French fries?'

'Yes, like potato chips.'

'Uh-huh.' Krish wasn't sure what exactly she was getting but was fine either way. In the US, when she ordered potato chips, she got potato wafers. Or at least that's what they called them in India growing up. Sometimes it was hard to remember what was what in all the code-switching between the two countries. Krish shrugged. Potato in all its forms was fine with her. Especially fried. But she was even more thankful when what did come out on a plate were French fries.

'Ah, potato chips!' Krish smiled and reached for one with tomato ketchup.

'How's your book coming along?' Anaya asked, munching on a fry.

'I think it's going OK. It changes and evolves. I am a pantser, so I have some plot, but mostly I just write by the seat of the pants. Some days I follow the story along a rabbit hole. Some days I steer it to the shore.'

'What day was today?' Anaya asked curiously, her eyes keen.

'I'm not sure. You want to read and tell me?' Krish offered.

Anaya looked flabbergasted and ecstatic at the same time. 'Uh, yeah!'

Krish opened her laptop and pressed Print and Anaya ran to the printer. She picked up the four pages that had printed up and sighed happily.

'I can't believe it. I get to read a work in progress of Krish Mehra. How cool is that!'

'You can't tell anyone, OK?' Krish looked at her seriously. Krish didn't usually share her work in progress with anyone but she felt like she had gotten to know and trust Anaya over the past few days.

'Yes, of course. I promise,' she said and sat down to read.

After about twenty minutes, she emerged. She looked at Krish with complete adoration. 'Oh my god! Wow! I mean, I totally didn't understand how any of this relates to your story or what your story is, but what a great rabbit hole to go down through. I loved it.'

Krish smiled and took the papers from Anaya. As she put them in her satchel, Anaya asked, 'So how does this relate with your story? Will it end up in the book? What do you do to all the stuff you write that doesn't end up in the book?'

'I have a document called "Manuscraps". I put all the extra stuff in it. Some time after publication of the book, I open my Manuscraps and read them to see if there is any interesting idea. This book stemmed from one of those manuscraps. I'm not sure where it will lead me. But so far I'm enjoying the process.'

'By the way, can I tell you how much I love the name Manuscraps? I am totally copying it.'

'You can "totally copy" it because I "totally copied" it from someone else,' Krish said using air quotes, and grinned.

'So you don't plot your story at all?' Anaya wondered aloud.

'I usually have a general idea as to where I want to go and a little of how I want to get there. But that changes sometimes.'

'So this new book, it's a period drama, right? I mean, there were bows and arrows and princesses.'

'Yes, I think so.'

'I promise I won't tell anyone,' said Anaya with sincerity.

'All right. Anyway, I should go back home now. My mother will be waiting for me.'

'Will you be here tomorrow? Can I come work with you?'

'Don't you have homework?' *Do kids nowadays not have the same amount of homework,* Krish wondered. She was buried in her books all evening when she was in school.

'I wake up early in the morning to finish it, so I can come work with you after school. I spoke to my mom. She said that as long as my grades don't slip, she's fine. And my father likes that it's here … in public.'

Krish could tell that Anaya felt embarrassed by her dad's outdated ideas and thoughts. Krish's face fell a little and she tried to hide it, but Anaya caught a glimpse of it.

'I ... I explained to them,' Anaya stammered, trying to clarify. 'I explained to them that I have never got a predatory vibe from you. You're just not like that.'

'There is a difference between being gay and being a paedophile. Your parents know that, right?' Krish frowned, shaking her head.

'Of course, of course. I just ...' Anaya was close to tears. She didn't know how to handle this.

'Don't worry,' Krish said, mellowing as she saw the kid freaking out. 'It's OK. Just makes me appreciate Karan a little more.' Thinking about all the trolling Karan Raichand had endured for so many years because he couldn't hide who he was from the public.

'Who?' asked Anaya, confused.

'No one,' said Krish as she placed the brown satchel on her shoulder and started towards home. That evening, Krish went for Thai with her mom to a restaurant near their house.

'Ma, when we were younger, this place was an Indian restaurant, right?'

'It's been an Indian restaurant, a Chinese restaurant, a pizza parlour ... Last year it was a Mexican restaurant. And now it's Thai.'

'Considering this food, I think next year it will be something else.'

'Maybe Indian again!' They both laughed.

On some evenings they had roadside chaat. The days soon became weeks.

One day, right after her taekwondo session, her face flush from the workout, her muscles feeling the burn, Krish headed out and there, in the hallway, she saw Mahi in workout clothes headed to the main gym. Mahi smiled when she saw her and nodded before she went in through the doors that led to the gym. Krish had stopped breathing. She hesitated, wondering if she should go in and talk to Mahi. She walked in the direction of the gym but at the last minute turned around and walked out.

≈

Summer was almost over and it was almost time for Krish to start heading back to the US, back to her own life, her own routine, her own shower. Krish thought about the heavenly water pressure and how she didn't really think about being grateful for such small things in the US.

When Krish came home from her writing session at the Soho Club that evening, Ma was waiting for her. She was in the mood for pani-puri tonight. Krish quickly put her work stuff away and they headed out. As they waited for their turn with the pani-puri seller, Ma got particularly chatty. 'How is your work with that kid?'

'Anaya. It's good. She's a quick learner. I think her writing has improved greatly.'

'Good. I am glad to see you work with others. Sometimes I worry about you.'

'Why, Ma?' Krish asked as she popped a pani-puri into her mouth.

'You shut out the world. You retreat into your head and you make no friends. You don't go out. You do nothing besides taekwondo. Even that you do alone. It's not good to be so isolated, Krishi.'

'The world sucks, Ma.'

'No, it doesn't. And I know you don't think it sucks either. You know how I know that? Because your book has a happy ending. In the end, the lovers find a way.'

Krish said nothing. She just smiled.

'You know, Krish, I can't wait for it to be a movie. I can't wait to watch it in the theatre and see Mahi in it. Are you going to work on the screenplay? Maybe that will get you talking to people. You need to work with people, beta. All this alone time is not good.'

'I haven't decided. We have an offer from a Hollywood studio.'

'Arre, what do those Hollywood studios know about a desi love story?'

'But the money is good. I doubt Karan Raichand can offer that.'

'You never know until you ask, right? Besides, he has something that those studios will never have.'

'What?'

'Mahi! I know it's stupid, but I can't see anyone but Mahi play the role of Meher.'

'Ma ...' Krish groaned.

As they walked home, her mother felt a bit unsteady on her feet. Krish took her hand and guided her. Later that night, when Krish and her mother watched TV, her mother complained about a headache.

'Take some medicine,' Krish said and went over to get a glass of water for her mother. When she came back, her mother was writhing on the floor.

12

⁃╱╿╲⁃

MA WAS ON THE FLOOR CONVULSING. KRISH LOOKED AT her mother in shock as she ran to her. 'Ma, Ma! What happened?' Krish knew she had to act soon. But, gosh, she didn't even have Ma's doctor's number. And she couldn't call 911. How does one call an ambulance in India? Shit. Why didn't she know such basic stuff? Should she call a hospital? Or call her mother's doctor? Could she look up his phone number on the internet? Her mom was on the floor in excruciating pain and Krish felt so fucking helpless. She quickly took her mom's phone and started searching for her doctor's number. As she went down to find Dr Mahesh, she found Mahi. Without thinking, Krish dialled her number. Mahi picked up on the first ring. 'Mahi, Mahi! Ma … She's having a seizure, I think. Mahi, help … Please.'

'Move her to her side and I'll send an ambulance right over.'

Krish moved her mother to the side. She knew that. Why hadn't she thought about it? And in a few minutes, Mahi called back. 'Ambulance is on its way. It will take you to Lilavati Hospital. I'll meet you there, but don't ask for me.'

In a moment Krish's world had turned upside down. The rest of the evening was a blur. The ambulances, the doctors, the intake. Ruchi, Mahi's assistant, was there taking care of paperwork, the money and the deposit. The doctors started work on Ma. They started an IV and ran tests. Krish waited as if in a trance. Minutes became hours. Krish waited alone, anxious. She messaged her friends on the group chat and let them know. They were shocked but offered positive thoughts. Krish felt so hollow in that moment. She knew her friends couldn't help. Heck, Krish barely knew how to help her mom. Eventually, a team of three doctors came out and spoke to her. Mahi magically appeared by her side as the doctors sat them down. Krish realized in that moment that she was getting this five-star treatment because of Mahi. She was extremely grateful for it. But right now she couldn't think about any of that.

Right now she focused on the doctors present.

'Right now what we know is that the patient,' the doctor checked his chart again, 'Mrs Mehra, has suffered a seizure. Her brain may have sustained damage from the loss of oxygen during the seizure. We're not sure of her prognosis at this point but we are monitoring the situation. We've intubated and sedated her.'

'What could have caused the seizure, doctor?' Krish asked.

'It could be a stroke. Or a malignant glioma or meningioma. We're not sure at this point. Once the patient comes to, we will run some more tests and re-assess the situation. We will have our neurologist, Dr Vikas Shah, take a look at her tomorrow as well.'

'Dr Vikas Shah?' Mahi stepped in. 'Isn't Dr Nalin Pandey available?' Dr Nalin Pandey was a world-renowned neurosurgeon based in Mumbai.

'Dr Pandey has his daughter's wedding. He won't be coming in for a few weeks.'

'I see.' Mahi glanced at Ruchi and she started typing away on her phone.

'The overnight shift will monitor the situation closely. We will come back around 10 a.m. and check on her. And give you our next update.'

'Thank you, doctor,' Mahi said.

'Yes, thank you, doctor,' added Krish. She got up but the doctors were focused on Mahi.

'It's a pleasure, Ms Mahek. Can we ... can we please get a selfie with you?' one of them asked sheepishly.

'Yes, sure.'

Mahi led them outside and took selfies with doctors, nurses and several hospital staff members.

After a few minutes, Mahi walked back into the room. Her eyes were gentle.

'Thank you so much for everything, Mahi,' Krish gushed. 'I am so sorry for calling you. But I had no one else to call. I didn't even know her doctor's number. I am sorry for involving you in all this. I know it's not your problem ...'

'Krish Mehra, don't ever say that. Ma is as much my mom as she is yours.'

'Still, we had fought. I had no right to call you.'

Mahi assured her that she was really glad Krish had called and that she could help her in some way. She could see Krish was feeling rather raw and emotional with this turn of events. She stepped closer and Krish just crumbled into a heap in her arms. She started sobbing. 'I am so scared. I don't want to lose her. What will I do without her?' Krish cried.

'Hush ... Nothing will happen to Ma, OK? You have to keep faith.'

Mahi led her to a small couch that pulled out for the family of the patient. Mahi put her hand around Krish's body and held her, rocking her back and forth. Krish whimpered softly. Mahi wanted to make it all right. For her, for Ma.

'Don't worry, Ishq. Whatever it is, we'll handle it together, OK? I'm in Mumbai the next few days. I'll be a phone call away, OK? Look at me, Ishq, look at me.'

Krish was crying.

'What is this? Every time I see you, you're crying?' Mahi joked, trying to add some levity to the situation.

Krish laughed through her tears at the joke and stopped crying. 'It's just ... I feel so useless.'

'Don't worry, I've got this. I've done this with my mother, remember? I know the lay of the land.'

Krish felt grateful and guilty at the same time. She said, 'You don't have to do this.'

'Don't worry. I'm not doing it for you. Ma asked me.'

'Wait, what?' Krish's eyes were wide with shock.

'Your mother ... remember when I came to your house and she sent you to get paan from the neighbourhood paanwalla?'

'Ah ha! I knew you guys were up to something.'

'She made me promise that if anything happened to her, I would be there for you. And I'd take care of you. And ...'

'And what, Mahi?'

Mahi said nothing. She wouldn't make eye contact. 'Mahi? What is it?'

'She made me promise her we'd get back together again ...,' Mahi added hastily, 'As friends.'

Krish shook her head and smiled, amazed at her mother. 'Why were you scared of telling me that?'

'The last time I met you, you said you hated me,' Mahi said softly. How much she hated hearing that. It had been hurting her ever since.

I wasn't wrong. Loving you wasn't wrong. You were wrong for leaving me. You were a coward. You are still a coward. I hate you, Mahi. I hate you.

'I'm sorry I was so angry the last time … we …' Krish started. She was embarrassed.

'It's OK.' Mahi got up and picked up her Prada bag, getting ready to leave.

'Mahi,' Krish reached for her wrist and held it. 'Mahi, stop. Please listen. I didn't want to stop talking or go our separate ways. I was happy to talk to you. To see you. I just … I needed to say things too. It doesn't mean …'

Just then Krish's phone rang. Mahi saw it was Allie. She looked Krish in the eye and said, 'Take it.' And left the room.

When Krish was done talking to Allie, she got out of the room and saw Ruchi. 'We have a car to take you home,' she said.

'No, it's OK. I can get an Uber.'

'No. Mahek Madam has arranged it. The driver will park the car at your house while you pack your clothes and he will bring you back to the hospital. He will stay with you from now on. He has a phone and can contact me at any point if you need to get in touch.'

'I see,' said Krish.

The ride home was quiet. When Krish opened the door to her house, she realized how much silence there was. The house felt odd without Ma's presence. Krish packed her bags and went back to the hospital. She couldn't sleep. She got her phone out and texted Mahi, thanking her for arranging the driver. Krish held the phone between her ear and her head as she contemplated a follow-up to Mahi's 'you're welcome' reply. She took a deep breath and wrote, 'Your thoughtfulness never ceases to surprise me.'

Mahi didn't reply. Krish waited for a response. She updated her friends about the situation with her mom and eventually fell asleep.

~

'Krish, sweetheart. Wake up.' Krish woke up to Mahi nudging her gently. Krish looked startled. Her first question was if Ma was OK. Mahi patted her and calmed her down. She assured her that everything was fine and pushed her off to brush her teeth and comb her hair, so that she was ready to talk to the doctors on their morning rounds.

'Shoot, It's 9 a.m. already?' Krish said, looking at her phone to check the time. There were messages waiting for her. She'd check them later. 'Thanks for waking me up. I couldn't fall asleep last night.'

Krish looked so scared and dishevelled. Mahi resisted the urge to run her fingers through her short hair. When Krish got ready and came out, she saw that Mahi had got her breakfast. Krish was really touched. By the time Krish finished her sandwich, the doctors came. Her mother was still not responding, but they would run tests today to figure out what had happened.

'What does this mean?' Krish looked worried. Mahi reached for her hand. Just then the door opened and Dr

Pandey walked in with his team. He was a tall, bald man with a commanding presence.

'Hello, Mahek.' He went straight to her. 'I am Dr Pandey … We spoke last night.'

'Thank you so much for coming, Doctor. I really appreciate it. This is my childhood friend, Krish Mehra. Ma, Mrs Mehra, is her mother. But she raised us both. She's like a mother to me. So we really appreciate your coming here to help us.'

Krish shook the doctor's hand too. 'Thank you so much, Doctor. You have no idea how grateful I am you've decided to take our case.'

'Ms Mehra, may I call you Krish?'

Krish nodded.

'Krish, we will give it our best shot, OK? Please don't worry. Once Mahek Singh called, I told my wife that I have to do this. My team is going to get started on tests and we will keep you updated every six hours. All right? You're in safe hands now. I've got your mother.'

And saying this, Dr Pandey and his team left the room.

Mahi was about to leave too, when Krish said, 'Mahi, please listen to me. Thank you so much for everything. You have been a life-saver. When I called you—I called you because you were the only person I knew, whom I could trust. I didn't realize that Mahek Singh and all her superstar powers came with it. I wasn't trying to take advantage of you. I hope you know that.'

Mahi nodded.

'I am truly grateful for all your help. Especially for getting Dr Pandey here. I don't know what strings you pulled, but I couldn't have done it.'

'Krish, stop. I told you, I promised Ma I'd be there.'

'I'm just saying thank you. That's all.'

'And I'm saying she's my Ma too.'

Mahi picked up her handbag and headed out the door. 'I'll come this evening. If there is any update, they will text me, but you can call too. OK?'

≈

Krish spent the morning updating several relatives, her Mama and Masi and other sundry kin and all neighbourhood aunties. They had moved Ma back to the room, so Krish could see her, but she was still sedated. She looked so frail. That afternoon Krish spent figuring out the costs and deposits that Ruchi had made on her behalf. She knew Mahi would never bring up money. But she could afford to pay for Ma's care. She didn't need Mahi's help there. Ma had invested wisely and Krish had made some money from her novel. And worst case, she would sell the rights to the book for getting the money up front.

≈

That evening, Dr Pandey gave them the bad news. 'It's an experimental procedure. Still very new. And expensive. But I think it's our best chance to get to the glioma—the brain tumour.'

'What are the chances of survival?' Krish asked nervously, tapping her foot. Mahi reached over and put her hand on Krish's lap. Krish gripped her hand and squeezed it.

'It's low. About 5 per cent. But this is her best shot. We don't have too many choices in the current situation.' He was gentle, breaking the news kindly.

'What about chances of recovery?' Mahi asked.

'If we are successful, she could make a full recovery. But it all depends on how much of the tumour we can get out successfully—we will only know that once we go in. If we can't get it all out, we will have to follow an aggressive radiation treatment. I've studied her CT scans, PET Scans and MRI results, and I think it's worth a shot. I know this is a lot to take in. And I'm sorry about that. Why don't you think about it tonight? We're going to lower her dosage so she will be conscious shortly. I would suggest you talk to her. Once you make a decision, just notify my team and we'll make a plan for the operation. But it will have to be soon. I can't take many more days—my daughter will kill me.'

After this, Dr Pandey spoke to Mahi in hushed tones. They looked at Ma and at Krish. Then she thanked him and he left.

≫≪

'What was that about?' Krish was curious.

'He said that if we need to say our goodbyes, we should. You know, just in case. The survival rate is low. So we need to prepare ourselves.' Mahi knew Krish would appreciate the truth.

Krish was silent for a bit. Then she said, 'Can you imagine a world without Ma? Because I can't. I mean, how does such a world exist?'

'I know, Krish, I know. It's not easy. But I'm here, OK?' Mahi held her.

'You know, I barely knew my father. I mean, I have faint memories of him. I am not even sure if they are real or imagined. My Ma was my everything. She was my sun and my moon. She was my constant, my North Star. First Pa, then you and now Ma. Everyone is leaving me. How does one live all alone? I don't want to be all alone.'

Mahi had tears running down her face. 'You're not alone. You're never alone, Ishq. I am here for you.' She held Krish and they stayed like that for a long time. There was nothing else to say.

13

━━━

THEY WERE BOTH ASLEEP WHEN MA CAME TO. BUT MAHI woke up immediately. She called for the nurse at once. Krish woke up too.

'Ma, Ma. Are you OK?' Ma looked at Krish. She gave her a weak smile and nodded. Words were hard. She looked at Mahi and Krish.

Mahi came forward. 'I've got her. Don't worry. I'll take care of her. Just like I promised.'

Ma smiled. Then she rested.

━━━

Mahi said, 'I'll tell Dr Pandey we'll do the surgery.' She left soon after. Krish spent part of the night talking to her mother, holding her hand. Allie called later that night. Krish left the room to talk to her on FaceTime. 'I'm so sorry, Krish. I wish I could be there with you.'

'It's OK. We'd both be pretty useless with the Indian method of doing things. I can't make head or tail of most processes.' Krish smiled weakly.

'I'm sure they'd be just as flummoxed by the American medical system.'

'True.'

'Anyway, like I said, I'm sorry I can't make it. But I have given Lauren and Chelsea some of my travel miles and they are heading over.'

'What? Are you serious?' Krish said excitedly. Her friends were like her family. They had seen her through thick and thin, sick and sin.

'I am.' Just then Lauren and Chelsea called from the New York airport. Krish patched them in. 'Can you believe it, bruh! We are coming to see you!'

They both sounded excited.

'Wow! This means so much to me. Thank you, all.'

Krish had tears in her eyes.

≫

The next morning Mahi arrived again with breakfast. Krish and Mahi had almost formed a routine. It felt comfortable. Like an old sweater. As they ate, Mahi said, 'I am wrapping up work early today so I can come here. We'll have dinner together?'

Krish nodded. 'Thank you. Masi is coming soon. She said she'll cover the day. So I'll go home for a bit after this. I have to get the guest room ready. Lauren and Chelsea are coming this evening.'

'Your friends Lauren and Chelsea?'

Krish nodded.

'From New York?' Mahi's eyes widened.

'Yes.'

'Are coming here this evening?' Her volume an octave higher. She was unable to hide her surprise.

'Yes. Allie couldn't make it, so she gave them some of her travel miles. They paid the rest.'

'Wow. That's very sweet. Most American friends want to come for weddings. True friends come for a parent's hospitalization.'

Krish agreed and, with a smile on her face, talked about how lucky she felt to have all this support that had come together for her and Ma. Masi, the neighbourhood aunties, her friends and, of course, Mahi. How did she get so lucky? But Mahi was thinking of more logistical issues. 'So I need to get dinner for four tonight? Do they have any dietary restrictions?' Mahi asked as she got out her phone and started tapping away.

'Right. Dinner. Yes, for four, I guess,' Krish said, scratching her head.

'Oh, did you not want me to come? Oh, right! Of course you'd want to spend time with them. I don't have to come. I can still send food over.' Mahi wondered if she had been presumptuous.

'You don't need to do that. Mahi, I'd love for them to meet you,' Krish said, now taking the lead.

'No, no. You guys probably want to catch up. What was I thinking? I can meet them tomorrow.'

'Actually, I'd rather you to meet them tonight. Tomorrow is the surgery and I'd rather you guys not meet at the hospital. I don't want any drama here,' Krish explained gently.

'Drama?' Mahi's eyebrows went up.

'They're my best friends. Don't worry, I've got your back, OK?'

'Hmm.' Mahi said nothing more but left soon after. She got her phone out and dialled Karan. 'I need your help. Where are you?'

~

Allie FaceTimed. She had sent a beautiful bouquet for Ma with a get-well-soon card. She apologized once again and wished she could have been there in person but work was hectic and she had some big deadlines looming. In reality, Krish was glad that Allie and Mahi were not in the same room together. She wasn't sure she could handle that or that her relationship with Allie could survive that. Krish shuddered at that thought. Then she heard Allie say, 'I have a new client based in Bangalore. I'll let you know if I'm coming there in a few weeks once the dates are finalized.'

Krish placated her and told her it was fine and that she didn't need to hurry. She explained that she had taken FMLA (family leave) from her university and would be here to take care of mother for her recovery after the operation. That things were all right. 'We're really lucky to get Dr Pandey working on Ma's case. He's the best in India and he's doing us a huge favour.'

Krish explained how Mahi had managed to get Dr Pandey to agree to do the surgery, even though he had taken leave for his daughter's wedding. To which Allie wondered, 'I'm still not sure how you guys are working that stuff out—especially with all that history?'

'I don't know. We're managing. It's been bumpy but we're friends now … I think. Ma wanted us to be friends again.'

'You guys are friends now? After all these years? Like nothing happened?' Allie asked incredulously. Her face was a mix of horror, anger and disbelief, topped with a lot of scepticism. 'Krish, I hope she doesn't break your heart again. I'm not sure our relationship can survive that.'

'How can she break my heart? We're not together.'

'That doesn't mean she doesn't have your heart.'

'Touché,' said Krish.

~

Later that morning, Masi arrived at the hospital. Krish was grateful to see her. When she thanked her, her Masi was quick to reply, 'Arre, you've become so American. Thanking me for coming? *Hain!* You can't thank relatives for coming. She's my sister. Of course I'd come. *Yeh bhi kya poochne vali baat hai?* Accha, now you go home and sleep. You must be so tired.'

As Krish got up to leave, her Masi called out. 'Beta, eat something, OK?'

~

That evening, Krish ran errands before heading to the airport to pick up Chelsea and Lauren.

'How are you doing?' Mahi had been texting and checking in on her every few hours. Krish knew she shouldn't get used to it, but it always brought a smile to her face. She wondered how her friends were going to react to meeting Mahi tonight. Mahi, on the other hand, was asking housekeeping questions. Krish explained that they were going to stay in a hotel but she had suggested they stay with her, at her home. That she had cleared the guest room for them.

'Do you have fresh towels and bedsheets for all of them?' Mahi asked.

'I found some in Ma's drawer. I didn't have time to go buy new stuff.'

'You pick them up, I'll have Ruchi take care of your house.'

'What's to take care? I've got it.'

'Yeah. I know,' Mahi replied but Krish could already hear Mahi typing away on her phone.

'I love it when you get this way.'

'What way?' Mahi asked. 'Like in charge, I guess. I always liked you in charge.' Krish smiled at the idea.

'If I had waited for you to do anything, we'd still be waiting now, wouldn't we?'

'That's not what I meant …. Anyway.' Krish shook her head. Just then Krish heard, 'There she is … Krishiiiiiiiiiiiiiiiiii!

'Got to go. Love you,' Krish said without thinking and disconnected the call.

≈

Mahi looked at her phone in surprise. Wait, did that just happen? Did Krish actually say 'love you'?

When they were younger and they would talk on the phone late into the night, they used to end with 'I love you' but if someone was around, they'd often just say 'Me too' and the other person would know what it meant. But what did this mean?

'What is it?'

'Huh?' Mahi looked up at Karan's curious face.

'You look like you're trying to make sense of something. And I'm guessing it's about Krish. Your *Ishq*.' Karan smirked.

'Stop!' Mahi said as she looked around.

'Don't worry, no one is around,' Karan smirked. 'I … umm … her friends have come down for her mom's surgery.'

'From New York?' His eyebrows arched in surprise.

'Crazy, right? They seem very close. Apparently, Allie gave them some of her miles since she couldn't make it herself.'

'Allie is the girlfriend, na?'

'Yeah. That seems like a big gesture, right? I mean, maybe they are serious.'

Karan tried to placate her. 'I wouldn't worry about it too much. I mean, Krish didn't even acknowledge her in her acceptance speech.'

'True. But maybe that will change after this,' Mahi wondered aloud.

'I doubt it. I'd worry about meeting her friends. When are they coming?'

'She's at the airport picking them up. I'm meeting them later.'

'Oh, drama!' Karan said, clapping his hands in excitement. Oh, how he lived for such moments.

'She said the same. Why would there be drama?' Mahi asked, baffled.

'You realize that you're the villain in her story, right? The one who spurned her. Her friends have never met you, they don't know how sweet your love story really is or how you almost killed yourself.'

Just then there was a knock on the door. Akash, Karan's very capable personal assistant, came into the room, letting him know the director was ready for the meeting. Karan postponed it by telling him to wait for a few minutes and turned his attention back to Mahi, who now looked worried.

'Right, so where were we?' Karan wanted to continue this juicy thread.

'You were telling me how her friends hate me.'

'Right. Oh, I wish I could be there tonight. You think you can record it?' Karan joked, and received a prompt thwack on his arm.

'Heyy!' He rubbed his arm melodramatically. 'Anyway, is that why you were looking surprised? That doesn't make sense.'

'No. Krish was talking to me from the airport and when she hung up, she said, "Love you." Do you think she meant it? I mean, we used to say "I love you". And I've heard her say "Love you" to her mom. So I don't know …'

'Hmm … that is tricky. It could just be old habit.'

'Do you think she actually could still …' Her voice trailed off at the idea. It was so incredible that Mahi couldn't even verbalize it fully.

'Only one way to find out, no?' Karan offered as he got up for his next appointment. 'Love you, Mahi,' he said as he left.

'Shut up, Karan!'

14

➳⟨⟨

'SHHH, SWEETHEART. IT'S SO GOOD TO SEE YOU. AND I'M so sorry about your mom's hospitalization. Just hope the surgery works out OK. We love Ma. You know, she is so awesome. So chilled out, so cool.'

Chelsea and Lauren hugged Krish tightly, conveying love, support and excitement all at once.

'Yeah, way cooler than you,' said Lauren as they started walking to the car.

'You remember that time when she came ziplining with us? Man, she was always up for fun!' They reminisced about their memories with Ma as they got to the car. The driver got Chelsea and Lauren's bags.

'You have a driver now? Since when?' Lauren looked surprised.

'This is not my driver. Mahi has appointed him for me. Temporarily.'

'Mahi? As in Mahek Singh?' Chelsea's eyebrows were touching the roof of the car.

'Shh … talk softly. I don't want a scene in the airport parking lot.'

As they got into the car, Lauren started, 'Krish Mehra, you better start explaining soon.' Lauren's dark brown eyes glared like hot coals. Chelsea's blue eyes were no better. Krish sighed. She had been dreading this. She knew they wouldn't understand the complicated history Mahi and she shared. They had only seen one side of it. Hers.

Now

Lauren had been her room-mate at New York University. She was a tennis player from Florida and had come to New York on a scholarship. They had been assigned a room together in their diversity and inclusion housing. She had heard Krish crying late into the night for the first few days. Krish didn't talk or mingle much. All first-year students were attending parties and events, and Krish was just cooped up in the room, crying. After two weeks, Lauren asked Krish, 'Are you not happy to be here? If you want to switch rooms, we can. You don't have to stay with a ...' she hesitated, 'you know, a lesbian if you don't want to.'

Krish remembered laughing for the first time since Mahi had left.

'I am gay too.' Krish felt the words leave her mouth and it was almost like doves flew out of her soul. It felt freeing—uplifting, even. 'I am gay,' she repeated.

Lauren still looked puzzled, so Krish explained, 'I'm not unhappy about being here. My girlfriend just left me. I ... I don't know how to live without her.'

'Fuck that. There will be lots of girls here. We're in the gay capital of the US—we're in New York City, baby!'

'I can't. I love her.'

Krish had tried to contact Mahi after that fateful day when they had been caught. She had tried calling her, sending her letters, reaching out to her friends at school. Krish even showed up at her school several times. But Mahi had gone incommunicado. Her brothers, however, had not. They had come several times to the house. They had threatened Krish, hit her, roughed her up and even threatened to rape her. After the first time, Krish and her mother didn't open the door. They would knock loudly, kicking and screaming outside. They cussed a lot, calling her and her mother all kinds of things. Krish remembered trembling inside and Ma holding a knife, ready to attack if they broke down the door. They changed the house arrangement so that they could quickly put a big desk against the door and hide if it ever came to that. Ma hadn't said a word to Krish. Krish was too oblivious to sense Ma's quiet support. All she cared about was seeing Mahi again. Krish had thought that, somehow, their love would prevail. That Mahi would choose her. She had gone to the airport four hours early, her eyes peeled for Mahi. Krish had waited and waited. And now she continued waiting for Mahi in New York.

Lauren would drag Krish out to parties and events. She took her to the LGBTQ alliance. There they met Chelsea at the first pride meeting. Chelsea was a smart, vivacious redhead with beautiful curls, a striking personality and a killer smile. Everyone was floored by Chelsea. They wanted to be Chelsea—they wanted to do Chelsea. Except Krish.

'Why do you not want to sleep with me?' Chelsea had asked over Brooklyn pizza slices and Mexican Coca-Cola. This was their second year at NYU and all three of them had become fast friends. Lauren and Chelsea had had a brief fling, but nothing had come of it. Lauren had moved on and was now in a serious relationship with a young Mexican grad student, an artist named Marisabel.

'Why do you like Mexican Coke?' asked Krish as she studied the glass bottle.

Chelsea looked at Krish and made a face that said, 'Don't sass me.' But she answered, 'Mexican Coke is made with real sugar. It tastes better.'

'Hmm, who knew … ' said Krish. 'I learn something new every day.'

'That doesn't answer my question!'

'Chelsea, the whole world wants to sleep with you.'

'Except you!'

'Except me. Because God figured you would need at least one friend in your life. Not an ex—because God knows you have enough of those—not a future lover waiting in line for her turn. Just a regular friend.'

'First of all, God doesn't exist. And second, why are *you* not waiting for me? Do you not find me attractive? Am I not sexy? Have you seen my sexy face? My come-hither moves.' Chelsea was acting them out, much to the amusement of Krish.

'So a) God does exist, and b) I have seen your sexy face several times. Almost daily, one might say. Either you are trying to convince me or you are actually using it on someone. And it's not …'

'It's not what? Sexy? Because it sure as hell is. What's wrong with you?'

'I am only human,' Krish grinned sarcastically.

'Exactly my point.'

'Look, Chelsea.' Krish suddenly grew serious. 'I like you, but you're not my type.'

'Your type? What you're really trying to tell me, without using her name, is that I'm not Mahi.'

Krish sighed. She took a big sip of her Mexican Coke, made with real sugar, to deflect conversation. But Chelsea wasn't letting it go. 'That is exactly why you should have sex with me. Because I'm not Mahi. She isn't here. I am. She isn't coming back ... Krish.'

'Yes, she is. Mahi loves me. I love her,' Krish said defiantly. Chelsea just shook her head.

A few months later, one evening in her dorm room, Krish saw an article about Mahi starring in Karan Raichand's latest film. She cried in the shower, put on her best jeans, and a black shirt, which hung nicely on her body. She was not wearing a bra. And she knocked on Chelsea's door.

'Let's go out tonight. You are my wingman. I need you to get me laid.'

Chelsea didn't make jokes. She didn't suggest herself. She took Krish to Henriette Hudson's and got her drunk. Once Krish was sozzled, she told her about a girl dancing on the floor. 'She's been looking at you. Want to go dance?'

'Umm .... I'm not sure. Maybe this was a bad idea.' Krish was getting cold feet. Oh god, how would she explain it to Mahi?

'Come on, you're a tiger, right? Isn't that what your mom calls you? *Sher?*'

Only with her accent it sounded like Cher. Krish chuckled. Chelsea motioned to the bartender. 'Two shots of tequila.'

She turned to Krish. 'Let's do this. I have never once failed to score. I am not breaking my streak tonight. We are both going to get laid.'

'Yeah,' Krish said, feeling pumped up.

'Fuck, yeah! Now drink up.'

Chelsea and Krish got to the dance floor. Chelsea found several women vying for her. Krish danced with the cute girl Chelsea had pointed out. Soon, the girl was grinding with her, and Krish, who had raging hormones and hadn't had sex for over a year, was ready to let loose. But Mahi. Mahi was still on her mind. But then the cute girl looked at Krish and Chelsea just happened to bump into Krish, so she was pushed into the girl. The girl took this opportunity to kiss Krish. Krish closed her eyes and kissed her back. It felt surreal and wrong. Her lips smelt different, tasted different. Her body pressed differently against hers. But kissing was good. If she had to move on, she had to kiss someone. Kissing was the first step. Krish considered it a win. She was moving on.

≈

A few months later, Krish met Noelle. Noelle was a grad student doing her MFA at NYU, and they were in a class together. Krish liked Noelle. She liked looking at her, her long legs, her long dark hair. She was different and eclectic, but not in a ditzy way. She had read books Krish hadn't even heard of. She introduced Krish to poems by Adrienne Rich and Elsa Gidlow, and books by Jeanette Winterson and Alison Bechdel. One day Krish mustered up the courage and asked Noelle if she wanted to go out for coffee. Noelle laughed. 'How about some tequila tonight instead? There is this club I go to. You might like it.'

The club turned out to be a fancy New York hotspot for artists and writers. Krish looked around in awe. 'How did you get in here?' Krish wondered out loud.

'My father has a stake in it,' Noelle said simply. That night she introduced Krish to Añejo tequila. And later her bedroom.

Noelle had her own apartment. And in a few months, Krish had practically moved in with her.

≈

Chelsea, Lauren and Krish still met regularly for lunch. 'So what's happening with Noelle?' Lauren asked one day a few months later.

'She graduates next month. But she's going to continue living in New York and is going to focus on her writing,' said Krish over Venezuelan arepas and Mexican Coke.

'If only I had so much money,' said Chelsea. Lauren and Krish laughed.

'You know, Chelsea, I'm surprised you haven't found yourself a sugar momma yet. You could totally be sailing in money,' said Lauren.

'Yuck. I am not interested in sagging boobs.' They all laughed.

≈

By the end of that summer, Noelle decided she wanted to go to Japan to find her inspiration. Their break-up was amicable.

'So Noelle is where now?' asked Lauren over Vietnamese Banh-Mis and Mexican Coke.

Krish scrunched up her face, as if to remember where Noelle was when they last spoke. 'I think she's in Bali.'

'I thought she had gone to Japan.'

'She was in Japan but she met some folks there and they were going to Bali. So she's in Bali now.'

'Oh, I bet she is loving that,' said Lauren, clearly jealous.

'Who wouldn't?' said Chelsea.

Krish just shrugged.

Lauren got serious. 'Are you not sad she's gone? You guys were together for a year or so.'

'Yeah. And I am happy she's finding herself,' Krish said nonchalantly.

'But, I mean, don't you miss her?' asked Lauren, her eyes piercing into Krish.

'I miss the sex,' Krish said, grinning, trying to deflect the question. 'And the nice apartment. I came this close to finding a sugar momma. But then I remembered the sagging boobs and changed my mind.'

They all laughed.

'I know, but you seem to feel no grief, Krish. I mean, when you first came here, you cried every day. For, like, a whole year.'

'Are you comparing Mahi to Noelle?' Krish looked at Lauren, incredulous.

'Why not? You were, in effect, with both for about a year, right?'

'Are you crazy? I was with Mahi for twelve years of my life. I had loved her for twelve years. Mahi is my soulmate.'

'There is no such thing as a soulmate,' Chelsea interjected.

'Fine. No god, no soul, no soulmate. Is there a heart? A sun? A moon? A universe? Mahi is all the stars in my sky.'

'Even after all these years?'

'Till I die.' Krish felt tears welling up in her eyes. She hadn't imagined she'd still feel so strongly about it. But when Chelsea would poke her about Mahi, she would feel this simmering rage that would threaten to burst like a volcano.

'So what about Noelle and other future relationships you may have?'

'I like women. I like sex. I am monogamous. I would never cheat on someone or hurt them on purpose. But if they are looking for a soulmate, I'm not available. Noelle wasn't looking for a soulmate. We had a good time. It was fun. It ended. We've moved on.'

Lauren looked at Chelsea, who shook her head.

'Fine.'

And they dropped it.

≫≪

Four years later, at graduation, when Ma had come over, Lauren, Chelsea, Krish and Ma had packed into a rental and gone to Niagara Falls. Krish and Ma also toured DC, Vegas, LA and San Francisco, and visited relatives in San Jose and Atlanta.

'Ma, can we go visit Savannah?

'What's in Savannah?'

'Nothing. Mahi always said she loved the way it sounded. We're so close. It's near Atlanta. Maybe I can rent a car and we can go visit?' Krish looked at Ma expectantly.

'Of course, beta. Why not?' Ma smiled sadly. She wondered how long it would take her daughter to get over her first love.

On the streets in Savannah, Krish felt like Mahi was with her, walking with her, holding her hand. Together they were roaming the streets lined with oak trees draped in Spanish moss on a blue, sunny day. Talking, laughing. Krish felt the soft, warm sun and could almost feel Mahi kissing her face, her soft, sweet kisses flooding her senses. Would she ever forget Mahi?

∽

That changed soon after she read the news of Mahi and her new boyfriend, Kabeer Agarwal. Something broke inside Krish that day. She had carried this kernel of hope that their love would prevail one day. That they would find each other and be together somehow. Even though Mahi's steady rise in the film industry had made it seem almost impossible. But when does love listen to rationale? Now, as she saw the pictures of Mahi in a bikini with her arms around Kabeer and his hot, toned body and six packs on some exotic beach, it was undeniable. Krish had been a blip in Mahi's life. Mahi had moved on. Maybe Krish had been a youthful fling, an experiment for Mahi. And while Krish had also been in a relationship since coming to the US, in her heart, Mahi was still her soulmate. Can soulmates change? Did soulmates not exist? Was Chelsea right?

Krish looked at the pictures of Mahi and Kabeer again. Anger and shame bubbled up inside her. How could she have been waiting, crying for Mahi for all these years? Mahi had not looked back a single time. She had clearly moved on, wanting nothing to do with Krish. She had broken all contact. Would she even recognize Krish today? Would she even acknowledge their friendship? Their love? Their relationship? And the answer that came from deep within was a resounding no. Chelsea and Lauren had agreed. And with their strong encouragement, Krish started a new journey, one in which she tried to move on. Really move on.

Krish opened herself to the idea of a love that wasn't Mahi. To not trying to find someone that reminded her of Mahi. Or felt like Mahi. But someone who was her own person and happy in her own existence. And it had been hard. But eventually Krish had stepped out of Mahi's shadow. Sometimes, when Krish was alone at night and saw the stars, she murmured her favourite line from the poem 'The More Loving One' by W.H. Auden. It said, 'If equal affection cannot be, let the more loving one be me.'

But Krish really did move on. Or at least she tried hard.

15

⁓⁊⁊⁓

Now, at the airport

Now that Mahi was back in Krish's life, and her two best friends Lauren and Chelsea were looking at her with eyes blazing, she had to explain. 'Well … we met on the plane.'

'What plane?'

'When I was coming to India. Remember that first-class flight that I was so excited about? Guess who was sitting in the seat next to me?'

'Krish Mehra—didn't tell us any of this.' The two women glared at her, astounded that their friend had kept such a big secret from them. 'We just saw your photos with Mahi at the award function and you said you gave her the cocksucking line.'

'Right. I did. But Ma invited her over to our house. Look, guys, I know this is not what you want to hear but she has been the reason everything has gone so smoothly with Ma. I know nothing and no one in India. And she opens doors like no other.'

'And then, after your mom's surgery? What? You go to Allie and she goes back to Kabeer?' Lauren looked at Krish intently.

'Oh, will he be coming to the hospital too?' Chelsea asked enthusiastically.

Lauren thwacked Chelsea.

'What? Come on, even you agree he's hot. I mean, they are both so hot.' Chelsea just couldn't help herself.

As they got closer to Krish's house, she explained, 'Anyway, listen. It's Ma's wish that we be friends. So, please, be nice.'

Lauren and Chelsea entered the house. It looked beautiful and not at all like Krish's house. There was a vase with bright yellow flowers in the room. The house had been cleaned. It was usually cleaned by the maid but this was better than the usual maid's cleaning. It smelt fresh and fragrant. The guest room had got new bedsheets, new towels for the girls, new shampoo, soaps and toothbrushes, and even new toothpaste.

Krish looked around. Wow! This is not how she had left it. She texted Mahi, 'Thank you. I am assuming you had Ruchi do this.'

'Ruchi got herself an assistant. But I'll tell her you liked it.'

'Liked it? I love it. I didn't even realize my house could look like this. Thanks to you, Ruchi and her new assistant.'

'You're welcome. I'll see you at 8.30 p.m.'

'You amaze me,' Krish texted. She hesitated before pressing 'send' but then pressed it anyway. Whoosh.

For a few seconds there was nothing. Krish wondered if she should have sent that text. There was no way to get it back now. Shoot, maybe it was a bad idea. Why did she care? Why was she panicking? *It's not like she's your girlfriend,* she thought.

Krish remembered what Allie had said, that she'd break her heart again. And Lauren and Chelsea had warned her of the same thing: What happens after the surgery? Do they go their own ways? Krish hadn't been thinking about Mahi and now suddenly that was all her brain was processing. When Krish wasn't worried about Ma, she was thinking about Mahi. Mahi had taken over all her thoughts. Like she was sixteen again. And she didn't need that heartbreak again. Fuck this.

Just then her phone beeped back. She quickly checked the text. It was Mahi and she had texted back, 'XOXO.' Krish got a big-ass stupid grin on her face. Shit. So much for her resolve to fuck this.

'Why are you smiling?' Lauren asked as she walked into the kitchen.

'I'm not.' Krish hurriedly put her phone away.

'It was Mahi, right? She said something sweet?'

'She *is* sweet. You should have seen the house when I left it. All this …' Krish motioned around the house, at the new pillows on the couches and the new rug in the living room and all the updates to the guest room. 'All this is her. She made it all happen in hours. Because she wanted you guys to be comfortable.'

'She's going to break your heart again,' Lauren warned.

'I'm telling you what I told Allie. We're not together so how can she break my heart this time?'

Chelsea joined them. 'What did Allie say to that?'

Krish blushed. 'She said, "That doesn't mean she doesn't have your heart."'

Lauren and Chelsea laughed. 'We knew it! Allie, my girl, she's the real deal! I knew she wouldn't fall for your BS!'

'Yeah, whatever. We'll cross the bridge when we get to it. Anyway, tomorrow is the surgery. I'll be spending the night at the hospital. Masi will be here with you tonight, OK?'

They nodded.

'Oh, by the way, Wendy sends her love for Ma too. I know she'd love to be here too but, you know, work and budgets and all, especially with the wedding planning. Anyway, I have promised her that once we get married, we'll come to India someday.'

Wendy was Lauren's fiancée. They were planning to get married in four months in Provincetown and they had both saved up for the wedding. Lauren was in real estate and flipped apartments from time to time. Wendy was an economist working at a think tank.

'That's very sweet of her. Thank you.' Krish smiled and nodded. She was thankful for her friends.

Just then the doorbell rang. It was 8.30 p.m. and Mahi was standing outside Krish's door. She had been pacing nervously for the past five minutes outside, but she'd been pacing in her mind since Krish had said 'love you' that morning. And then the text. She had panicked when she had seen the text from Krish that read, 'You amaze me.' What does one reply to that coming from your ex-girlfriend?

She sent it to Karan. 'What do I do?'

Karan called her back right away. 'Tell me everything,' he said. 'I love living vicariously through your drama. My love life is so boring!'

'Your love life is not boring. It's sweet and, come on, Karan … what do I reply to this?'

'Hmm … Can you text "Love you! I want to marry you and have babies with you?"'

'Really? Karan, her mother is in the hospital, heading into surgery. Also, you know, Kabeer!'

'Yeah, yeah. All right. How about just XOXO? Plain and simple but lovey-dovey too.'

'I'm not sure you're helping or hurting,' Mahi said, part jokingly and part sceptically as she texted it to Krish.

'You will find out later tonight, right? Oh, not tonight. Tonight her friends are going to make your keema! I will miss out on all the fun.' Karan gave an exaggerated sigh and hung up.

16

―ィↂヽ―

So HERE WAS MAHI, WITH HER THE SECURITY DETAIL
outside, as she entered the house, nervous about seeing
Krish again and scared about meeting her friends.

'Hey! Come in.' Krish's smiling face greeted her as the door
opened. 'Thanks for coming and bringing us dinner.'

Krish picked up the box from one of Mahi's guards. Oh,
right! Mahi had completely forgotten about that. The food she
had ordered and brought for these women who were going
to make her keema tonight. Mahi stepped in and removed
her scarf, sunglasses and hat and before she could say hello,
Chelsea exclaimed, 'Oh my god! Krish, you were right! She is
really more beautiful in real life. I didn't think it was possible.
But, I mean, you are!'

Lauren looked at Chelsea, annoyed for fraternizing with
the enemy. Mahi looked at Krish, who was leaning across
the door frame and shaking her head in amusement. Mahi
and Krish shared a smile as Lauren gave Chelsea and Krish a
rather stern look.

Chelsea continued, 'I mean … we still hate you for what
you did to our friend, who, by the way, is wonderful and
loving and kind and intelligent and a total catch …'

'For Allie,' Lauren interjected.

'That's right, for Allie,' Chelsea continued. 'Because, you know, she's with Allie now.'

Krish had thrown up her hands by now. 'All right, people. I think she understands.'

'Mahi, this is Lauren. She was my roommate at NYU. And this is Chelsea. We've all been best friends for the past ten years now.'

'Hello. Very nice to meet you two.'

After they all greeted each other, Mahi looked at Krish and said, 'How about we open that bottle of wine now?' She sure could do with some alcohol right about now.

'Great idea,' said Krish and went to get glasses and the corkscrew to open the wine bottle Mahi had brought along with her.

'So, what do you do?' Mahi asked Chelsea as they settled into the living room. Chelsea was wearing blue shorts and a white T-shirt. Mahi could not help noticing how her legs just went on forever.

'I work in an advertising agency. I'm a senior media planner,' Chelsea answered.

'Oh, that sounds fun,' said Mahi.

'It's fun sometimes. Most days it's just work,' replied Chelsea.

'Yeah. That's how I feel about my job too,' said Mahi.

'And I keep wondering how she can say that. When she travels to all these exotic locales,' Krish added as she walked out of the kitchen and joined the conversation. Mahi felt better with Krish around. At least there was someone to defend her.

'Yes, but then we're working there. Performing steps for some random romance number, mostly. Lots of aerial photography and wind blowing in your face. And mostly I'm just cold.'

Mahi remembered all those helicopter shots and the wind and the thin saris. Yeah, she didn't particularly enjoy much of that.

'Yeah, why is that? Why don't they have the actresses wear more clothes?' asked Lauren.

'That's what I am saying,' Mahi said, smiling. 'Maybe Hollywood should start that trend.'

'Touché,' said Krish and raised her glass to Mahi. Lauren and Chelsea couldn't help but agree.

'Umm … this wine is delicious,' said Lauren.

'Thank you,' said Mahi. 'I'm partial to wines from Napa. I got this from my personal stash.'

Yeah, she was sucking up and didn't mind winning some points that evening.

Chelsea licked her lips. 'Well, it's very good. You have great choice in wine. Not so much in lovers.'

'Speaking of which, how is Kabeer?' asked Lauren. Lauren's wrath was rather focused and her jabs were quite deliberate.

Mahi stiffened. She wondered how long this would go on. 'He's fine,' she said, and turned to Krish. 'Krish, he sends his best wishes to Ma. Both he and Karan wanted to come to meet you and Ma but I figured it would become a media circus. So I told them not to come and that you'd understand.'

Krish had stiffened too on hearing Kabeer's name. But she softened a bit after she heard Mahi. 'Thank you. That is very thoughtful of you and them. I would prefer it be about Ma. I'm not sure how to deal with your presence. I mean, I know absolutely, certainly, that Ma would want you there. But the people and their cell phones …' Krish looked like she was having trouble figuring it out.

'Don't worry. I'll be covering my hair and wearing large sunglasses. My security will be there if things get out of hand. I can't stop them from taking photos of me but hopefully it won't be too bad. We'll be waiting in the room anyway. I really want to be there the whole time, but if it gets too distracting, I'll leave and wait here. All right?' Mahi looked at Krish, wanting to make everything right.

'All right. Thank you so much, Mahi, for understanding.' Krish felt relieved. Mahi nodded, smiling. She looked at Lauren and Chelsea, who looked like they were not sure how to react to that interaction.

Soon, it was time for dinner and they all sat down to eat. Lauren and Chelsea thanked Mahi for the wonderful spread in front of them, realizing just how hungry they were.

'I'm starving too. Dig in, folks,' said Mahi, hoping maybe the tide was turning.

'So, how did you guys meet?' Mahi asked Chelsea. 'I met Krish at a pride alliance meeting. I was friends with Lauren and she told me about her roommate, who had been crying her eyes out for three months straight. She figured maybe if I slept with her, it would cheer her up and she'd forget this bitch who had broken her heart.'

Mahi almost choked on her food.

Krish came to her rescue. 'Guys … stop … Anyway, Mahi, long story short, since that day Chelsea has been trying to bed me and is a little sour that you got what she clearly hasn't after ten years of trying.'

'I see.' Mahi smiled and reached for her glass of wine.

Chelsea added, 'Honestly, Krish. After seeing Mahi, I'm wondering how you ever managed to get the most beautiful woman in India. Now that I think about it, I think I'd rather pursue *her*.'

Before Krish or Mahi could answer, Lauren jumped in. 'She's with Kabeer.' Lauren glared at Chelsea. They were clearly playing off one another and their goal was to get as many hits as possible.

'Do you bat for both teams, Mahi? Or was Krish an experiment?' Lauren asked Mahi.

Krish got tense. 'Guys … come on. I told you …'

'Mahi can answer. She does interviews for a living,' said Chelsea.

Mahi was expecting this. Though she didn't expect it to be so direct. 'Krish was the love of my life.'

'So then why did you leave her?' Chelsea asked.

'It's a complicated issue. I know I'm the villain in your story. I get that. You saw your friend gutted. But I can tell you, life hasn't been a cakewalk for me either. Sure, I am famous and have money today. But I have no life, no friends, no family. I'm all alone.'

'Except Kabeer,' Lauren pointed out.

'Yes. Except Kabeer,' Mahi said as she wiped her mouth with a napkin.

'So if you loved her, why didn't you contact her? All these years … didn't you want to know how the love of your life was?' Lauren asked again, pushing further.

'At first I couldn't because my mother and my brothers were monitoring all of my contact with the outside world. After that time had passed, I was scared. I knew I had let her down. And I couldn't bring myself to face the hate I knew she must be feeling. I also thought that maybe she had moved on. And maybe forgotten me. And I didn't want to see that either. I know I was selfish. But, honestly, it was self-preservation too. Her memories were all I had. I didn't want to taint them.'

Mahi's forthcoming confession and her sincerity touched everyone. Lauren and Chelsea looked at each other and decided to stop attacking her. As much as they hated Mahi, they had to admit she wasn't all that bad. They had another sip of the wine.

Krish looked at Mahi. Her eyes were brimming with tears but were gentle with understanding. She reached for Mahi's hand under the table, like they used to. Mahi squeezed Krish's hand and smiled.

After dinner, they sat in the living room with dessert. Mahi ate from her own bowl this time. Krish looked at her as she picked up her own bowl, and their eyes met. It was almost as if they both realized they were thinking the same thing. That Krish wanted to share her dessert with Mahi, like they always did. And that Mahi wanted the same. Krish shuddered. How were they falling into old habits so easily? Why was it so 'natural' that everything else seemed alien? Maybe Allie was right. Maybe this was going to end very badly for her.

17

~/|\~

THE NEXT MORNING, LAUREN AND CHELSEA WENT TO THE hospital with flowers and wished Ma a speedy recovery. It was an effort for Ma to speak, so she smiled and nodded. Masi and Ma spoke briefly. Masi nodded along. She was crying. Just then Mahi entered the room in sunglasses and a scarf. Masi exclaimed in excitement as she quickly wiped her tears. Mahi bent down to touch her feet and Masi could barely contain her excitement at the idea of India's number one actress doing so. She hugged her.

'*Isse kehte he sanskar*,' Masi said admiringly. Lauren and Chelsea looked at Krish for translation. 'Loosely translated,' she said, 'this is what good upbringing means.'

'Ah.' They both nodded.

Mahi went to Ma's bedside and spent a few moments alone with Ma. Krish saw her whisper a few things in Ma's ear and she stepped away to give them their privacy. Ma spoke to her for a bit. Eventually, Krish stepped up to her mother's bedside and took her hand. 'I don't know how to do this, Ma.'

Ma was serious. She said, 'Krish, I love you. I'm so proud of you. You have to promise me—don't hate Mahi any more. And be happy. Don't be so angry. Life is short. Be together.'

Krish looked at Mahi and nodded.

'I don't think I have any final words to you, Ma. Because I'll be talking to you for the rest of my life. I don't know any other way. I love you, Ma. You are everything. Promise me something, Ma. Promise me you'll stay with me forever.' Krish gently touched her mother's face.

The orderlies wheeled Ma in.

～

They waited in the room. Lauren and Chelsea shared anecdotes from their college days with Mahi. Of them looking for cake at four in the morning, of going to Niagara Falls with Ma.

'Hey, guys, I'm super hungry. Can we please go get breakfast?' Chelsea proposed.

'Yes.' Masi, who had been hanging around in the background, jumped on the bandwagon, and Lauren, Chelsea and Masi went to the hospital cafeteria. Everyone agreed it was probably not a good idea for Mahi to go down to the cafeteria too.

'Do you want us to get you anything?' Lauren asked.

'Yes, why not? We have all day to kill.' Mahi looked at Krish.

'You can go to work. You don't have to stay here,' Krish said gently.

Mahi just p@ed her and discussed breakfast options with Lauren.

Once they were gone, Mahi and Krish were alone in the room. No one said anything. Mahi picked up her phone and started replying to messages. Krish walked around a bit and then said, 'So ... what did Ma tell you?'

'Why?' Mahi looked up from her phone, an eyebrow arched.

'I dunno. Just. You both have always been so close. I think it really hurt her when you stopped talking to us.'

Mahi's eyes dimmed. She looked down at the white and beige tiled floor.

'Sorry, sorry. I didn't mean to upset you. I'm so sorry, Mahi … You've been amazing. I mean, I am truly, deeply grateful for your presence in our lives right now. You are the reason that doctor is operating on Ma right now. So who cares about what happened ten years ago?'

'You do.'

'Not any more. I can't hate you any more, Mahi. I have promised Ma. No more hate. No more anger.'

'Hmm.' Mahi liked the sound of that. A slight smile escaped her lips.

'So?' Krish prodded. 'What did Ma tell you?'

'She told me she loves me, that she is proud not only of my career but also the person I am. And asked me to take care of you …. and … she asked me to take her puja ghar … if something happened to her.'

Krish remembered the times she had sat next to her mother as she was performing puja in the mornings. Krish used to like performing puja too, like doing aarti. Like most kids, she loved the prasad. Now she imagined the puja house being moved to Mahi's house. She imagined Mahi performing the same puja. Would her kids be with her as she did so? Where was Krish in this scenario?

'Oh!'

'It's just …'

'I know. I don't believe in God.' Krish looked away. 'Is that all?'

'Yes,' said Mahi.

'Ha … OK!'

'What?' Mahi asked.

'I know there is more. I could always tell when you were lying.'

'How did you know?'

'You can be Mahek Singh all you want, but I know Mahi. The one that lives here.' Krish stepped closer to Mahi and pointed to her heart. 'That Mahi could never lie to me. I know her better than anyone else in the world.'

Mahi said nothing.

'Besides, you have a tell. You scratch your neck when you lie.'

Mahi looked up at Krish. Something in the air changed between them. Krish took one more step. This time she got into Mahi's personal space. Mahi was surprised by Krish's boldness and took a step back. Somehow, this only emboldened Krish, who took another step forward. But as Mahi stepped back again, she hit the wall. Mahi looked at Krish, her big, hazel eyes wide in surprise and anticipation, not sure what was going on in the other's mind. Krish's eyes bore into Mahi. 'So, what else did she say?' Her hand reached for Mahi's waist.

Mahi's breath hitched. 'She said she had always hoped I would come to your house as her daughter-in-law,' she whispered, looking Krish in the eye. They were so close. Krish could smell Mahi's perfume. She could feel Mahi's body heat. But hearing those words made Krish hesitate. Her face fell, her eyes dimmed. This time Mahi's hands reached for Krish's face. She gently cupped her chin, raising her face, which had sunk, as if lost in the hurt from the past. 'Ishq …'

Just then, the door opened.

18

-/1\-

LAUREN WALKED IN WITH FOOD. HER EYES FLEW OPEN AS she took in the scene playing out in front of her. She saw Mahi in her white embroidered top pinned against the wall, with Krish's hands on her waist and Mahi's cupping Krish's face. Was Mahi planning to kiss her?

'Oh ... umm ... excuse me?!' said Lauren, not sure of what to say.

Krish and Mahi quickly moved away from each other.

'Food! Yum! I am starving,' said Krish, as if nothing had happened. Chelsea and Masi entered carrying more food, oblivious to what Lauren had just seen.

Soon, everyone started eating. From time to time, Mahi caught Lauren glaring at Krish. To dissipate the tension, Mahi started a conversation with Masi.

'Masi, how is everyone at home? How is Sonia? And Manav?'

'Arre beta, they are all very good. Sonia has a six-year-old now, and Manav is soon to be engaged. We have just finalized his rishta with a girl from our neighbourhood. They were in college together. They won't believe you were here. I'll send them a photo later.'

Masi turned to Lauren and Chelsea. 'You know, these two girls were best friends. They played together all the time. All day. Play, play. I can't believe the little girl who used to play with our Krishi has now become such a big superstar!' Now she turned to Mahi. 'Beta, we love watching your films. We go as a whole family to watch your films. I tell everyone that Mahek Singh used to play with our Krishi …We are all so happy for you.'

Mahi smiled. Masi continued talking to Lauren and Chelsea as if she were educating them on the Krish–Mahi history. 'When my eldest daughter got married in Meerut, my sister and Krish came for the wedding, but Mahi came along too. We had so much fun together. *Itni dhamaal ki ke pucho mat.*' Masi looked at Krish for interpretation.

'We had so much fun. It was a blast!'

'These two girls were so close. They were like …'

'Best friends,' Mahi offered quickly before Masi could say 'sisters'.

'Like best friends. But closer. They did everything together.' Mahi's eyes darted to Krish, a deep flush rising in her cheeks. Krish was unable to make eye contact with anyone. She, too, was blushing rather furiously. Lauren and Chelsea looked at the two girls. 'Surely there is more to the story …' their eyes seemed to convey.

Masi, who was oblivious to all of this, kept going. 'They danced on *Bole Chudiyaan* from *Kabhi Khushi Kabhie Gham* … I am sure Sonia has kept the video. Mahi was so talented. Everyone who came to the wedding still remembers your dance. You were too good, beta.'

Chelsea years perked up. 'Video? Of Mahi and Krish dancing? On *Bole Chudiyaan*? Can we see it?' A mischievous smile appeared on her face.

'Haan, haan, why not? I'll message Sonia right away.' Mahi and Krish both glared at Chelsea, who was clearly enjoying their mortification. Masi left the room to call Sonia. And Chelsea couldn't resist saying, 'So, what really happened in Meerut between you two "close friends"?' Chelsea used air quotes.

'Nothing. We all just had fun. Wedding and all. It was a short trip. Just four days.' Krish was giggling now.

Mahi started giggling at the memory too. 'And?' Chelsea tapped her feet impatiently. 'Man, it was epic! We ...'

'Krish Mehra! Don't you dare!' Mahi warned. Her eyes were wide.

'Come on, Mahi. They are my best friends. Besides, it happened over ten years ago.'

Mahi folded her arms. Krish waited to see if she would object, but with nothing forthcoming, Krish turned to Chelsea and said, 'We had just gotten together. And this was our first trip together. We did it everywhere. Like rabbits. We did it on the train, at their house, in the bathroom, in the shed.'

'In the haystack,' Mahi supplied.

'Shoot, I forgot all about that one!' Krish chuckled.

'With good reason. That one was not fun. Hay is a lot more pokey in real life.' Mahi winced at the memory, remembering the red welts on Krish's back after Mahi had pushed her on the stack. Mahi had cried when she saw the welts but Krish hadn't complained. It was worth it, she had told Mahi, refusing to make her feel bad.

'We were twenty-five people in a three-bedroom house, and the kids all slept all in one line in the living room. And Mahi still managed to do it. With everyone around. It was freaking epic!' Krish was smiling so hard from the memory her cheeks hurt. 'Oh my god, and you were not discovered by anyone?'

Lauren looked horrified.

'People don't necessarily think of these things when they see two girls together,' Mahi explained.

'You forgot the rooftop terrace.' Mahi offered another memory. That bittersweet memory was special to her. Krish's eyes widened as she remembered. A soft moan escaped her lips.

Meerut, back then

'The bride looks so beautiful, no?' Mahi admired Sonia in her red wedding dress. Mahi got no response, so she turned and jabbed her fingers into Krish's shoulder.

'Answer, na?' Mahi prodded.

'Ouch, stop. I had food in my mouth. Can't you wait two minutes for an answer? No, everything has to happen as soon as Madam wishes for it.'

'Sheesh … relax … why are you being so grumpy?'

'*Kya yaar*, Mahi? You got to sleep in. I had to wake up early morning for the *grah-shanti* puja. And I couldn't tell them my girlfriend kept me up half the night.' Krish yawned. 'I'm so sleepy.'

'Tch tch, my darling. Let me get this right—your problem is that you're having too much sex … that, too, with the most beautiful girl at the wedding? People would die for such problems.'

'Come on, Mahi. We've done it six times in the last twenty-four hours. That's not human.'

'Fine. Maybe I'll find someone else.' Mahi baited her. And Krish fell for it.

'Achha, go! Go. I'll see what you find.'

Mahi wasn't wrong about being the most good-looking at the wedding. In her red and orange ghagra choli, and her shimmering dupatta, she looked resplendent. She wore long earrings but kept her neckline empty. She didn't need heavy jewellery because her luminescent skin was dazzling enough. Every eligible boy was eyeing her. Most uncles' eyes trailed after her. And most aunties wished for her as a daughter-in-law. But Krish and Mahi had been so into each other, Krish probably didn't realize it. It came as a hard slap when she did.

'Fine, I'll show you!' Mahi got up from the table in a huff and walked to the dance floor by herself. Chintu, a boy from Masi's neighbourhood, seeing the opportunity, sidled up to her and started dancing. Mahi, by this point in her life, was aware of the effect she had on men. She didn't care to use it, but she could wield her charm if she wanted to. She couldn't fathom how easy it all was. All she had to do was give a wide, doe-eyed smile and the men would do almost anything for her.

Chintu was joined by Deepu, another boy from Masi's neighbourhood. Mahi danced away seductively, her eyes on Krish, teasing her mercilessly. Krish looked at the scene unfolding in front of her. Soon several men were gyrating erratically around Mahi. Their eyes traveling all over her body. Ma was right there, as were several wedding guests, so no one tried anything untoward but Krish's face turned a beetroot red with rage. She could feel her nerves twitch. She knew she couldn't just go up on stage and snatch Mahi away and kiss her, announcing to the world that she was hers. *She loves me. I love her. We are together.* But she just watched the men try to stake their claim on Mahi. Krish felt impotent, aggravated by society and everyone around her. Her eyes narrowed and her breathing became laboured.

When the song was over, Mahi looked for Krish but she wasn't there. She was gone.

Shit! Mahi leapt off the stage, her eyes frantically searching for Krish. But now she had a bunch of boys following her. She ran towards Ma and sat down with her. The boys kept their distance, waiting, hoping …

'Ma, have you seen Krish?'

'Beta Mahi, calm down. Sit for a bit. Have some water.' Ma offered her a glass of water.

Mahi's breathing slowed. But she craned her neck, searching all nooks and crannies for Krish. 'Where is she, Ma?'

Ma shrugged. Mahi huffed, clearly unsatisfied with this answer.

'What were you expecting would happen?' Ma eyed Mahi. Her face showed stark honesty and a note of disappointment. 'It is already hard. Your … love. Did this make it easier?'

Mahi's eyes widened in horror. Ma knew! Shit.

'How long?' Mahi asked demurely.

Ma smiled but didn't answer.

'I'm sorry, Ma. I shouldn't have. Please tell me where she is.'

Just then Manav and Krish came back to Ma, holding a bag of rice.

'Great, Manav beta, let's take this to your mother. She'll need it during Sonia's *bidaai*,' Ma and Manav took the bag and went to Masi. Krish turned to leave, but Mahi caught her wrist. 'Please, I am sorry.'

'Why should you be sorry? I am sorry. I dared you. You showed me … You were right. I was wrong.' Krish's eyes brimmed with tears and her voice quaked. 'I only told you, na, to go. You sure showed me. You can have any guy in the world.'

'Ishq, I'm sorry, sweetheart. I shouldn't have teased you liked that. I promise I'll never do it again.'

'No, you go. Go have fun. Look, they are all waiting for you on the dance floor.'

Krish again tried to leave, but Mahi had pinned her hand. 'You're not leaving me, Krishna Mehra,' she whispered so fiercely that Krish sat back down.

'How far is the house?' Mahi asked. Her voice indicated that she was not to be meddled with.

'Two lanes away,' Krish answered.

'Take me home,' Mahi declared.

'The wedding?'

'Take me home. NOW.'

Krish and Mahi got up and quietly walked home. Masi's house was dark, since everyone was at the wedding. Mahi quickly ran up to the terrace with Krish, still holding her hand. Once there, she led them into the little alleyway between the water tank and the house. Krish was quiet. Finally Mahi let go of her fierce grip.

'Now what?' Krish huffed as she massaged her wrist.

'Close your eyes,' Mahi said softly.

'Mahi, I don't want any jokes. I'm not in the mood. And I definitely don't want you to kiss me. I don't want you to touch me.'

'I promise. I won't touch you or kiss you. Now close your eyes.'

Krish closed them. And waited. A few moments later she heard Mahi whisper, 'Open them.'

Krish gasped. She looked around wildly. 'What are you doing?' Krish exclaimed. 'Are you out of your mind?'

Standing in front of her was a very naked Mahi. She was naked except her jewellery. Somehow this odd mixture of her naked but bejewelled body intensely excited Krish. And even though it was an insane idea, Krish couldn't help but admire her soft, beautiful curves, her bountiful perky breasts, the slight outline of her ribs, her flat stomach and her gorgeous womanness.

'I'm yours, Ishq. I always will be.' Mahi stood there naked on that warm summer night, giving herself absolutely to the woman she was in love with.

Krish was speechless. She was not expecting this.

'Now I know that I had promised that I wouldn't kiss you …' But before Mahi could finish her sentence, Krish's mouth was on hers, crushing her with emotions. So many emotions. Their lips met ferociously, violently. Mahi's fingers lightly raked Krish's scalp. Krish opened her legs and let Mahi in, trying to drape as much of her naked body with hers. She cupped Mahi's breasts and took a nipple into her mouth. Usually Krish was super gentle, but today she let her teeth graze a little.

'Ohh, Krish … Ohhh.' Krish loved Mahi's moans. She kissed Mahi's bare stomach, her hands staying firmly on her breasts, kneading them, tugging on her nipples. Mahi pulled her back up and started kissing her neck and ears, while she started working on Krish's salwar, trying to get it loose. It fell to the floor.

'Krish …' Mahi pulled her up to her lips. Kri

kissing her neck. Her kisses were going to bruise Mahi. 'Ishq,' Mahi whispered again, 'Ishq, I want you in my mouth.'

Krish looked deeply into Mahi's eyes as Mahi went down on her knees. Mahi gently pushed Krish against the door, carefully so as not to inflame the welts from the haystack that she had put aloe on earlier. Krish lifted her long tunic, so she could see Mahi as she went down on her. Mahi's eyes never left her as she kissed Krish's thighs. She could smell her want. Krish was ready for her.

Mahi looked up and said, 'I love you, Ishq.' Her tongue sought the sweet nectar from Krish. Her tongue circled Krish's centre, teasing her. She licked her. Once, twice, thrice.

'I need you so much,' Krish groaned. Mahi pressed her hands against Krish's butt as she buried herself in her wetness, now licking and sucking vigorously. Krish's fingers were in Mahi's hair, gripping them firmly to show her need. She desperately needed release but also wanted it to last. But tonight was the night she was going to last long. Krish jutted her mound out so she could lift Mahi's face up to look at her again as she licked her. Mahi's eyes met Krish's again. Mahi could feel her thigh twitching. She knew Krish was close … so close. She eagerly attacked Krish's wetness. A throaty sound released from Krish and waves of pleasure coursed through her body, giving her the most intense orgasm she'd had. When she opened her eyes, Mahi was still looking at her, gently holding her palm against her mound, releasing the last ripples of her orgasm against her palm. Krish fell to the floor softly. Mahi held her and they rocked back and forth.

'I'm in love with you, Mahi. You are my everything.' And then, quickly, before Krish was even aware of it, Mahi got up and put her clothes back on.

'What? What happened? Why are you getting dressed?'

'It's bidaai time. They must be looking for you. Let's go.'

'Huh? What about you?' Krish asked as she tied her salwar.

'Later.'

'Are you sure?' Krish asked as Mahi hustled her out of the terrace.

'I promise. Don't worry, I'll take my pound of flesh.'

'Undoubtedly,' Krish said, laughing out loudly.

Now, at the hospital

Krish was standing against the wall, looking down in Mahi's eyes as she sat on the chair opposite her. The same memory was coursing through both their bodies. Maybe it was a distraction from her mother's surgery or the need for a life-affirming moment but the memory created a want so deep, so guttural, it made Krish shudder. Their trance was broken when Lauren loudly cleared her throat. She and Chelsea were wide-eyed and scrutinizing Krish. Mahi was so flush, she decided to escape Lauren and Chelsea's watchful eye and went out to make a phone call. Lauren couldn't stand it any more. She looked at Krish pointedly.

'So … ?'

'Huh?'

'Don't pretend like nothing happened, Krish. I saw what I saw! You guys were practically dry-humping when I walked into the room. And right now, you guys were totally reliving the Meerut memories. I could *see* you orgasm in your minds. How can you go from hating someone so much to suddenly wanting to get married and having kids?'

Krish sighed. 'We don't want to get married and have kids. And you know we didn't break up with each other because we hated each other. I hated her because she broke up with me. And now that things are ... I don't know ... normal-ish, it's kind of hard to resist the chemistry and the past sometimes. I know this doesn't make sense, especially because of Allie and Kabeer. But we've always fit. We've always made sense. Remember I used to tell you guys that she was all the stars in my sky, that she's my soulmate.'

Mahi, who had entered the room during this conversation, cleared her throat. Lauren and Krish turned to stare at her. 'Umm ... just finished the phone call.'

Shoot, had she heard them? Mahi pretended that nothing was different or that Lauren hadn't just interrupted them in an intimate moment or that Krish hadn't just talked about her being her soulmate.

Masi joined them in the room. Krish went to check if there was any news from the surgery. She waited patiently as someone from Dr Pandey's team came out to give her an update. 'Dr Pandey said it is going well.' Krish breathed a sigh of relief. When she came back to the room, Masi was showing their video of *Bole Chudiyan* to Lauren, Chelsea and Mahi. Everyone looked very amused. 'Oh my god. You guys look so young, so cute,' said Chelsea.

'Oh my god, look at my make-up. How horrendous,' Mahi stated emphatically. Krish thwacked her lightly. 'You were the best-looking at the wedding! Except the bride, of course.'

'And the bride's mother!' said Masi.

Everyone laughed.

Hours passed. Masi took a nap. Lauren and Chelsea went home for a bit and took a nap too. They were jet-lagged. Finally the doctor came.

'Good news. The surgery was successful. In fact, it was better than we expected. We were able to get all of the tumour. We will be running tests tomorrow to confirm. My team will be doing all the follow-ups. I'll come check on her in a few days. Don't worry, they will keep me posted. I have my best team on the job.' Saying this, Dr Pandey shook Krish's hand.

Again, he whispered something to Mahi, who nodded. And then he left.

When Mahi turned, Krish was sobbing. 'Oh, thank God. Thank you, God! You know, Mahi, I was so scared I was going to lose Ma too. I was so scared I'd become an orphan today. I'm so glad she's OK!'

'Shhh ....' A hand reached around her back and hugged her. 'It's OK, Ishq. I'm here. I'm your family. You are my family. We've got each other.'

Krish turned around and hugged Mahi back fiercely. Mahi was petting her, holding her lovingly. She kept saying, 'I've got you, Ishq.' Krish just cried and cried.

When they got back to the house, Lauren and Chelsea were relieved to hear that Ma was OK but confused by their friend's appearance. Krish's face was botchy and swollen, her eyes were red and puffed up. Relief and fatigue had claimed her mind and body. 'I just want to sleep,' she said and lay down. Lauren and Chelsea looked at their friend curiously but didn't say much. Masi was on her way to the hospital with one of the aunties from the neighbourhood.

Mahi tucked Krish in and was walking out of the door when Lauren came out of the kitchen with a bottle of water.

'How is she?' Lauren asked.

'Relieved, I think. She was just so stressed. I think it all came crashing down. She probably just needs some rest,' Mahi answered.

'Look, Mahi. I know you're only trying to be nice. And I know she needs you right now. I get it. But what's your end game here? It took her years to get over you. She wouldn't date for the longest time. And then she only dated girls who looked like you or smelt like you or whatever.' Lauren flicked her hair in annoyance. 'After I don't know how many years of that nonsense, she finally, finally learnt to move on. I'm worried that when you break her heart again, she's not going to recover from it.'

'What do you mean by break her heart again?' Mahi asked.

'You're with Kabeer, right?' Mahi didn't reply but bit her lip.

'Krish is with Allie. And they make a great couple. A wonderful powerhouse in their own right. Krish is happy. Not like the way she is with you, but she's happy … And now you're back in her life and no woman is going to come close to the incredible, perfect Mahi. And it really doesn't help that you look like this! I mean, come on … how does anyone compete with this?!'

There was a moment of silence. Then Mahi asked curiously, 'How is she different when she is with me?'

'What?'

'You said, "Not like the way she is with you." How is it different?' Mahi waited for an answer.

Lauren thought about it for a few moments, 'When you're around her, there is another Krish altogether. This one has more angst. I mean she was always brooding, but here she's more …' Lauren tried to find the right word, 'teenage-y, almost. And this Krish needs you like hunger. This hunger feeds off your presence, your voice, your heartbeat. Like she can't exist without possessing you, consuming you. But it's not one-sided. You're both like that with each other. I am worried both of you will burn your lovers in your all-consuming passion. And that's fine. I'll tell Krish to leave Allie if she wants to pursue you. But if you want Krish, you must leave Kabeer.'

Mahi bit her lip again.

'Can you? Can you, superstar Mahek Singh, be in a lesbian relationship? How would that impact your career? So is this really a choice between your career and Krish again? Because we know she lost that race ten years ago. And now you have something tangible to lose. Then you were a newbie funnelling your mother's ambitions, but now you're a superstar in your own right. You have millions of dollars banking on your career, and a handsome dude like Kabeer by your side. So you see how I'm worried about my best friend?'

'Yes, I do' was all Mahi said. And then she turned around and closed the door behind her.

19

⟶ʼ⟨⟨⟵

'YOU MISSED HER AGAIN.' THE NURSE SAID AS KRISH walked into the room. Lauren and Chelsea were behind.

Ma was doing well. Her surgery had been successful. The new scans showed they had indeed got all of the tumour out. And Ma was recovering well.

'What? Are you serious?!' The disappointment on Krish's face spoke volumes. Lauren felt bad for her friend. She knew Mahi had started avoiding Krish since they last spoke. Should she tell Krish? She looked at Chelsea, who shook her head. This was not the time or place.

The next day Krish took her friends to see Mumbai. They saw Juhu beach, Haji Ali, Victoria Terminus and Rajabai Tower. 'I feel I haven't seen this much Mumbai in all the eighteen years that I lived here,' Krish announced as they got back home.

'I get that. We often don't recognize the beauty of where we live, right?' said Lauren.

'Except New York. I feel we've really explored our city,' mused Krish.

Krish thought about that for a moment. Was New York her city or was it Mumbai? New York was where she had been for these past ten years. But now Mumbai, with Mahi in it, was calling to her like a siren song. One that would lead to a heartbreak yet again. Krish shook her head. No. Lauren and Chelsea were right. She needed to focus on her work and going back to New York.

Why, then, did that thought make her feel so empty?

Over the next few days, as Ma recovered, Lauren, Chelsea and Krish made time to go to the National Gallery of Modern Art, the Jehangir Art Gallery and to some other local art galleries.

'Wow. That was a lot of culture. Let's balance it out with dinner at McDonald's,' Lauren suggested.

That evening, as they were eating McVeggie and McAloo Tikki burgers along with Piri Piri fries at McDonald's, they discussed the burgeoning art scene in India.

'I love how more artists are experimenting. I love the juxtaposition of the old scriptures and stories with multimedia and other forms,' Chelsea said as she bit into her Filet-o-Fish. 'Yum … it tastes just the same,' said Chelsea, nodding approvingly at her burger.

'I don't understand how the real estate market is not crashing. It seems imminent,' said Lauren as she reached for a fry. 'These are so good, we should seriously sell this stuff in the US.'

'I know, right?!' Chelsea exclaimed.

'Wait, I thought we were discussing art.' Krish looked a little confused.

'Are you in your own world again?' asked Lauren.

'Is this your book world or your girl world? Because the look on your face … that's telling me it's not about a book.'

'It is very much about a book,' Krish lied. Lauren let it slide. So Krish changed the topic. 'Anyway, how does the real estate market impact the art market?'

'The art market will be impacted by the real estate market. You need a house to put a painting in, right?' explained Lauren. She loved talking about real estate. No matter where the topic started, Lauren could bring it back to real estate. Chelsea just shook her head and rolled her eyes. Krish smiled.

'Anyway, I'm bummed you won't be joining us,' said Chelsea, touching Krish's arm. 'It will be odd seeing Delhi and Agra without you. We've talked about it for so many years. And now we'll be two white girls all alone in a dangerous city.'

Krish smiled. She had enjoyed their company and was truly grateful that they had come for her, for Ma. But Ma needed her attention and care. Though, she wondered, how much of that care would be filled with Mahi. Would Mahi come back into her life when her friends were gone? Krish missed Mahi. *You're my family.* Those words reverberated in her mind from time to time. She felt them in her heart. But she worried about whether Mahi would go away again.

'I wish I could join y'all, but I have to coordinate Ma's physical therapy, her check-ups and need to be around for general care. I have to deal with the medical expenses too. The sooner Ma gets better, the sooner I can come back home to New York City.' 'Home' now sounded unfamiliar on her tongue. *Stop it, Krish. You're just setting yourself up for failure.*

'And to Allie,' Chelsea interjected.

'Yes, back to Allie.' Krish smiled a bit more resignedly this time.

'Krish …' Chelsea started, 'look, if you're not feeling it with Allie, break it off with her. You and Mahi seem like two trains on a collision course. Lauren and I can see it. Mahi can see it. If Kabeer and Allie had seen you two together, they would see it too. The question is not if, but when.'

'That's not true. I've never cheated in my life. I won't start now. Heck, I didn't even cheat on Mahi after she had dumped me,' Krish said defensively.

'We know!' replied Chelsea and Lauren.

'Look, I get it. You're not a cheater. But this is Mahi you're talking about. I know you're already counting down the hours till we leave for our morning flight tomorrow. You'll drop us at the airport and you'll message her. And she'll come running. You will pretend to talk. You may cry. She'll comfort you. And by afternoon, you'll be naked in bed.' Lauren's eyes dared Krish to defy her.

Krish blushed deeply. Her friends sure did know her well. 'Well, she's not in town tomorrow. So there …' Krish faltered. That sounded bad. She knew it.

'Really, your denial is based on the fact that she's not in town? It's not even, oh gosh, how could you insinuate such a thing? I'm with Allie. She's with …'

'Shh …' said Krish. 'We're in public.'

'All right. You know what I mean, though.' Lauren gave Krish a hard look. 'Buddy, you've picked up a gun and you're heading towards a cliff, where either you'll shoot yourself or you'll fall off the edge. We can't bear to see either happening.'

Chelsea nodded gravely. Krish said nothing.

On the other side of town

Why had Mahi agreed to do this short film? She couldn't quite recall. The make-up artist finished work on her face.

The director came in. He explained the scene. Mahi listened intently, taking in the small details.

'Are you good with the dialogue?'

Mahi nodded. 'Yes, I looked it over yesterday.'

'Do you have any questions? Do you have any thoughts or suggestions? I'm open to your ideas.'

'Ah.' Now Mahi remembered why she had agreed on the cameo. The young director was attentive and respectful. But, more importantly, while he seemed to have a clear vision, he was open to new ideas. Mahi and the director chatted for a bit and then he went to start the shooting.

Mahi's scene went off effortlessly. They did it in three takes—with varying intensity, so the director had a few options for later.

'Would you like to see more? Nirali is next. You can hang back. I've got a chair here for you,' the young director asked Mahi. She wondered if he was being serious or just flirting with her. She texted her hairdresser and mentioned the young director. Her hairdresser was often the one she went to for gossip. She replied that he was probably flirting (because who could resist flirting with Mahek Singh?) but was harmless. He was apparently happy with his wife.

Mahi was relieved. She waited to see the next few scenes. She sat next to the director and watched. Nirali was playing a village belle in a family drama. After the third take, there was a short break. Nirali came and sat next to Mahi.

'Hey, Mahek. How are you?'

'Hey, Nirali. Nice to see you!'

They air-kissed.

'So what did you think?' Nirali asked.

'It hardly matters what I think. The director's notes are all that matter.'

'Yes, but it matters to me. You're my senior in this field. I would love to get some pointers.'

'I have a question about your role. Just because your character is a village belle, why does that make her stupid?'

Nirali looked unsure. 'Huh?'

Mahi explained, 'Just because she's not from the city doesn't mean she is a simpleton or that she is stupid. You are the voice of this girl. If the character is supposed to be stupid, that's one thing, but why are you portraying her as stupid?'

Nirali thought about that for a moment. 'Hmm ...'

Mahi put her hand on Nirali's shoulder. 'Just think about it. It's free advice. Take it for what it's worth.' Saying this, she got up from her chair and headed out to her car.

As she walked out, she called Karan. 'I saw her. I don't think you should take her.'

'Are you sure? She will look regal as the navy captain.'

'I'm saving you a lot of heartache. Pick Zara or Tanisha.'

'All right. I trust your judgement. I'll make the calls. Are you and Kabeer going to be available tonight for drinks?'

'No, tonight we have to go do a jig at that wedding I told you about.'

'Oh ,right! You're such a good friend, Mahi.'

≈

The next morning, Krish waved Lauren and Chelsea goodbye at the domestic airport and, just as Lauren had predicted, she was on the phone with Mahi on the ride home.

'When do you get back?' Krish asked anxiously. Why was she so nervous?

'I'm not sure—my calendar is in a flux. I took a few days off with all the stuff happening, so I had to move some dates around to accommodate the producers and all. We're dubbing for that action film soon, so I'll be back in our recording studios in Mumbai for that.'

'OK. Well, let me know. Maybe you can come for dinner one evening. Or lunch. Whatever works with your schedule.'

'Yes, sure.' As if changing the topic, Mahi asked, 'Ma is looking better each day. Have you set up her PT?'

'Yes. I am meeting the physical therapist the doctor had recommended later today. This morning I'm heading over to the bank to figure out the finances for paying these bills.'

'I don't envy you at all. I wish you'd take my help. Ruchi is excellent at dealing with these things. And she's got an assistant now.'

'I love that you have an assistant for your assistant.' Krish laughed.

'Well, she is taking care of two people right now. So she needed help.'

'Well, I'm very thankful for her help and yours.' Krish was truly grateful. 'Can I pay for part of her salary or her assistant's salary?'

'Oh, have we become so formal now that you're offering me money?' Mahi asked, sounding offended.

'I didn't mean to offend you. And I know you make a ton of money. I just feel bad that you're having to incur all these expenses because of me. I know you've footed all the hospital bills and I want to make sure I make you whole.'

'Please, if we were married, wouldn't this be yours too?'

'Wishes-horses-beggars-ride,' Krish replied wryly. 'Besides, if we were married, you wouldn't be India's darling heroine. Our PM's favourite actor.'

'What would I be, then?' Mahi asked.

'My wife. Like I'd be your wife,' Krish replied merrily. Mahi could hear her smile all the way through the phone.

'And what would we eat?'

'Hmm … that's a good question. Would we be two random employees at some multinational company? What a waste that would have been of your talent, Mahi,' Krish said contemplatively.

'And yours too, Ishq.'

'Hmm … maybe Ma was right. Maybe we're both successful because we were apart.'

Mahi said nothing.

Krish continued, 'Mahi, do you think we're better off apart? That we can't be successful together?'

Mahi sighed. She had thought about this question after meeting Krish again. She gave a thoughtful reply. 'It's indisputable that we've reached incredible heights without each other. And perhaps we couldn't have achieved that had we been together back then. But now things have changed— times have changed. And we're at a point in our lives when maybe we can make each other even more successful.'

'I guess we're back to wishes-horses-beggars-ride. Anyway, I should go. I have reached the bank and I have to go deal with our wonderful bank bureaucracy and find out how I will pay for this experimental procedure.'

'Are you sure you don't want Ruchi's help?' Mahi asked.

'I'm OK. I really have no handle on Ma's finances and it's best I learn for myself. But I really appreciate you making the path smoother for me. You've been a lifesaver.'

'I'm so glad I could do this for you. And for Ma. It means a lot to me.' Mahi words were genuine. Krish didn't know Mahi any other way. Maybe Mahek Singh was used to dealing with fake people and crazy fans, but Krish only knew Mahi—pure, simple, always genuine Mahi.

And then Krish surprised Mahi when she asked, 'I need a favour from you.'

20

-)|\\-

KRISH STEPPED INTO THE MAIN OFFICE ATRIUM. PICTURES of Raichand House's famous films adorned the walls. Krish remembered going to see some of them with Mahi and Ma. It felt like a lifetime ago. How quickly time passes, she thought wryly. It had been more than a month since Ma had her stroke. Lauren and Chelsea were back in the US. They were in touch regularly but were busy with their own lives. Mahi had been missing in action, off working on various projects. Krish felt that she might be avoiding her. Maybe their little relationship was only till everything was happening around Ma. To be fair, Mahi had been incredibly helpful and Krish had no right to expect more. She had helped Krish tremendously during that difficult time. *You're my family.* Krish remembered Mahi's arms around her after Ma's operation. Krish wondered if those emotions were just temporary or if she really meant it. Krish was tired of wondering and guessing. This was not what she wanted. She wanted a simple life. And she was ready for that again—the normalcy that New York offered her, her old life, her apartment, her shower and its water pressure and, of course, Allie.

Here, in India, Krish had been busy with Ma's treatment. She had got a five-month family leave from her university, which allowed her to deal with the post-operative treatment and therapy that Ma needed. Thankfully, she was recovering well, and that was all Krish could ask for.

Mahi had promised to come for dinner with Ma soon. Maybe next week, she had said. Mahi had been travelling to the Czech Republic and to Italy of late. There had been delays and some other trips. She had finally come back yesterday. Krish knew this because they had been in touch almost every day. Mahi might have been avoiding Krish but she hadn't really let go of her either. Mahi texted her every evening to check in. Krish had asked for Mahi's help to set up a meeting with Karan. And here she was, standing in his office.

Karan got up from behind his desk and came around to greet her. Krish's body language was still pretty clear—it would still just be a handshake.

'Hello, Krish.' Karan offered his hand. 'I am glad your mother is feeling better now. We wish her a speedy recovery. Mahi keeps us updated. She talks so fondly of Ma.'

'Thank you. We received your flowers and note. Ma says thank you too.'

'Of course,' said Karan. 'Not every gay child has someone like Ma. Though they all should. So I understand how lucky you are.'

'Thank you. I'm grateful, trust me,' Krish said and smiled.

After a few seconds of silence, Karan said, 'Shall we walk to the conference room?'

'I'll follow you,' said Krish, picking up her brown satchel. As they walked to the room, Karan asked, 'How did the visit from your friends go? It was very sweet of them to come to India to be with you. Most Americans just want to come for weddings.'

'Yes. They are very good friends. And I hope someday they will come for my wedding too. Though I doubt it will be here.'

'Why not?' Karan's eyebrows arched in question.

'I only have Ma here. I'm sure we can fly her there,' said Krish. For some reason, at that moment Krish remembered that Ma's last words before her surgery to Mahi were that she wished she had been her daughter-in-law.

Karan opened the conference-room door. Krish saw there were a few people waiting for them. They all got up. 'Umm ... Krish, I've got a few people here. Viren is our lawyer and he's here with his team, and Hitesh here manages our accounts.'

Krish nodded and shook hands with the men. She then introduced her own lawyer, Sunaina, who had been arranged by her agent. Sunaina introduced her team, who were all lawyers working on this account. 'Why she needed so many I don't know,' wondered Krish but kept the thought to herself. Her agent had said the bill had been taken care of and Krish hadn't bothered asking for more information. Sunaina had already negotiated the price of the book with Viren and Hitesh. As they sat down, Sunaina explained that, based on the way the rights of a book worked, she would have to get final approval on some pieces from the main office in New York but some decisions would be up to Krish alone. They all nodded and sat down to discuss the points.

Krish had been hoping she'd see Mahi at the studio's main office. She looked around and through the conference room's glass doors, her eyes searching for Mahi. But she didn't catch a glimpse of her.

Karan saw Krish looking distractedly around. 'Umm ... Krish. It's just us today. I hope that's OK,' he said softly.

Krish nodded. Earlier she may have been embarrassed that Karan had figured out whom she was looking for, but nowadays she didn't feel such emotions. Life was too short to be embarrassed.

'Anyway, Karan, as you know, I'm not really the business type, so I'll leave those points to Sunaina and her team. I am here only for one reason. My last conversation with Ma before her stroke was about you. Can you imagine?' Krish gave a dry chuckle.

'Anyway, she really wanted to see my book as a Karan Raichand film. And she specifically wanted Mahek to play Meher's role. I know we are both on the same page about this based on our previous conversations.' Krish looked at Karan for agreement and he nodded. 'However, Ma had one more thought and I am not sure how you feel about this ...' Krish paused. She could feel all eyes in the room on her. 'Ma wanted me to work on the screenplay along with your team.'

Maybe Karan was expecting something more bizarre, because Krish was certain she saw him exhale. He smiled. 'I think we can work out an arrangement. It really depends on how much veto power you expect with the screenplay.'

'Of course. I understand screenplay writing is very different from writing a book. So I am definitely not planning to lead the process. I'm just happy to work on the team. I'm not sure about the veto power thing. Let me think about that and we can iron out the rest of the details. I believe Sunaina has worked with other authors who have helped write their screenplays for production houses, and I have seen some of those agreements. They seemed reasonable to me.'

Karan nodded. 'All right. I think we can do this.'

He got up and shook hands with Krish. 'Welcome to the Raichand family. We would like to announce this soon.'

Krish shook hands with Karan. Someone came in with champagne, flutes and mithai, and everyone started congratulating each other. The associates were happy to drink free champagne and eat free sweets. Krish hung out for a few minutes and then nodded to Karan, picked up her brown satchel and left the room.

As she waited for the elevator in Karan Raichand's tasteful and very expensive office reception, she heard two interns talking. The taller intern was asking if the shorter one was waiting for Kabeer Agarwal. Krish's ears perked up, wondering if Mahi would be around. The other replied in the affirmative, saying there was a meeting with a director for narration and that she had to escort him to the smaller conference room. The taller intern was practically drooling now, coming up with scenarios that included the couch in the smaller conference room, Kabeer Agarwal and ice cream. Both the interns giggled, but the shorter one reminded the taller one that these thoughts were only good for dreams. There was no way Kabeer Agarwal was going to cheat on Mahek Singh. 'Not unlike,' she said, and here she lowered her voice, 'you know who ... who can't seem to keep his hands to himself.'

'I heard that. His poor wife. Anyway, I can't imagine how lucky Mahi is. They are such a perfect couple. They will make such pretty babies.'

At this point, the shorter one lowered her voice again, as if telling the other a secret. 'I heard there has been wedding talk. I heard that Kabeer is going to propose to her soon.'

Krish braced herself at this piece of information. Her throat went dry. She pushed the elevator button again. Where was the damn elevator? Of course—they had been together for the past five years. Why wouldn't he propose? Mahi and Krish hadn't spoken about Kabeer much. But Krish knew her outdoor shoot was at a beach destination—was it the Amalfi Coast?—with Kabeer for their upcoming Razia Akhtar film. Krish wasn't even sure she could pinpoint where the Amalfi Coast was, forget visiting it. She imagined them getting all cosy after a day of shooting at the beach. Mahi in a bikini, Kabeer in his swimming trunks. Them showering together, getting all the sand out. His hands on her body. Her moaning as he touched her. Krish was breaking out into hives at the idea of Mahi having sex with Kabeer. Where the fuck was this damn elevator? *Fuck it, I'll take the stairs.*

The two interns were staring at her open-mouthed when Krish realized she had scratched her face. Red welts started appearing on it. Just then the elevator reached the floor Krish was on and the doors opened.

∽

They were mid-laugh when the doors opened. Mahi's hand was on Kabeer's arm for support as she doubled over from the funny story he had just told her. Mahi looked up and saw Krish's blanched face. Krish looked like she was going to throw up. Oh, this is not how Mahi would have done this. But there was nothing they could do now. Introductions would have to ensue.

Kabeer stepped out, smiling, and said, 'Hello, Krish! We haven't met yet. I am Kabeer. I am ...' He stopped and looked at Mahi, as if for confirmation.

'Mahi's boyfriend. I know,' Krish said, trying not to grit her teeth as she said it. 'Very nice meeting you. I was just waiting for the elevator. I guess I should go now.'

The intern tried to interrupt and hesitatingly informed the actor that the meeting was soon and that she had to escort him to the smaller conference room if they had to keep to the schedule. Kabeer waved the intern off. Then he put his arm around Krish's shoulder. 'I've heard so much about you. I am so happy to meet you finally.' Kabeer was being friendly, but Krish's body tensed and coiled tight, years of taekwondo training kicking in. Without moving she was ready for an attack. She narrowed her eyes and glared at him so strongly that he moved his hand away. 'Anyway, how is Ma? Mahi talks about her all the time.'

Krish was polite. 'She is well, thank you for asking.'

He continued, 'I keep telling Mahi that I think we should have dinner soon. Mahi, will you please coordinate?' With that, he started walking towards the intern and where she was leading him. Mahi groaned inwardly. This was the last thing she wanted. She knew Krish wouldn't react well to Kabeer. Kabeer was a sweetheart but sometimes he could be so clueless. He had poked the bear without realizing what he was doing. As he left with the intern, Kabeer turned around to look at Krish curiously. Krish felt his eyes on her and thought maybe he was judging her. Her short-cropped hair, her yellow shirt and blue tie, with her dark blue jeans and her brown satchel. In New York City, Krish didn't particularly stand out. It was New York City—who would? But here, in Mumbai, she stood out like a sore thumb sometimes. All Krish wanted was to go back to her home in the US. This constant judging, the eyes, the looking up and down, the light-bulb moment when they figured it out, and then more judging—all of it was grating. She knew that things had changed in many societies and many educated elites didn't do a lot of judging any more, but as soon as she stepped out of those small circles, it was as present as the scorching hot sun.

Mahi was looking at her. 'Hey!' she said quietly. She looked ready for a day at work. Her hair was freshly blow-dried, her nails were done in a subtle pink shade, and her face was glowing and tastefully made up. She was wearing skin-tight jeans and a short crop top with a large Prada bag. Mahi looked gorgeous, as always. 'Fancy running into you,' Mahi said as she stepped into the foyer in her high heels. Her eyebrows raised, a concerned look in her eyes, Mahi studied the red welts on Krish's face. She gently put her hand on Krish's arm. Krish relaxed to the touch. Her body uncoiled. Words were not necessary with Mahi, were they? Krish took a deep breath.

'Hey, Mahi … Mahek!' Krish finally said. 'I'm just heading out.'

Sometimes, for a writer, Krish could be very abrupt, Mahi mused.

Krish was waiting for the elevator again. It had closed and moved to another floor when Kabeer had stopped to say hello.

Mahi stepped a little closer to Krish, so they could talk to each other softly. 'I'll see you for dinner soon?' she asked, her big hazel eyes looking expectantly at Krish.

'Umm … OK,' Krish said. She sounded like she just needed to be home now.

'All right,' Mahi said as she decided to leave Krish to be by herself. She hovered around the area, chatting with the receptionist as she saw the elevator doors open and Krish hurry inside. Their eyes met one last time. And then the doors closed.

≈

'Congrats on the film contract. You'll be raking in millions now.' Mahi sounded happy.

'Money I'll be using to pay Dr Pandey's very high bills,' Krish said, laughing. 'Ma wanted to confirm you're coming for dinner tomorrow. She wants to thank you for all your help during her surgery. Honestly, without your help, Ma wouldn't have got his attention and his world-class team. So we both want to thank you. I'm making baingan ka bharta, so you'll join us tomorrow night for dinner, na?'

'Once you add baingan ka bharta to the equation, it makes it an easy yes, no? Of course I will. Is 7.30 p.m. OK?'

'Umm ... Mahi.'

'Yeah?'

'Ma was wondering if Kabeer wants to join. She said she'd like to meet him.' Krish loathed saying those words out loud. She held her breath, hoping, praying even, that Mahi would say no. 'That's sweet. I'll tell him. But he can't join me tomorrow.

He has a prior commitment. I'll let him know, though. We'll make a plan for another day once Ma is better, OK?'

Krish exhaled. 'OK. See you tomorrow.'

Mahi could hear Krish breathe again. She sounded so relieved. Mahi smiled too.

≈

That evening, when Krish was writing with Anaya, the seventeen-year-old, at the Soho Club, she couldn't concentrate. Krish had liked the routine they had set up and after a few days of her mother being back from the hospital, they had started writing again. But today was different.

'Dude, is everything OK?' Anaya looked at Krish, a little alarmed.

'Hmm … yes,' Krish replied, as if coming back to earth from a faraway world. 'Why do you ask?' She looked like she was in a daze.

'Because you're clearly not here. Are you in another world? Hopefully the one from your book?'

Krish looked at Anaya and smiled. 'Why do you say that?'

'Well, you've been muttering something about Kabeer all evening under your breath. And you're typing only one word on your laptop. Repeatedly.'

Krish looked at her screen. Anaya was right. She had written nothing all evening, except 'Mahi'. This was not helpful. Krish selected all the 'Mahi's on her screen and was about to delete them, but paused. Gosh, she couldn't even delete them. What was happening to her? She was going insane. Mumbai was making her crazy. She couldn't be with Mahi and she couldn't live without her. This had to end. She selected it all and pressed delete, and watched it all disappear in a flash.

Anaya looked at Krish and asked, 'Krish, is this Mahek Singh?'

Krish froze. She didn't say anything. Her fingers were still on the laptop.

'You guys were together, right? As kids? She's Meher in your book, right?'

'Why do you say that?' Krish asked, as she glanced around the room. Thankfully it was a quiet day and there weren't too many guests yet. No one had heard Anaya. Anaya realized Krish wanted privacy. She continued quietly.

'Your eyes. They light up when you see her. They are constantly searching for her. Even here, every day when you come, you first look for her. I saw you at the award ceremony, remember? Then I saw pictures of you guys at the event in the papers. Am I wrong?'

'Have you spoken to anyone about it?' Krish asked quietly.

'No. Not even my mother.' Anaya looked scandalized that Krish would think she was callous enough to out someone.

'OK.' Krish relaxed visibly. 'Look, it was a long time ago. She's with …'

'Kabeer now, I know. But you still love her, right?'

Krish wasn't sure what to say. She said nothing.

∽∽

That night Krish FaceTimed Allie. 'Hey!'

'Hey, sweetheart. It's good to see your face. I miss you so much.' Allie was having coffee, getting ready to go to work. She was dressed in a white and grey business suit, with a soft green–blue Hermès scarf.

'How are you doing?' Krish asked.

'I am well. I have some great news. I am coming to Mumbai next week.'

'Next week! Wow!' Krish's face registered surprise, excitement and anxiety all rolled into one.

'Yes. I have a client meeting. I figured I could take a few days off and we could be together.'

Krish said nothing.

'Krish, is everything OK?'

'Yes. That sounds like a great idea. I would love it. I'm so glad,' Krish paused. 'It will be great to see you again. That was very nice of you. Thank you.'

Allie smiled. 'Of course, Jaan. I'm here for you.'

Krish hesitated and then asked, 'Hey Allie, would you like to have dinner with Kabeer and Mahi when you're here?'

'Mahi and Kabeer? What? We're friends who have dinner now? Krish, what's going on with you and Mahi? All the time I've known you, you've hated her. And now you're friends? Who dine together with their significant others?'

'I haven't. I keep explaining—I didn't hate her. I hated that she broke up with me and cut off all ties with me. I was in love with her. It hurt,' explained Krish.

'So it doesn't hurt now?' Allie prodded.

'You know, it doesn't. I've been seeing things from her perspective. And honestly, she's been so helpful with Ma's surgery and illness and all. I know it's confusing. I can understand how you are confused by these developments. Honestly, I am confused too sometimes.' Krish was trying to explain her perspective as honestly as possible.

'How do you imagine it working out once you're back in the US?'

'I dunno. Hopefully we can be friends.' Krish had been wondering about this too. But she had no idea how it would all work out.

'So she's not interested in you?' Allie asked bluntly. She knew there was no point beating around the bush about these things.

'Mahek Singh? The most talented actress, the most beautiful woman in India—maybe even the world—interested in me?

Leaving her hot, sexy nice-guy boyfriend? No, I don't think so. I think he's going to propose to her very soon. That's what I heard, at least. She'll probably be married in a few years. I met him today—Kabeer. He was the one who suggested we have dinner. I guess I can let them know we're not interested?'

'Not interested! That's not what I meant. I think we should do it.'

'Wait, I thought you didn't want to.' Now Krish was confused.

'No. I was just confused about your relationship status with Mahi. I am totally on board with having dinner with the hottest couple in Bollywood!'

'Where did you get that?' Krish started laughing.

'What? I have clients in India. I read stuff. I'm up on Bollywood gossip.' Allie grinned. Allie had read about the proposal rumours between Kabeer and Mahek Singh. She had wondered if Krish's presence had caused it. Allie wondered how all of this would shake out eventually. She looked at her watch and realized she had to leave for work. Allie worked at McKinsey & Company, one of the world's largest and most prestigious consulting companies. With Krish's success and Allie on her way to becoming partner, Lauren had been right, they were quite a power couple in their own right. But that was in New York. Power couples were a dime a dozen in Manhattan. Manhattan. Krish thought about life in New York with Allie. There was a certain anonymity New York offered that was very appealing to Krish. Krish couldn't wait to get lost in the crowd again. Her work in India was almost over.

'E-mail me the details. I'll come to the airport to pick you up.'

21

~⁘~

MAHI WAS TREPIDATIOUS ABOUT GOING BACK HOME TO Krish and Ma. She took a deep breath before entering.

But Krish got Ma out in her wheelchair and there was a warm loving welcome waiting for her. Ma smiled at Mahi. 'How are you beta?' Her speech was slightly slurred.

Mahi hugged Ma tightly. 'It's so good to see you.' Ma and Mahi sat down in the family room.

'I'm just finishing the cooking. Food will be ready in 10 minutes,' Krish said as she headed to the kitchen. Mahi got up to go to follow Krish into the kitchen but Ma stopped her. 'Sit. I want to talk.'

Mahi wondered what was on Ma's mind. 'I know I said this before I went in for surgery but I mean it. I'm very proud of you Mahi. What you have accomplished in life. But also what you did for me. You are thoughtful and kind and considerate and caring. Many people forget these things when they become famous. But I see them shining brightly inside you. And it makes me very happy.'

'Come on Ma. I didn't think twice. You deserved the best care.'

'I know. I wish...'

Mahi looked at Ma expectantly. But she stopped. 'What is it Ma?'

'I wish you both hadn't been separated. I begged and pleaded with your mother. You may not know this, but after your mother gave you the ultimatum, I went to speak to her. I pleaded for you and Krish. I thought perhaps we could talk about it, mother to mother. She blamed Krish for corrupting you. For leading you astray. But I had seen the way you looked at her, it was the way Krish's father, my husband used to look at me. So I knew the fire was on both sides.' Mahi listened. Tears brimming in her eyes.

'Yes, I was worried about your safety in our society then. And I was especially worried when your brothers came to our house to threaten Krish. Did you know that? They roughed her up pretty bad, they kicked her, beat her pretty bad. We had to go to the hospital. It was the reason she is now a Black belt. She promised me that she'd never get hurt again. But she was talking about physical pain then. She didn't know that the emotional pain of having her heart broken was going to break her irrevocably. I don't blame you for it though. Please know that. You did what was right for you, in your circumstances. I understood that then and I tried to explain it to Krish too.' Ma patted Mahi's hands. Mahi had tears streaming down her face. 'But to Krish you were the flower and the nectar, the bee and the pollen. You were the beginning and the end. When I explained this to your mother, she refused to believe it…Anyway, I am telling you all this because when your mother was near her end, she came to visit me. She wanted to apologize for breaking you up. She said she had tried to do what was best for her daughter, but had ended up losing you altogether. Neither you nor Krish were the same. Your mother had extinguished your happy, carefree smiles, your beautiful puppy love. She had just come back from your house and realized her mistake. She knew then but it was too late. I didn't tell Krish any of this because Krish had moved on too and you were with Kabeer.'

Mahi nodded.

'But Krish doesn't really know how to move on, does she? I thought maybe with time she had gotten over you. She has tried but I think, in her heart, she is still stuck at that airport, waiting for you to come, like she was all those years ago.' Mahi's face reflected her pain at this idea.

Ma quickly changed course, 'Anyway, all this long story to tell you, forgive your mother now. I have got a second chance to be your Ma again. I want to make sure you give her a second chance too.'

'Food is ready,' Krish came out of the kitchen triumphantly and she saw the two of them. Mahi was crying. Ma was petting her. 'All OK? Why are you crying Mahi? What happened Ma?'

Neither of them answered.

'Whatever I did, I am sorry. I promise I won't do it again. Please don't cry.'

This brought a smile to Mahi's face. She got up and hugged Krish. 'You didn't do anything wrong.'

'Then why?' Krish looked befuddled. 'It's just between me and Mahi.'

'Ma, this is not fair. How come you guys don't tell me anything!'

'Why are you so jealous Krish!?' Mahi teased.

'Yes, Krishi! Anyway, you're not my only daughter!' 'Ma, please don't make Mahi my sister.'

Mahi and Ma both chuckled.

≈

That evening after she got home, Mahi got into her pyjamas. She had cut her visit short. But she had a lot to think about. She knew Krish had wanted to talk to her but she couldn't. Not tonight. So she had dined and dashed. Leaving behind a confused and frustrated Krish.

Now Mahi was tucked in bed, her cocoon. She snuggled in her warm blankets and tried to process Ma's words. Mahi remembered the time her own mother had come unexpectedly to see her. She just showed up one day, out of the blue. Mahi had a set rule when it came to her family, she never made a scene. So when her mother showed up, she let her in. She served her coffee, which they drank in silence. Her mother tried asking her questions, 'How are you Mahi?'

No response. Instead Mahi got up and led her to her office. She shut the door to ensure complete privacy. No assistants, security, or servants. Just her and her mom.

'Do you need money?' were the first words that came out of Mahi's mouth. She didn't even feel bad about it.

'No, beta. I…I just came to see you,' her mother said gently. 'What do you need?' Mahi asked again. Not understanding why her mother was here. At her house. In her private sanctum.

'I need you Mahi. How many years are you going to punish me? Not talk to me. Not acknowledge me. I gave birth to you, I raised you. You've thrown away your whole family, for what? For whom?'

Mahi got up and looked outside the window. The view from her apartment was quite amazing. She seldom saw

Minita Sanghvi

it nowadays. Life had been so busy with the movies and shootings and movie promotions.

'Come home Mahi. I need you. I am old now. I need my daughter,' her mother seemed distraught. But then, she was an actress too. Mahi smiled at that thought. After a few minutes of silence, Mahi checked her watch and then started heading out to the door. Her mother reached out and held her hand, and stopped her. Mahi's eyes blazed fire. 'Don't. Touch. Me.' Mahi said menacingly. Mahi reached for the door of her office to get out.

'Mahi, I'm dying. I've got stage 4 throat cancer,' her mother said in anguish. As if she had left this information as her last ditch attempt to get her daughter back.

Mahi stopped. She turned around slowly, 'How long?'

'I have a few months to live. Please come back to me, Mahi,' her mother beseeched her.

'Do you remember how many days I cried? How many times I told you I love her, please let me go. How many times, I begged you, I pleaded with you?'

Her mother nodded, 'Maybe I was wrong. But I was doing it for your best. Look at where you are in life. Look at your success. Aren't you glad I stopped you from going to USA? Now you've got Kabeer. Isn't he making you happy?'

Mahi's eyes raked her mother over coals, 'You have never cared about my happiness. You only wanted to achieve your dream. Look, mother. I am all that you hoped I would be and more. All that you couldn't be. Are you happy in my success? What do you tell your friends, when I don't come visit for Diwali?'

'Let it go. Why are you so angry?' her mother cried.

'Angry? You took away my only happiness. You took away my oxygen. You took away my life,' exclaimed Mahi.

Her mother looked shocked. Realization was dawning on her, slowly.

'Krish was my dream, she will always be my dream. She's the only person I love mom. Mahi's eyes went over to the photos of her and Krish on the wall. Her mother's eyes followed. Her mother walked over to the photos on her wall. There was a photo of her and Krish as little children. They were holding hands. Another of Krish and Mahi when they were teenagers. Mahi was on the swing and Krish was sitting in the swing next to her. One couldn't see Krish's face but one could see Mahi's reaction to something Krish was saying. It was pure love writ large over her face. Her mother looked at Mahi and Krish in the photos.

Then her mother looked at Mahi and she looked at the photo frame again.

'You're right. I am sorry,' said her mother gently and she left quickly.

Mahi wished she didn't care but I mean, it was her mother. Mahi visited her mother every week from that day onwards and then towards the end every day. At first they didn't talk much. But every visit, her mother said sorry to her. Every visit Mahi cried a little. And somehow eventually, all that anger towards her mother had washed away and they had found solace in each other. At the end, Mahi had finally found the family she had wanted. Only it was too late.

Mahi sighed. She thought about Krish again. There were so many emotions to process. Her memories kept going back to their last summer together. The summer that changed their lives forever.

Back then

'Krish, are you sleeping?' 'Depends.'

Mahi turned her over coming face to face with a smiling Krish. Oh how she loved that smile.

'I have a question for you,' Mahi said as she snuggled in. Krish enveloped her body into hers and asked, 'Hmm. Bolo?'

'What's our future?'

'Huh?' Krish looked surprised at this line of questioning. 'You know marriage, children, all that.'

'Hmmm….do you want to get married?' Krish looked crestfallen.

'Don't you?' Mahi wondered what was going on in her mind.

'I mean…' Krish took a long breath, 'only to you.'

'Whom do you think I was talking about? Imran Faiz? You idiot. I was talking about getting married to you too.'

Krish's face lit up with a wide smile. 'Oh. Our marriage. Ohh!!!!'

Mahi shook her head in disbelief, 'For being so smart, how are you such a duffer?'

'I mean, we can't get married in India, no? I think Ma might be OK with it. But your family will toh totally freak out. Not to mention all our relatives and society and all that. No, Marrying you in India is toh not possible.'

'Hmmm…' Mahi was imagining her brothers and their reaction. Ugh. That was not going to be pleasant. 'So then?'

'We could go live in the US. It's legal in some states there. We can get married in California, and Massachusetts, and some other states. I can do some research when I go there in a few months. Mahi, you can join me when I go to New York.

We'll live there, get married, have children, buy a house, get a dog…Ma can join us too!'

Mahi smiled at that thought. 'Children?' 'We want children, no?'

'Achha, how many children do 'we' want?' Mahi smirked with her air-quotes.

'I was thinking we should have three children,' Krish grinned.

'Three children? I'm not getting pregnant three times!' 'Why are you assuming you will have them?' Krish

furrowed her eyebrows, questioning Mahi's assumptions gently.

'You mean, you will?' Mahi appraised Krish in a new light. She hadn't imagined Krish as a mom.

'I am a woman too, you know! Don't be so stereotypical. Just because I dress butch doesn't mean I am not a woman.' Krish had just read Stone Butch Blues and she was beginning to form her own identity, one that accepted labels and yet refused to be trapped by them.

'I know…you don't like labels,' Mahi rolled her eyes.

'I don't. I think they are very reductive. Anyway, I was thinking we'll each have one. And then we can flip a coin for the third one.'

'Or….we can each have one and call it a day,' Mahi grinned. She couldn't believe they were discussing children. It made her so happy – the idea of a little Krish running around the house.

'Alright, fine!' Krish conceded.

'What will we call them? I'm assuming if you've thought of how many, you must have thought of their names too!'

Krish looked like Mahi had caught her red-handed. She murmured something.

'What? I didn't catch it. What did you say?'

'Rehan and Neev,' Krish replied, a little loudly this time.

Mahi thwacked Krish with her pillow. 'You've named them already? What the heck Krish!'

'I'm sorry. But I'm not. I did. I named them. I have imagined a whole future for us. I'll go in August. You make some excuse and join me quickly. We'll get married. We'll find jobs. It will be hard at first, but we'll manage. Can you imagine, someday we will have our little house, with a white picket fence, and beautiful green lawns and a swing set and our kids…Rehan and Neev…are playing and it's spring and the sun is shining and the flowers are blooming and Ma is telling them a story and we are all one happy family!' Krish was off weaving dreams till she noticed that Mahi had tears in her eyes.

'What is it?' Why are you crying?' Krish looked concerned.

Mahi hugged her tight. 'Nothing. It sounds perfect.'

Their last summer was idyllic. They spent all day and often all night together. Her mother had been shooting on location and Mahi had spent weeks with Ma and Krish. But now Sujata was back and she and Ma were headed to a temple early that morning. Mahi, who had stayed over the night was sleeping in Krish's room. She heard the main door close and waited for a few seconds. The house sounded empty. Then she nudged Krish to wake her up. 'Wake up, sleepy head. They're gone. We are all alone.' They had been busy the night before and Krish was tired. 'Let me sleep, Mahi!'

But Mahi started kissing Krish, her tongue was soon trailing Krish's back.

Krish turned around and put the pillow on her head, effectively shutting Mahi out.

'Fine,' harrumphed Mahi. She got up and left the room.

And there was silence.

After a few minutes, Krish could hear her in the kitchen, making coffee. Mahi was humming a sultry song that she knew Krish particularly liked, as she stirred the coffee in her mug. Krish opened one eye. Her ears had perked up to the song. Mahi was a siren call that Krish could just not resist. It would be her undoing, she groaned. Within a few minutes, Krish got up and joined her outside. Mahi was sitting in the dining room on a chair sipping coffee, her legs pulled up so she was resting the coffee cup against her knees. Krish loved looking at those legs. 'Is there any sugar in the coffee,' Krish asked. 'Or should I make a fresh cup?' Mahi liked her coffee strong and often didn't add sugar.

Mahi didn't answer but smiled sweetly, 'Taste it and find out.' She took a big sip from her cup and looked up at Krish, provocatively.

Krish smiled as she shook her head from side to side. 'Of course.'

She reached over to taste Mahi's lips, but she found Mahi pushing for a deeper kiss, driving Krish's mouth open with her tongue. Krish felt sweet, hot liquid pour into her mouth. Oh gosh! Only Mahi. As she gulped the coffee, a moan escaped Krish's lips. Only Mahi could get her worked up so fast. Mahi loved to hear Krish moan. It drove her crazy. But Mahi was not done, she slipped her hand into Krish's tank top, seeking her nipples, rubbing them. Krish took a few steps back from the surprise and arousal that was now coursing through her body and mind. Mahi's ministrations on her breasts were not only to get Krish worked up, but also to show Krish, how much Mahi wanted her.

Mahi took Krish's hands and put it on her breasts, offering them to her. Krish started fondling her nipples, which were already awake and responding to her touch. 'Ummm....Ishq, I love you touching me,' Mahi removed her top, needing more of Krish's touch, more of her affection. Krish started kissing Mahi's breasts, sucking her nipples and leaving tiny love bites around her areola. She knew Mahi loved to look at them when she was away from Krish, all alone in her bathroom.

Mahi pushed Krish against the wall and nibbled gently on Krish's ears and whispered, 'Are you going to make me beg?'

Mahi didn't need to tell Krish what she wanted. Krish knew exactly what Mahi wanted. She got down her knees, needing Mahi in her mouth just as badly. Her own body was searing in need. Krish was on her knees, Mahi's face was contorted in an orgasm and screaming Krish's name when the doors opened. Mahi's mother had forgotten her purse and they had come back. The two mom's looked as their kids as they scrambled to make it seem like what they had witnessed was not true. Mahi's mom was in shock. She face hung open, her eyes narrowed, and if her eyes could throw flame balls to incinerate Krish, Ma would have been left with a pile of ash.

'Mahi, let's go,' her mother said so loudly, it made Mahi jump.

Mahi looked at Krish and then at her mother. Tears started streaming down her face. She went quietly to Krish's room and got ready. She picked up her duffel bag and her books and got out. She was crying but Krish didn't dare say anything. It was only when Mahi was leaving that Krish couldn't stop herself, she said, 'Mahi'

But her mother turned and said, 'Nahi.' There was a finality to the voice. Mahi didn't look back. She just left. There was going to be hell to pay.

'Kya gandh macha rakhi hain (What is all this dirty business), Mahi?' asked her mother once they were alone. 'Woh ladki. Woh gandhhi ladki. Usi ne tujhe uksaaya hoga. (That girl, that dirty girl, she must have incited you). Bloody unnatural girl. You are not going to see her again.'

'Mummy, please. I love her.'

'Shut up Mahi. Tere future ki soch. Think about your future, that girl will amount to nothing.'

'What are you talking about mom? She is one of the top rankers in her school. She has got a scholarship to go to NYU in Fall.'

'Very good,' her mother said with a vehemence. 'Let her go to USA. We don't need people like her in our country. Yahaa pe khaamakha gandh phela rahi he (She's just spreading her filth here).'

'Mummy, please. I love her. I can't live without her. We'll go to the US. You never have to see us again. Please don't separate me from Krish, mom. I can't live without her.'

Now

Mahi looked at the picture of Krish and her by her bedside. It was them after Krish's 17th birthday. They were very much in love. Krish is dressed in a suit and Mahi is dressed in a dress. They were heading to some party and Ma had taken the photo. Krish was smiling shyly. But Mahi could see how proud she was of the fact that Mahi was on her arm. Next to that old photo, she had put their new one from the awards night. The one whose copy she had sent to Krish.

Mahi thought about what Ma said to her again. Mahi had stood by Krish, helped her with all the hospital stuff. When the gossip columns started wagging their tongues, Kabeer had bought off their silence with the story of proposing soon. Mahi knew that Krish would be going back to the US soon. If she had to say something, this was the time. She had spoken to Karan earlier in the day.

They were drinking wine in his office on the lounge. 'She's going to leave soon. I am not sure what to do. We've moved from hate to being friends again. But…do you think I should say something or do something?' She asked him apprehensively. They had had some form of this conversation since Krish had come into her life. She was tapping her ring on the wine glass nervously.

'Stop doing that! You're driving me crazy,' Karan put his hands on hers to stop her. 'Do you think she will understand?' He looked at her inquiringly, his eyebrow raised. 'There are many lives and many crores of rupees at stake here. It is not just about the two of you. If it goes badly, it could impact all of us.'

Mahi took a deep breath. 'She won't say anything. I have unqualified trust in her. But I am not sure how much she will understand. Or want it.'

'Oh, she wants it. Her eyes search only for you. They are such sad, soulful eyes. And the mere mention of your name, and they light up. Mahi, you really did a number on her! You heart-breaker!' Mahi knew Karan was teasing her. Karan had seen her after their breakup. He knew how hard it had hit her.

'I'll try broaching it soon. We'll see what happens,' Mahi decided.

'Finally. I can't wait for all the details. Even the sordid ones. And definitely the raunchy ones! Leave nothing on the table,' Karan laughed. Just then Kabeer walked into the room with his charming swagger and cool persona and asked casually and cluelessly, 'What are we talking about?'

'Tera pataa kaise kaate,' Karan chuckled.

22

⁓⁄⁊⁊⁓

MAHEK SINGH WAS LOOKING GORGEOUS IN A shimmering red saree at a party for the short film's release. Nirali's performance had been praised for her role in the short film as the village belle and she had received a lot of critical acclaim. 'Nirali's performance was sharp yet funny without being derisive. The laughs she earned were genuine and heart-felt.' Another review said, 'In a world where actors use stereotypes for cheap laughs, Nirali's performance is a breath of fresh air.'

Nirali reached out to her right away. 'Thank you so much your advice. Did you read the reviews' She asked as she hugged Mahek.

'Of course. I read the reviews. Congratulations.' Mahek offered warmly. Nirali was happy to share the credit for her success. She gushed about how Mahek's advice had been invaluable and what she was working on for another role in an upcoming film when another actress and Nirali's friend, Mia joined them. They were all chatting when Mia remarked, 'Look who's here.' Kabeer joined the girls and Mia and Nirali looked at Kabeer hug and kiss Mahek. There was an involuntary sigh. Mahek and Kabeer excused themselves and went over to mingle with other guests. Mia turned back to Nirali, 'Arre wah, Nirali. Teri toh chal padi! Moving with all the movers and shakers' Mia stated. There was a hint of bitterness in her compliment.

'Don't worry Mia. Those two movies don't mean anything. Everyone goes through the ups and downs of flops and hits. You should talk to Mahek. She gave me some great advice!'

'Mahek gave you great advice? You mean, like the way she torpedoed your chance for that Navy captain biopic?'

'What? She wouldn't do that!' Nirali looked flabbergasted. Why should Mahek help her and then hurt her? It made no sense. Mia filled her in.

A few drinks later, Nirali saw Mahek was leaving the party. She decided to find out if what Mia had said was indeed true. She confronted Mahek outside the party, right in front of the papparazzi. 'Is it true? Did you recommend to Karan not to give me the Navy biopic?'

Mahek looked surprised and horrified. She was not expecting this. And Nirali had decided to do it in the worst way possible. Flashbulbs went off all over the place. Mahi tried to calm Nirali. 'Nirali, let's talk about it tomorrow. OK?' 'What was it? Did you want the role for yourself? Or could just not see anyone else succeed? The gorgeous and talented queen bee can't give us an inch to succeed!' The paparazzi were having a field day. They clicked away. Cameras were rolling capturing every interaction for salacious TV and gossip rags. Ruchi called the car right away. She opened the door for Mahi.

'Nirali, call me tomorrow,' Mahi said and tried to get into the car. But Nirali grasped her wrist, trying to stop her. 'I want answers, Mahek!'

Mahi looked around. She usually kept a low profile. She hated all this drama. She let her wrist loose from Nirali, who was crying now, and got into the car.

'Chalo driver.'

They got out of the hotel driveway.

Ruchi spoke, 'Mahek Madam, if you want, I don't have to go home right now. I know that's what the plan was. But it's OK. I can help contain the…'

'What's to help? It was all captured on camera. It's already on Twitter.'

'Where to Madam?' The driver asked.

'We'll drop Ruchi to her home in Andheri and then head to our house.'

After she dropped Ruchi, Mahi realized she wasn't ready to go home yet. Besides the paparazzi might be waiting for her there. She decided to she had to escape. And only one thought came to her mind. 'Driver, please take me to Krish's house.' She texted Krish. 'Are you awake?'

Krish replied immediately. 'Yes.' 'Can I come over?'

'You don't have to ask. Of course you can.'

Something about that reply brought a huge smile to Mahi's face. How she missed this unconditional love!

∼

Krish waited for Mahi anxiously. She quickly jumped into shower. Just in case she was smelly. Now Krish looked at herself in the mirror. She was wearing dark blue jeans and a black shirt. They were her good going-out clothes. She smelled her arm-pits. No smell. But she put some cologne on anyway. No harm. She had even put on socks for the occasion.

Why was Krish so nervous. Things were finally good with Mahi. They were communicating. They were… working together. She knew Lauren, Chelsea and Allie didn't particularly get it. And it was hard to explain. But for the time being, they were sort of like friends. Mahi's help had been invaluable with the hospital and surgery and everything else. Mahi's assistant had helped a whole bunch dealing with hospital bills and all when Mahi was on shoot. Krish had got Ruchi a Rs. 10,000 gift card as a thank you.

Tonight, Krish wanted to thank Mahi too. She wasn't exactly sure how. She wanted to express her gratitude and maybe, talk. Talk about their past, their present and maybe their future? Krish's hands felt clammy at the idea. She rubbed them against her thighs on her jeans. Calm down, Krish. She was practicing deep breathing when the bell rang.

Krish opened the door and Mahi came in quickly. She was in her shimmering saree and full make up. Oh boy! Thought Krish. Mahi's eyes searched and found the wonder and joy and lust and longing she was looking for in Krish's eyes. Mahi knew how much Krish liked her in red.

Deep breaths. Kabeer is going to propose to her soon. But then why is here, teasing me? Why is she wearing red? thought Krish.

Krish went into the kitchen and poured some cold water for Mahi and herself. Heaven knows she needed to cool down, thought Krish.

'Thank you,' Mahi said as she reached for the glass of water. Even the way she was sipping her water was so sexy to Krish today. What the heck, Krish. Control yourself.

'You were out at an event?' Krish asked.

'Yes. It was going well till…anyway. It will be in the news!

I don't want to talk about it, OK?'

'OK.' Krish's face showed so much love and concern. Mahi knew she was really OK here. Mahi looked around and asked if Ma was sleeping. Krish replied she had gone to sleep a while ago but that she was doing well. 'She walked the community compound today. 5 times. Apparently that's a kilometre. So that's good.'

Mahi sat down and got comfortable. She asked about Krish's writing. Krish's eyes perked up and she talked about how it was going well and she was happy with the progress of her second book. Mahi loved seeing Krish talk about her writing. There was pure joy on her face. 'How's the kid, your writing partner?'

'Anaya? She's good.' Krish smiled, 'She's a good writer but so excitable! Did we get excited as easily at that age?' Krish wondered aloud.

'In which way?' Mahi teased. 'You used to get plenty excited.' Mahi giggled.

Krish blushed, 'Sheee, not like that.' Krish sent a pillow flying towards Mahi, 'And if I remember correctly, so did you.' 'Oh, you liked that even more,' Mahi laughed. They sat there smiling, lost in their memories for a few moments. This felt good. But also odd. There was so much tension and with Ma fast asleep, it was almost like there was nothing stopping them from ripping each other's clothes off. Except, themselves.

And Allie and Kabeer. As if sensing the awkwardness, Mahi changed the subject again.

'Is there any food?' Mahi asked as she got up to go into the kitchen. Krish got up too and followed her into the kitchen, 'There are no left overs. But I can make you some poha quickly. Would you like that? It will only take me two minutes.'

Mahi teared up. 'That's very sweet of you, Krish.'

'Come sit. You talk, I'll make the food.'

'Did you have a fight with Kabeer?' Krish asked tentatively. Her eyes not meeting Mahi's eyes.

'No! Why?' Mahi asked innocently, wondering what was bothering Krish.

'You looked upset.'

'No. He is never one of my problems!' Mahi said absent-mindedly. Her phone was blowing up. Karan called. Mahi went outside to talk to him. 'So much drama!' His voice crackled with excitement.

'Tell me about it! Do you know who told her?' Mahi asked. 'I think it was Mia. But that's just conjecture on my part.' 'That was a stupid move on her part!' Mahi sounded irritated.

'Ohhh...she won't know what hit her! She's not seen Mahek Singh on the war-path!'

'Forget Mia. We'll handle her later. Can you help set up a talk with Nirali. I want to clear all misunderstandings before it gets out of hand.'

'Are you sure?' 'Yes.'

'I thought she'd be on your blacklist after tonight.'

'Karan, her rise is inevitable. She is talented. But not ready to carry a whole film on her shoulders yet. No point being a villain in a story when you know its end. She's better an ally than an enemy.'

'Alright. We'll have Akash and Ruchi talk to her person. Anyway, where are you? How did you get into your building? It must have been a hot mess.'

'I'm actually at Krish's house.'

'Ooohhhh! Booty call!' Karan was chortling in positive delight.

'Shut your mouth Karan!' Just then Krish came out carrying a tray of steaming hot poha and some cold coffee. 'Anyway, I have to go now.' As she hung up the phone, she could hear Karan saying, 'I want details.'

'Hey!' Krish said. 'I made some cold coffee. I know it's not those fancy lattes or anything but you used to like it…a long time ago.'

Mahi tried it. Foam covered her lips making a moustache. 'Yumm. I still like it! Thank you!' This is why she had fallen in love with Krish. There was no judgment, no questions, no expectations. Just love.

'Umm…you have…' Krish looked at her lips…and involuntarily bit her own lip. 'You have…on your lips!'

'Oh!' Mahi giggled. 'Sorry.' She took a napkin and dabbed it on her lips. In previous times, Krish would have licked it right off. Part of Mahi wished she still would. They sat down and ate in silence for a few minutes. Oddly, it didn't feel weird. They talked about their days and their weeks. About work and politics and all things normal couples talk over late night poha and cold coffee. Mahi informed Krish that Ruchi had sent thanks for the gift-card. Krish insisted that it was her instead who should be thankful and that she couldn't have dealt with all the hospital bureaucracy without Ruchi's help. 'I'm glad it all worked out OK,' Mahi was happy she had been able to help Krish. Even if Ma hadn't asked, Mahi would have wanted to help. Their talk moved from people to movies and things from their past and present.

'No way you still like Govinda movies?' Mahi gaped at Krish in astonishment.

'Why does that surprise you?' Krish asked. 'I liked them then. I like them now.'

'I thought of you as the literary types, you know with more discerning tastes. More profound. More intellectual.'

'I am. But everyone loves camp. Govinda is quintessential Indian camp. Especially his movies with Karishma Kapoor.'

'Hmm…maybe you're right. That's what I like about you Krish. You're who you are. You like what you like. And you don't change it to suit other people's perceptions of you.'

Krish smiled. There seemed like a deep sorrow in her eyes as she smiled.

'What is it?' Mahi asked, wondering.

'I had no one impress. You were the only that mattered. In some way, it gave me a lot of freedom to do what I wanted to do, to study what I wanted to study, to be whatever I wanted to be. There were times I'd stop and think would Mahi approve, would she like this?' Krish looked at Mahi, who nodded. 'You know Mahi, the entire time I was at NYU. I just wanted to share it all with you. But I didn't really care to impress anyone else. And I guess by the time I got around to dating and all, I didn't care. I was who I was. It was a take or leave it package.' Krish shook her head, 'After meeting you again, I feel I've been unfair to everyone else in my life. You suck up so much of the air, no one else gets to breathe.' Krish chuckled ironically, 'Anyway, forget it.'

After Krish had taken their plates away, they sat on the couch. Krish opened a bottle of wine. They sipped from their glasses. Looking at each other. Krish said, 'Mahi I never really thanked you for all you did for me. With Ma. For Ma. That day when I called, you had the ambulance here right away. You were just so amazing with everything. With my friends, the surgery, with my relatives, with all those aunties.' Mahi and Krish chuckled.

'And I know I thanked you for my friends – but I know that wasn't easy. I'm sorry about that. They were just…looking out for me. They've seen me…mourn your loss.'

Mahi's eyes looked pained. Krish knew that something had been said between Lauren and Mahi. But she wasn't sure exactly what. She knew whatever it was, it is what kept Mahi away from her for so long. 'They aren't to blame. They haven't seen me happy with you. You…we are different.' Krish tried to explain.

'Lauren said that too,' Mahi said, biting her lip. 'What did she say?' Krish enquired.

'She said you're different with me than with Allie or your previous girlfriends'

'Aren't you different with Kabeer than you are with me?'

Mahi said nothing for a second. Krish looked at her. Her eyes boring into Mahi. 'It's different,' Mahi expressed finally.

'Exactly.'

'Anyway, forget Allie and Kabeer. As I was saying, I wanted to thank you so much for standing by my side with everything. I honestly don't know what I would have done without your help.'

'Don't be ridiculous. Since when did we get so formal? Ma is my family too.'

'I know, but still. Thank you.'

With that Krish leaned back on the couch. There was a finality in the air. Like this was it. Krish had said thank you. Now they had run out of things to talk about. They had to talk about themselves. Their past, their future. Their very present. They were both anxious. Looking at each other. Wondering who was going to initiate the conversation.

Alright, Mahi. This is the time. You can do it. Aar ya paar. She took a deep breath. 'So, ummm....you know, Kabeer and I....ummm....' Mahi looked nervous. She paused, 'ummm...' Krish jumped in, 'Yes, the dinner that Kabeer wanted to do, right? Are you guys free next week. Allie is coming. I thought we could have a double date.' Mahi's face fell, 'Oh!?'

'What is it?' Krish asked, 'Did I interrupt something you were saying? Are you engaged? Is that what you're trying to tell me?'

Mahi looked at her in bewilderment, 'Engaged? What? Where did you hear this?'

'I heard from some interns at the Raichand office,' Krish explained. 'I heard Kabeer is planning to propose soon. Congratulations.'

'Ohh. That's what I was trying to explain,' said Mahi. 'Oh, what about it?' asked Krish, her eyes on Mahi.

'Nothing,' said Mahi. 'Nothing. Forget it. Allie is coming?' Mahi looked interested. Or she could act really well.

'Yes. She will be here day after,' said Krish.

'Oh ok.' Mahi pouted her lips. This is not what she had planned.

There was silence again. After a few moments, Krish said, 'I am thinking of heading back to the US soon. I'm going to discuss it with Allie. She is coming for work but is planning to stay for a few days. I just have been away so long. And Ma is doing much better and we're going to see if Ma can come to the US for a bit and maybe continue her physical therapy there. Of course once Karan's team has been set-up, I'll work on the screenplay. I'd prefer doing it remotely but he said he'd prefer doing it in person. So we'll see about that.' Krish stopped and looked at Mahi nervously.

'So you're leaving?' Mahi looked miserable at the idea. She had gotten used to Krish being back in her life.

'Well, my agent, my work, my friends, Allie – all are back there.'

Mahi's face fell. She was quiet for a moment and then she asked, 'What about me?'

'What about you Mahi? I thought we were friends. Aren't we friends now?' Krish looked hopeful. 'Are you still upset with me?' Krish tried to make things right. She wasn't sure what exactly happened but Mahi looked disappointed.

Mahi teared up. She hid her face in her hands. 'Mahi, don't cry. I'm sorry. I didn't mean for you to cry. Look if you cry, I'll cry too,' Krish pleaded.

Krish moved to where Mahi was sitting. 'Mahi, please. Don't cry,' But Mahi was crying, silently but she was crying. She had hidden her face from Krish. Krish hesitated and then put her arm around Mahi, enveloping her body into a hug. Mahi leaned in to the hug, her body slackened and Krish scooped her up in the hug even tighter. Mahi rested her face against Krish's shoulder and cried. Krish put her hand on Mahi's head, petting her silky black hair softly. 'I'm sorry. It's OK. I'm here. I'm here with you.'

They sat there for a bit. Many moments passed. The closeness reminded them of all the memories between them. This felt good, familiar. Krish sighed. Mahi let out a soft moan. Then something changed. Krish could never resist that moan. The heat emanating from each other's body, the proximity to each other, her overwhelming sorrow on losing Krish again, their constant underlying longing…it was all too much. Krish's face turned towards Mahi and Mahi looked up from Krish's shoulder, their lips meeting. Softly at first, gingerly they found each other. It was as if the lips were recollecting their lost memories. Oh yes. Their lips apparently remembered just fine. And the needs that were just embers moments ago, now turned into a raging fire. Their mouths needed each other, their tongues craved contact. It was as if they had to make up for years of exploration they had missed. Do you still feel the same, do you still taste the same? Do you still moan the same? Krish kissed her ears, a tender spot that Mahi used to particularly enjoy. But Mahi pulled her back. Nope, my lips are not done with you, her mouth seemed to say. Krish was happy to go back to kissing Mahi. She could kiss Mahi for the rest of her life. Isn't that what they had both wanted for so long? Was this really happening? But Mahi and Krish were not planning to think tonight. Not about Allie or Kabeer or how this would make them both cheaters. Because if they thought they wouldn't do it, they couldn't go through with it. But they couldn't not go through with it. The need, the yearning, the sensations coursing through their body were so strong, so compelling. It was like being consumed by an inferno, so strong that it burned through any thoughts they had. No, tonight only their bodies were doing the thinking and the talking. And they had so much to say to each other, so much to show each other, show much to share with each other. Wordlessly, Krish and Mahi went to their room and made each other whole again. And again.

23

THIS IS SO GOOD!' ALLIE GUSHED AT THE LUNCH SPREAD at a famous five star hotel she was staying at. 'The food is definitely one of the reasons I love traveling to India. Especially since my home chef has been missing in action.'

Krish was sitting across Allie in a restaurant eating lunch. She smiled nervously. Allie had just come to India and met Ma and spent the morning at her house. Now they were getting lunch but Krish wasn't sure what to do. Should she tell Allie that she had slept with Mahi. That it had actually happened. It was not a dream, not one of her fantasies – it had actually happened. Flesh to flesh, they had lain together, all night. Till Krish woke up in the morning and there was a note from Mahi that said, she had to leave for a few days and that they would talk soon. But they hadn't spoken. Not because Mahi hadn't called or texted. But because Krish had retreated into a cocoon. She didn't know what to say to Mahi. And now she didn't know what to say to Allie. She was stuck between her two worlds. She had two choices. Her bird in hand and the bird that she really, really couldn't live without. The bird was her oxygen and yet that bird was not available. That bird might be getting married to another man soon.

Krish wondered why Mahi had slept with her. Did she want one last lesbian fling before she took her final step into the heteronormative patriarchy? Or maybe she slept with Krish, for the same reason that Krish, who was also in a relationship, slept with her. Because she was in love with her. Because she missed her.

'Another deep sigh!' Allie observed Krish. 'What's going on? You have been sighing a lot since morning. Is everything OK?'

Krish shrugged.

'Are you worried about Ma?'

'I'm always worried about Ma. I don't want to leave her here but she insists on staying. I don't know what to do!'

'Don't worry we'll try to convince her when I'm back, OK?' Allie was being so nice. So thoughtful. She had got Ma a beautiful Pashmina shawl as a gift. Said all the right things, done all the right things. Everything would have been perfect, if Mahi wasn't in her life. Why did Krish have to go and mess everything up.

'OK!' Krish sighed again.

'Is that it or is there something else on your mind?' Allie asked perceptively. Krish was different. Krish knew that Allie was not stupid. Allie had been nice to Krish, patient and loving. Krish had been open to the relationship but this relationship had the same problem that all of Krish's relationships had. Krish still carried the scars from her first relationship. And the night spent with Mahi didn't help any.

Just then the phone rang. Whew, saved by the phone! 'Hey Karan,' Krish answered the phone.

'Hey Krish, I have some good news. We are able to bring together the team to work on your screenplay. They are scheduled for the next 3 weeks. Does that work for you?'

'Oh…' Krish paused. 'Alright. Yes, that works. Will that be enough time?'

'Yes. I think so. We will sort all major issues by then and then we can continue and you can join us on Zoom.'

'OK. Then let's do it,' Krish said.

When she finished her phone, Allie had finished the food in front of her and was checking her phone. 'Allie, I wanted to talk to you about something.'

'Is it important? I have to leave in a few minutes. How about we chat after I come back from Bangalore in a few days.'

'Yeah, OK. Let's do that.' Krish said. Whew. Maybe she could think of something to say by then.

'Oh, when is that dinner you promised me with me the world famous couple, Mahek Singh and Kabeer Agarwal?'

'Ummm…I am not sure. I will have to check.'

'Are you kidding me? I thought you had set it up.' She looked miffed.

'I had.' Till I slept with one half of that couple. Krish chuckled nervously and took out her phone to text Mahi.

'Allie is here. She wants to know when we're all having dinner together.' The text beeped into the ether-verse.

There was no answer.

Krish and Allie looked at the phone, waiting for it to beep back. 'Ohh, come on Krish. Don't back out on me now. I told everyone! They were all so jealous.'

'I'll make it happen. I promise.'

Krish sent another message to Mahi. It simply said, 'Please.'

∽

Mahi looked at the text that popped up from Krish. Finally, she thought as she opened her phone hurriedly. She had trying to get in touch with her for days. She had called, texted, tried facetiming, and there was just radio silence. And now finally…wait. What the fuck!

Mahi was so angry when she read the texts that she literally threw the phone across the room, 'For fucks sake!'

The production team had been doing various things around her. Suddenly the whole room went silent. Mahi was not known as a temperamental actress. She didn't make life hell for her staff, didn't make unnecessary demands or throw temper tantrums. She was known in the industry as the most hard-working actor. So when Mahi looked around the room she saw everyone had shocked faces. She took a deep breath and motioned to Ruchi and said, 'I think I need a new phone.' 'Of course,' said Ruchi as she hurried out to get her a new phone.

Within the hour, Ruchi had given her a new phone complete with her contacts and messages and all. Mahi sat with Karan at the end of the shoot. She still hadn't replied.

'So? What are you going to do?' Karan asked. 'I've got her staying here for another few weeks. I've bought you more time. But now you need to…'

'You know what I had planned to do. But then … '

'You guys let your bodies do the talking instead,' Karan sneered.

'And Allie is coming, remember?' Mahi said, irritated. Mahi hated the idea of seeing this woman who called Krish, Jaan in front of her. How dare she call her Ishq, Jaan. But then Mahi softened, 'What if this is her person, I don't want to screw it up for her?'

'You know and I know that is not true. There is only one person for her. And that's you.'

'Why are you doing this? What about Kabeer and his career?' Mahi questioned.

'What about Kabeer. We discussed it already. We've got a plan,' Karan waved off that question.

'You're right. I'm just getting cold feet. We have a plan. Once Allie is done with the visit, right? OK,' said Mahi decidedly, 'We can do this. Let me send her the text – How about you and Allie come on Saturday at 8:00 pm at my house?'

'THANKS SO MUCH!' Krish replied right away.

Then Mahi's phone pinged again with a text message. 'What about the other thing? Should we talk before then?'

'The other thing? Really? Is that what we're calling it now?' Mahi typed back.

'Well, you know what I mean,' Krish's message read.

'Isn't Allie with you right now?' Mahi asked. 'Are you guys…?

'She's in Bangalore,' Krish replied.

'Oh.' Mahi felt so much better. She had been driving herself crazy imagining Allie and Krish together. 'What did you want to talk about?'

'I mean…' Krish texted.

'Yes?' Mahi wasn't going to make this easy for Krish. Not after the radio silence she'd been getting for the past few days. 'I don't know. Are you planning on telling Kabeer? I have

to tell Allie. I'm not sure how and when. I feel so terrible.' 'What about us, Krish?'

'Huh? What about us?' Krish texted back, clearly unaware of what Mahi was talking about.

'Before we think about Kabeer and Allie – don't we have to sort us out?' Mahi explained.

'I don't even know where to start to sort us. Where do we begin?'

'WTF Ishq. Say it.' Mahi needed to hear it.

'I love you. I have always loved you. Some days I feel I have loved only you. The rest just exist.'

'Me too,' replied Mahi. She had a wide smile on her face. 'So, now what? What about Allie and Kabeer?' The phone pinged back. Mahi looked at the phone, wondering what to answer.

24

~⁄|\~

KARAN AND HIS TEAM MET KRISH FOR THE SCREENPLAY in the conference room. 'We've all read and enjoyed the book,' Karan started the meeting. 'We're lucky we have the author of the book willing to work with us on the screenplay.' Some people groaned at the idea. 'Don't worry, she's not under any illusion to write the screenplay. So Shreya Mathur here will be leading the project. I will assist. As will Krish Mehra, the author. As the scenes get written, I want the storyboards set up.'

Everyone nodded in agreement. Shreya started the meeting, explaining the story line. 'We want to keep the magical realism within the book. Because without that it's just a plain love story. But we have to find ways of making it fit a reasonable time line. Let's start there. Any ideas?'

'Can we do it as punar janam (re-birth)?' One of the script writers suggested.

Krish cringed at the idea. Oh geez

'This is not Rishi Kapoor's Karz or Dimple Kapadia's Bees Saal Baad,' Karan interjected, dismissing the idea before it got any legs. Krish nodded to him, thanking him.

'Can we do it as a time warp, like that iconic scene in the 1962 Time Machine?' another person suggested. Some people nodded.

'Yes, but Rehan also lives many lives in that time period. It's not like she is just watching time run by her,' Shreya explained. 'Though, we can keep that as one option on the back burner.'

'What if we were to do it like that song Waqt ne kiya, kya haseen sitam from Kaagaz ke Phool? Where they exist but don't. Leading the parallel lives,' asked another screenplay writer.

'Kinda of like La La Land climax?' another one turned and asked her.

'Hmm…That's an interesting concept. I think we should explore it more. Alright, let's keep working on this. Let's also start developing the story boards for the story we do know.'

Karan nodded to Shreya, he felt satisfied that the team was moving in the right direction and he left the room.

Krish worked all day with the team. At first they seemed wary of her presence among them. But Krish watched and learned and just observed. She didn't argue when they consolidated characters. In fact, she agreed with them. Many were surprised by this. So, when Krish finally spoke, they listened. And sometimes agreed.

≈

Nirali, Karan and Mahi met in his conference room. Karan poured them a glass of wine. Nirali looked sceptical. She wasn't sure what to expect.

'Nirali, let me get straight to the point. What Mia told you was true. I did recommend Karan take Zara over you,' Mahi started.

'I knew it! Mia was right!' Nirali screamed. There was a moment of moral superiority. Of moral justification for her bad behaviour. She knew she had fucked up by making a scene at the party in front of reporters. But now she could justify it. And Mahek Singh had given her all the proof she needed.

On the other side of the table Karan glanced at Mahi. Mahi had just managed to get Nirali to confirm it was indeed Mia who had crossed her. He knew Mahi wouldn't have attacked Mia without confirmation. But now that she plied it out of Nirali, he knew she would take her down in an epic way.

Mahek trained her eyes on Nirali, 'Nirali, will you listen to me? I only wish the best for you. Will you believe me when I tell you that you were not ready for the role. It's not easy carrying a whole film on your shoulder. You're very talented. You will get there. Very shortly.'

Nirali flicked her hair and narrowed her eyes but said nothing.

'Look, actors are like a tree. If you harvest them too quickly, they are not ready give fruit yet. And if they do give fruit, it doesn't taste as sweet,' Karan explained.

'Please...this is such bullshit.'

'I knew you may not believe me. So I took the liberty to get the audition from the film. Let's watch it for a moment. Ok?' They all watched it together. Karan and Mahek giving commentary about certain aspects of the acting or direction.

Nirali could see why Zara made sense but she wouldn't admit it to anyone.

'Nirali, you're very talented. All you need is a little more maturity in your acting abilities. It's only a matter of time. And I promise you, there will be roles. Lots of roles.'

'Why are you doing this?' Nirali asked Mahek point blank. Mahek and Karan were a powerful team in Bollywood. They didn't need to explain themselves to anyone. So Nirali was surprised at this meeting. She thought she was going to get chewed out. Her defences were up. But instead, the meeting's conciliatory tone was surprising her.

'I'm trying to explain to you that I'm on your side.' Mahek expressed simply.

'But why?' Nirali was so confused. She was not sure if this was some elaborate take down or an olive branch.

'Because I see myself in you. I am not the enemy. I've been there. I believe in you. Besides, we need more strong female friendships in Bollywood. Enough of the cat fights. The men have their old boys' club. It's time women got together too, right?' Mahek seemed sincere. Nirali had to decide what direction she wanted to go in. And friendship with Mahek and Karan would only be beneficial. And maybe Mahek actually meant it. Nirali let out a deep sigh.

'I'd like that.' Nirali cracked a smile. 'Me too!'

'Me three,' chimed Karan. They all laughed.

After Nirali left, Karan asked Mahi what she was planning to do to Mia.

'Nothing,' Mahi answered flippantly, examining her nails. 'Come on! The last time someone took panga against you, their lives were destroyed. You're liked but also feared all over the industry.'

'Karan, I'm going to let you in on a secret. I actually do nothing to the people. I just make it known they have crossed me. And the rest is actually their own fears. Their own self-fulfilling prophecies. I just sit back and wait.'

'What? No way!'

'Seriously, you think I have the power to cause them harm? No, they inflict the harm upon themselves. Because they stop believing in others. When you're suspicious of everyone, when you think everyone is out to get you, you make stupid mistakes. They are responsible for their own downfall.'

'Really! You do nothing?' Karan looked flabbergasted.

'I promise!' Mahi smiled and went back to examining her nails.

That evening, Krish talked to Ma, 'You were right, as always.' Krish smiled wryly. 'Working on the screenplay and it's fun. I am enjoying the process. It's different. I wouldn't have thought I would have enjoyed it. But I did. How did you know me so well?'

Ma smiled. She looked tired.

'Did you do your exercises today?' 'Yes,' she said quickly.

'Here let me check how many steps have you walked today? The doctor said you need at least 8000 steps.'

Krish took Ma's wrist in her hand and tapped on her Fitbit. 'It says you only walked 6477 steps. Ma!!'

'I got tired, beta!' Ma looked so small and frail after the surgery.

'You said I should go work and that you were fine. And that you would do everything and that the aunties were there. I can't leave you like this Ma if you're not taking care of yourself…We're going for a walk after dinner. OK?'

Krish went into the kitchen and started cooking.

Just then her phone buzzed with a FaceTime call. It was Lauren.

'Shit.'

She shut off the stove as she pressed answer and then ran to her bedroom and closed the door.

'Hey Lauren.' Krish smiled. Unable to fully look her in the eyes.

'I thought so,' Lauren said, her eyes were all beady and narrow with I-told-you-so writ all over her face.

'Hey Krish,' Wendy said from behind Lauren.

'Hey Wendy. It's nice to see you,' Krish loved Lauren's fiancée and would take any distraction she could get.

'How's your book coming along?' Wendy asked sweetly.

She was clearly trying to save Krish from Lauren's wrath.

'It's good. I'm thinking of renaming my lead character after a kid I met here. It seems appropriate. This generation is so feisty. I feel it suits my character, all the way back to 2000 years ago.'

'Oh, that's sweet,' Wendy smiled.

'Yes. I thought so,' Krish smiled knowing they were just delaying it and that Lauren was probably going crazy.

Wendy giggled and said, 'Alright, I see Lauren throwing me dirty looks. She thinks I'm shielding you from her anger.'

'You are,' Krish smiled.

'Yes, not for long. Krish Mehra, HOW COULD YOU? You told me you're not a cheater. And now? What do you have to say?' Lauren bellowed.

Krish said nothing.

'It happened just like I said, right? She came over, you were crying, she hugged you and you two were naked,' Lauren had a gleam of I-knew-it in her eyes.

'No. She was crying.'

'Ahh. And that makes all the difference. For fucks sake, Krish!'

Just then Chelsea got on the call. As they patched her in, she said, 'Sorry all, what did I miss?'

'Nothing. Lauren was gloating about how she called it,' Krish said dryly.

'Yeah, she's been pretty happy about seeing the train collision – that everyone could see,' Chelsea rolled her eyes.

'Hey, that's not the point!' Lauren argued, wondering when did this conversation become about her.

'Lauren really loves gloating, doesn't she?' Krish pivoted. 'Oh gosh, yes,' Chelsea giggled.

Even Wendy joined in from behind, 'That's all she's been talking about.'

'That's not the point. Chelsea, and don't enable Krish,' Lauren was serious now.

'It's done, isn't it? Question is now what? Krish, do you have any answers to that? Now what?' asked Chelsea getting serious.

'I honestly don't know. I haven't spoken to Mahi since we…you know.' Krish answered.

'Yes, we know,' said Lauren, rolling her eyes.

'Her life is here,' Krish explained. She'd been thinking about this nonstop since that night.

'And your life?' asked Chelsea.

'Would it be wrong if I said it was with her.' Krish knew it would hurt Lauren and Chelsea when she said that but she was being honest.

'But Kabeer?' Lauren asked.

'I know. I know.' Krish sighed. 'I can't live without her. And I can't be with her. So it makes sense to go back to Allie, right?

I have really fucked up my life. The person I want, the person I'm with – all of it – it's just fucked up. I don't know what to do. How to feel. About her, about Allie…I mean, I'm not blaming Mahi for what happened. But shit. After that night, it's so hard to go back to Allie. I can't bring myself to be intimate with her. Shit. What do I do?'

'You're in deep shit,' said Chelsea.

'I know. The logical thing to do is to apologize to Allie. And hope she takes me back,' Krish shrugged.

'Hmmm. Apologizing to Allie is definitely the first step. Do you think she'll take you back?' Chelsea was sceptical.

'She may not. I'll have to try. We can go for couples counselling and I can work on getting over Mahi.'

'Maybe this will be ancient history soon. A summer fling. Once you're back in USA, everything will go back to normal?' Lauren suggested.

'Yes. Maybe. But how do I remove my soul from my body?' Krish asked.

Krish was back in Karan's office. Shreya was there too. They were having a screenplay meeting before the rest of the team arrived. Krish looked around the office. She liked the modern décor with the traditional elements. The office colours were red, blue and gold. It was Indian with a modern twist. Or maybe it was just Indian. India had changed so much in the last 10 years. Sometimes Krish had trouble keeping up.

Karan asked Shreya and Krish, 'How's the screenplay coming along?'

'We've still not resolved the magical realism issue. But work has been steady and we're coming along nicely.'

Karan turned to Krish, 'Are you happy with it?'

'I have a small issue. There is a scene where you have Mahi, I mean Meher take out her anger and frustration with her dancing and you have Rehan in the gym boxing. Well, I like the cinematic elements – the juxtaposition of how they are dealing with their anger and separation. but can we have a scene before that, that shows Rehan signing up for boxing class. Just a quick scene – words are not necessary – just a handshake or seeing a pamphlet or signing up or something. See, because during the separation Rehan is feeling physically and emotionally vulnerable and helpless. She can't defend herself, or her love. She's weak and she hates it. So she decides to go boxing. I think that element needs to come across more clearly.'

'I understand. We can definitely add it to the mix,' Karan looked at Shreya who nodded in the affirmative. 'Of course I can't promise what happens in the editing room.'

Krish looked a little peeved by that response. Like Karan was not taking her concern seriously.

'But I can definitely put in a note,' Karan placated her. 'Anything else? Any major concerns?'

'No, none. Shreya and team are doing a great job. I think this is what Ma wanted,' Krish was satisfied with the way work was going.

Shreya looked at her watch and said, 'I think the team is probably here. I'll head out. You guys can join me when you're done.'

'Alright,' said Karan.

'So, we're thinking of a small launch party next week. I think the team can continue working on the rest of the screenplay,' Karan said once Shreya had left the room. Krish was a little surprised by this news. 'The jyotish said there was a really good mahurat for a new venture. So we thought why not? Besides, we wanted you around for it,' Karan explained. Krish was overwhelmed by the gesture. She thanked him. Karan waved her off and changed the topic, 'You're happy with the screenplay then. Shreya said your suggestions are few and made sense to the plot. Without a lot of author interference, our team will belt this out in a couple of months. Don't worry these guys are all professionals,' Karan explained.

'I'm glad I'm not like other authors then,' Krish chuckled.

Karan laughed, 'Hey, while I have you here, do you know whom you'd like to play Rehan?'

'I don't. There was some discussion among the writers. One of them suggested it would be cool if Mahi played Rehan. I mean, any actress can play Meher, right?'

'But I thought your mom wanted Mahi to play Meher.' 'Yes. I mean, it's just a thought. I just figured it would be something different,' Krish shrugged.

'Yeah.' Karan's wheels were turning. Krish could see him figuring out the different permutations and combinations of actresses to figure out the best on screen pair. 'I'll get the casting director on this,' said Karan. Krish started getting ready to leave when Karan asked her if she was leaving for the US after the launch party. Krish nodded. Karan asked, 'Back to your life in USA?'

'It's not like I have a life in India, right?' Was Krish asking Karan for a sign about Mahi? They were close friends, after all.

'Au contraire, one could argue, your life is literally in India,' Karan smirked.

'My life is supposedly getting married to someone else very soon,' Krish replied without missing a beat.

'Where have you heard that?' Karan's eyebrows arched up. 'From interns in your office, Karan,' Krish said pointedly. 'Most of what you hear about stars is bullshit,' Karan waved his hands dismissively. 'Have you spoken to Mahi about her relationship with Kabeer?'

'You mean, how she chose him over me? No. I don't want to hear how he is better than I am. Or that he can give her something I can't. I'm not interested.' Krish didn't want that pain. No thank you. Somethings were better left unsaid.

Karan got serious, 'It's not what you think Krish. You should talk to her.'

Krish said nothing.

'I have a question for you. If Mahi was single, would you want to be with her?'

Krish chuckled wryly. 'That's like asking me, do you want to breathe?'

'Then maybe don't book your tickets just yet,' Karan's eyes seemed to dance with possibility.

'But Karan, it's not just Kabeer, right? It's also her career. Her movies. If she's with me, she has to come out. And I'm not sure how that will impact her career. How will the country react to Mahek Singh coming out? How will the prime minister react to his favourite actress being a lesbian?'

'Does she have to come out? Can you not be with her without her coming out publicly?' Karan countered gingerly. 'You mean, we'd exist like the known secret? Open to rumours, blackmail, and all kinds of innuendo? And she'd be happy in that existence? You've talked about the toll it takes on you. Why would you want her to go through that? No. If Mahi chooses me, she has to choose me. And everything that comes along with it.'

Karan looked at Krish sceptically, there was a little sadness in his eyes.

'She didn't pick me then. She's not going to pick me now, when she has so much to lose,' Krish sighed. 'Anyway, so launch party next week?' she asked as she got ready to leave to go to the screenplay meeting.

Karan nodded, 'Do you want to invite anyone?'

'You mean except Ma and Mahi. I guess I could invite those aunties who have been helping us. Is that OK? They may get a little star crazy.'

'Don't worry, we handle that every day. I'll make sure you get some invites.' Krish started ready to get up and leave and then she stopped. 'You know, actually, is it going to be an adult kind of affair? If not, there is this kid – she's like 16-17 years old. I'd like to invite her... with her parents, of course. Actually, you might know them. She's the minister's daughter.'

'Yes, of course,' said Karan.

25

⁓⁓⁓

ER CONVERSATION WITH KARAN HAD BEEN ricocheting in her mind, and Krish realized that the door to any relationship with Mahi was closing. Mahi would never pick her. It was an impossible dream. Krish had to reconcile her mind and heart to being friends with Mahi. And come clean with Allie. So that is what she had in mind when she picked up Allie from the airport.

'Hey Allie! Gosh, it's so good to see you,' Krish smiled as she hugged her. There was something pleasant and familiar about Allie. Maybe this is not so bad.

Allie was dressed in a grey suit and with a white shirt and her signature Hermes scarf.

'Hey sweetheart. It's good to see you too,' Allie kissed Krish on her cheeks. Allie was mindful of them being in India, at the airport in public.

'We have to be at Mahi's place around 8:00 pm. We have a little time if you want to change. Not that you need to. You look fantastic.'

'Aww. You're sweet. Yes, I'd like to change. I am not only meeting your ex, I'm meeting the most beautiful woman in

India. You couldn't have just, you know, fallen in love with someone more ordinary?' Allie laughed.

Krish smiled bashfully. As much as she wanted to move on, the mere mention of Mahi made her feel all gooey inside. Krish and Allie entered the hotel and as they started to head for the elevators, someone called out Krish's name. It was Shalini Baweja, the media mogul. 'Oh hello, it's nice to run into here,' said Krish. Shalini was wearing jeans and a white shirt, simple yet elegant. Krish noted she was still wearing the mangalsutra. This puzzled Krish. But she simply shrugged it off.

'Allie, this is Shalini, she is the CEO of Big B Books and media companies. I met her at the awards ceremony and we've kept in touch since then,' Krish made introductions. 'Allie is my girlfriend. She's visiting Bangalore for work but decided to detour to Mumbai to see me.'

'Ahh, hello! Nice to meet you,' said Shalini Baweja, happy to meet Allie. Krish exhaled a quiet exhale. She wasn't sure how it would go down when she actually introduced people to her girlfriend. It's one thing when you see a lesbian as a single person. Another when she's in a relationship. Krish was glad Shalini was open-minded and cool, despite the mangalsutra. Krish liked her even more now. And she made a mental note not to judge people so quickly.

'Nice to meet you too,' Allie smiled as they shook hands. 'So, congratulations Krish. I heard you're working on the screenplay for your movie with Karan Raichand,' Shalini said looking at Krish now.

Allie interrupted them before Krish could respond. 'Krish, how about you stay here and chat, I'll go and get changed, OK?'

'Alright,' Krish nodded and she started chatting with Shalini about their favourite topic, books.

Krish didn't realize how engrossed she had been for the past 20 minutes when Allie tapped her shoulder. Krish turned around and was stunned by her girlfriend. Allie looked gorgeous. Her hair which had been tied earlier was now open and had been blow dried and she was wearing a white and black dress that fit her curves beautifully.

'Wow. I feel so lucky,' said Krish as Allie put her arms around her waist.

'You should be,' Shalini laughed. 'Allie, you look gorgeous. Have fun you two!' And Shalini took leave. 'Krish, think about our offer!'

Allie arched her eyebrow. Krish explained, 'They are opening these writing programs around the country and they want me to do a series of workshops on writing. Kind of like an Indian Masterclass.'

'That sounds fun.'

'Yes, and the pay sounded good too. I just don't know if I want a job here.'

'You don't really need a job. Your book is still on the New York Times best-seller list.'

'I know, right?! Anyway, let's not worry about that tonight.' Krish offered her arm to Allie, 'Shall we?'

'I'm nervous,' Allie said in a rare moment of self-doubt. 'About meeting Mahi?'

'I mean, she's not just your ex. She's the Ross to your Rachel.' Allie said referencing a popular sitcom, Friends, that they had both enjoyed over the years.

Krish laughed. 'No. You're with me. And she's with Kabeer. And we're all having dinner. It's that simple.' I wish!

Soon, Allie and Krish carrying a bottle of wine, and a bouquet of lilies were standing outside Mahi's door. Allie nudged her at the sight of the armed security guards outside their apartment. Krish just shrugged, 'Crazy fans! Can't be too careful.'

Kabeer opened the door and welcomed the couple. Kabeer was wearing a dark grey jacket over jeans. His shirt was also dark grey, as were his leather shoes. His clean shaven face, his dark eyes, his glossy hair, and his 6 pack physique would have been alluring to anyone but the couple standing in front of him. Though, even they had to admit, he was sexy. They were gay, not blind. Kabeer took the wine bottle from Allie. He went to take the flowers from Krish but she was clearly not willing to give it to him. She turned slightly and waited. Kabeer's face registered surprise but I guess he had gotten used to Krish being different by now. He let her be and went to the wet bar to get drinks.

Krish took in the house, it was mostly white with white walls, white furniture and white marble, except for the large bouquets of pink lilies in the foyer and the living room. Large black and white photos adorned the walls. It was open space and the living room was two steps down from the hallway. Krish's eyes went to the door that opened as Mahi came out of her room, a vision in white. Krish gulped as Mahi headed down the living room hallway towards her. Allie followed Krish's open-mouthed gaze, and saw the object of her affectation. She saw Mahi's slight smirk, aware of the impact she was having on Krish. Allie noticed that Mahi's eyes were taking in all of Krish too who was standing there in the blue suit she wore to the Big B Dinner with a white shirt and yellow and blue checked tie. Hmmm....thought

Allie. The most handsome man in India was in the room but Mahi's gaze was only on Krish, lapping her up with her eyes. If there was any doubt in Allie's mind about Mahi's sexuality, this scene playing out in front of her removed them. Krish hadn't been an experiment. Mahi was gay.

Kabeer came towards Allie, with two wine glasses. Allie was in the living room, a few steps down from where Krish was standing. 'Some wine?' he asked her, showering her with his trademark smile.

'Don't mind if I do. Thank you,' Allie smiled back at Kabeer. 'Thank you for the flowers,' Mahi said as she got the lilies from Krish. Krish blushed. Allie wasn't sure she had seen Krish be coy before. Mahi's hands were touching and holding Krish's hands, a lot longer than necessary in the exchange of lilies.

'So, what brings you to Mumbai, Allie?' Kabeer asked amiably. Allie wondered if he was unaware of what was happening in front of him.

'Hmm...' Allie was distracted, her eyes on Krish and Mahi, who were still standing, their hands still touching each other. Mahi probably wasn't even aware of it but her fingers were caressing the back of Krish's hand. 'Umm ...' Allie forced her attention back to Kabeer who was waiting patiently. His eyes on Allie. 'I work at McKinsey. I had a client in Bangalore. So I came to Mumbai for a few days to spend some time with my girlfriend.' Allie said the last part of that sentence loud enough that Krish gave a little jump in the air. Almost as if she suddenly remembered she was here with Allie.

'Right,' Krish said as she hurriedly walked over to Allie. 'Hello Allie, Welcome, I've heard so much about you,'

said Mahi stepping down in the living room cradling her lilies. They air-kissed and Allie inhaled the Opium. She remembered how she had seen Krish go to perfume counters in stores and take a whiff of Opium. She'd seen Krish at the counter stand in that moment, as she shut her eyes, letting her olfactory senses take her down memory lane. Now the pieces of the puzzle were coming together for Allie.

'Before this evening goes any further, can I ask for a favor?' Allie asked. 'I've told my friends I'having dinner with y'all and they wouldn't believe me. Can I post a photo of the four of us on Insta?'

Krish was a little surprised. Allie hadn't told her she was going to make this request. And as well as she knew Mahi she would have never wanted to make such an imposition. Krish looked at Mahi and Kabeer, who thankfully were used to such requests and agreed politely. They put away their wine glasses and the four of them posed. Krish and Allie stood on one side, Mahi and Kabeer on the other side.

Krish, Mahi, can you please get closer, we're not getting you in the camera, said Kabeer as he angled the camera on the four of them.

Krish and Mahi scooched closer. Krish put her hand behind Mahi's back to pull her closer. Mahi looked at her, surprised. Krish shrugged. And mouthed sorry. And then they all smiled for the camera. Kabeer gave the phone back to Allie. 'I've clicked a couple, see which one you want to post.' Allie saw the one where Krish and Mahi were looking at each other, with Krish's hand around Mahi. Mahi looked happy. She scrolled through the others and then picked one where the four of them were looking at the camera and smiling, saying cheese. She posted it on Insta with the tag 'Hanging out with my girlfriend and her friends' and tagged Kabeer, Mahek and Krish.

Mahi, wine? Kabeer asked sweetly. 'Yes, please.' She said smiling at him.

'This is really good wine,' Allie complimented him.

'It's all Mahi. She's the wine connoisseur here. She is very picky about the winery and vintage and wine legs and all. I think she has the best collection in all of Bollywood. She has a whole room in the house dedicated to keeping it at the right temperature.'

Kabeer gazed at Mahi with pride in his eyes. She smiled back as Krish studied the marble flooring. He turned to Krish. 'Krish, what about you? Cab ok?' Kabeer asked holding the Cabernet Sauvignon from Napa Valley.

'Yes, sure.' Mahi noticed right away that Krish had a more guarded posture again. Her body coiling tightly as Kabeer kissed Mahi on the cheek as he gave her a glass of wine. Mahi gently and very discreetly pushed him away. She knew Krish was a ticking time bomb with everything going on between them and she didn't want to exacerbate the hurt.

Krish turned around and looked at the walls. There were some bookshelves and some old photos of Mahi. Krish walked over right away. She stood in front of the picture of the two of them together playing in their colony garden and smiled. Allie joined her and entwined her fingers through Krish's. She could see Krish's face had that same expression she had when she was smelling Opium at the perfume counter.

'Is that you?' Allie asked, pointing to the picture.

'Yes. That's us,' Krish smiled, waves of nostalgia on her face.

'Wow! That's…deep. Do you know when you fell in love?' Allie asked innocently. Krish looked around. She wasn't sure if Kabeer knew about her and Mahi. But he was in the other room. Mahi came over to where Allie and Krish were standing.

Mahi said, 'That's your girlfriend, right there. Wasn't she a cutie.'

'She sure was.' Allie smiled. 'I was just asking her, did she know when she fell in love with you?'

'Oh!' Mahi lifted her eyebrows in surprise. 'What did she say?'

'She hasn't answered yet.' Allie and Mahi now both turned to Krish.

Krish laughed nervously, 'I don't know - The first time she held my hand. I have no idea. I loved looking at her. I loved it when she smiled at me. When she saw me. We'd play chor police and she'd tickle me when she caught me. I loved it. I loved it when after she bought her textbooks for the new academic year, she'd come over to our house and give me her English reader.' Krish explained to Allie, 'Mahi went to a private school. Her school had better books, a better literature program than we did. So I'd read my books and then read hers too. She was always so thoughtful. And I loved it when she put her head against my shoulder and I fed her part of my dessert. And most when she hugged me.'

Allie looked at Mahi's face which was mirroring Krish's as memories from their past resurfaced. They looked so happy.

'Was there a definite moment for you Mahi?' Krish asked, smiling at the fond memories.

Now Allie turned her head to look at Mahi. Mahi blushed, 'When we walked together to my Bharat Natyam class and you would be reading your book while I danced. And sometimes when you thought no one was looking, you'd look up and see me dancing. And the way you looked at me. It just melted my heart. I was just smitten.'

'Haha,' Krish laughed. 'I never knew!'

'That's a sweet love story,' said Kabeer joining them by the photos.

Krish mouthed, 'does he know' signalling to Mahi with her eyes.

Mahi nodded, with an 'Of course.'

Hmmm, Krish was surprised. She wasn't exactly sure why. But she was. Kabeer announced, that dinner was ready. And he took Allie's arm to lead her to the dining room. Which left Krish and Mahi looking at each other. 'Shall we?' Mahi asked. 'Yes, of course,' replied Krish. Mahi stepped forward and instead of taking Krish's arm, she got closer to Krish's face, their eyes met, Krish's lips opened involuntarily. Mahi smiled, then slowly reached and fixed Krish's tie.

Krish inhaled deeply, 'That's not fair on so many levels.' 'And you not answering any of my calls or texts? Was that fair?' Mahi whispered back sharply.

'I didn't know what to do? I still don't. I have to tell her, right? I mean, I feel like I should feel so horrible. But I kind of don't. Is that terrible? I mean, I feel bad about them...' they looked over and Allie and Kabeer were chatting about the view. Kabeer was showing her the ocean.

'Anyway, let's do this,' Krish shrugged.

Mahi stopped her. 'What is it Krish? What's going on? Are you not happy?'

'Nothing Mahi. I just...I have a lot to talk to you about and now is not the time.'

'Soon?'

'Yes, soon,' said Krish. She headed forward but then hesitated, turned around and addressed Mahi, 'By the way, I wanted to tell you, you look breathtakingly ravishing in that outfit. I mean, I thought I loved you in red. But this luminescent white...ummmm mmm mmm.'

'Really?' Mahi's lips curved into a sly smile. 'I wanted to make sure I was more beautiful than your girlfriend today. Does that make me shallow?'

'No. She had the same intention,' Krish said. 'I'm not surprised,' Mahi giggled.

Mahi and Krish entered the dining room area and Krish looked at the beautifully laid table, but there was no food in sight. 'So where is the food?' Krish wondered.

'It's a sit down dinner, no Krish? Once we sit down, the food will come,' Mahi shook her head at Krish's naiveté.

'Oh ok. I didn't realize we're doing it all fancy!' Krish said. Sometimes she forgot Mahi was not just the girl next door anymore.

'Tch tch,' said Mahi as she sat on the 8 seater square table with another large floral arrangement. Kabeer sat next to her. Mahi had the table laid out in an L shape which meant, she could have Kabeer on one side and Krish on the other. Krish got the chair out for Allie and offered her a seat next to Mahi. Allie hesitated. And then she said, 'Why don't you sit here, Krish. I'll sit next to you here,' and she pointed to the seat next to Krish.

'Are you sure?' Krish asked, secretly delighted about the idea of sitting next to Mahi.

'Yes, I'm sure,' Allie smiled. 'It's your friend. You should sit next to her.'

'There is no such formality. You are welcome to sit here,' Mahi smiled. But her face too shared the delight about being seated next to Krish.

Gosh, why were they such school kids, full of puppy love?

As they sat down the waiter came out with wine. She poured the wine in their glasses around the table. Kabeer lifted up his wine glass and made a toast. 'So glad we could all be together tonight. To old friends and new friends.'

'Hear hear!' everyone sipped their drink.

As they all got seated, two waiters came out with the first course, soup. The chef came out and explained, that it was a Maharashtrian specialty called Tomato Saar soup.

'I've never heard of it,' said Krish, thinking how much of her own culture she had missed out on.

The chef explained it was made by boiling and pureeing tomatoes, which were then flavoured with tamarind, cumin, mustard seeds, curry leaves, peppercorns and coconut milk.

'Ummm…it tastes delicious,' said Krish as she took a spoonful. They all murmured their approval of the soup.

'So Mahi, do you have thoughts about a career path after films? Directing, maybe? We always need more women directors!' Allie asked Mahi.

'I would love that. I've been asking Karan to involve me more in script writing, editing, directing,' Mahi said. She had been seriously thinking about her post acting career. Especially now that Krish was back in her life.

Kabeer chimed in, 'You've been talking about becoming an assistant director to him for his next movie.'

'Who knows when that will be,' Mahi said.

Maybe it will be the movie based on Krish's book,' said Allie.

'Maybe,' Krish smiled.

Kabeer clapped his hands, 'That's a great idea Allie. Mahi, you should become the assistant director to When Doves Die's Hindi adaption, Jab Kabootar Parlok Sidhaare,' Kabeer cracked himself up at his own Hindi adaption of the title.

Mahi shook her head at him, showing her disapproval.

Allie looked at Krish for translation.

'Well, it really means when the pigeons reached the heavens or something like that. I think he mistook doves for pigeons. It was really lame.'

'I think it should be called Maahi Ve,' said Allie.

Mahi looked at Allie with a curious expression. Krish and Kabeer stared at Allie too. Mahi was trying to understand what Allie was up to. It was as if Allie was testing them. But Mahi couldn't figure out why. I mean, she could perhaps guess that Allie had figured out that they had slept together. Especially since Krish was probably avoiding getting intimate with her. Was Krish avoiding getting intimate with her? Mahi had never asked. Krish hadn't volunteered that information. Would Krish sleep with both of them, in the same week? I mean, it wasn't unheard of. And the circumstances were unique. But still....Mahi felt the room get hotter.

'Maahi Ve?' Krish questioned.

'I mean, it is your love story, right? So it seems fitting,' Allie explained as she took another bite of the food.

'I like it,' said Kabeer as he tried it out in his head.

Krish and Mahi said nothing. Krish shrugged, 'I guess that will be up to the screenplay writers and the director, right?' Krish looked and Mahi and Kabeer for confirmation.

'And maybe some jyotshi somewhere,' Kabeer laughed at his own joke again. This time everyone joined in. This one didn't need translating. Allie had head of Jyotish baba's from Krish.

Everyone was having a good time. Dinner was largely uneventful. That is until Kabeer asked about Ma.

'Hey Krish, how is Ma doing? How is her recovery?' Kabeer asked.

Mahi shifted uncomfortably in her chair. Krish noticed it right away but could not figure out why.

'She is fine. All thanks to Mahi and her magic with Dr Pandey.'

'Ya, I toh told Mahi. Krish's Ma is like our Ma. So if we have to go to Dr Pandey's daughter's wedding and do a little dance. No worries, sign me up!'

Krish's face registered shock and horror. Allie and Kabeer realized right away that Mahi hadn't told Krish about this side deal that Mahi had made with Dr Pandey to get him to take the case. The room was silent for a few minutes. Krish was still processing what Kabeer had just said. She had to hear it again. She looked at Mahi.

'Wait...you both danced at Dr Pandey's daughter's wedding...so that he would come and operate on my mom?' Krish articulated slowly.

Mahi didn't say anything but Kabeer interjected. 'Arre, it was no big deal. We do this every day. It's part of our life,' He tried to backtrack from his faux pas.

Krish turned to Mahi and waited for confirmation. Mahi nodded quietly.

'Mahi?! Why didn't you say anything? If Kabeer hadn't said something, I would have never known?' Krish exclaimed.

There was more silence.

Krish looked around the room but she was unable to meet Kabeer's eyes. He had danced for her mom's life and she had repaid him by sleeping with his girlfriend, and future fiancée. What an ungrateful wretch she was. How she had hated him. Boy, that tomato saar soup seemed to be bubbling right back up. She gulped. Finally she said, 'I…I am so sorry for all of this. I…don't know what to say. I can't begin to thank the huge favour you both did for my Ma. The surgery was lifesaving and I know it couldn't be possible without both of you going out of your way to help my Ma….Geez, I am so grateful for your kindness and generosity.' Krish was in tears. 'Without you,' she looked at Mahi, 'my mom would not have got the best care possible.' The she turned to Kabeer, 'Without your kindness and generosity, my mom may not have made it. I am truly indebted to you. Thank you so much. I don't know how I will ever repay your kindness.' Krish's voice cracked with emotion.

Kabeer looked embarrassed. 'Really, Krish, it was nothing.' Krish looked disconsolate, 'For you it may be nothing. But for me it was everything. And you both did it for me. And I repaid you…'

Mahi interjected quickly, 'Krish. Stop. Please. Really, it was no big deal.' Her eyes darted to Allie and then Kabeer. She tried to act casual but there was a hint of alarm on her face. The last thing she wanted was more drama in their lives. She knew Krish was already struggling with their night together. This was not going to help.

Allie noticed that Kabeer and Mahi shifted uncomfortably. Allie wanted to put Krish out of her misery. She raised her glass, 'To Ma.'

Kabeer and Mahi heaved a sigh of relief and raised their glass too, 'To Ma.'

Krish wiped her tears and smiled, 'To Ma.'

After dinner, they sat in the living room and drank some more wine. The waiters brought them dessert. Krish's eyes immediately went to Mahi as she picked up her own bowl. She looked at Krish and as if daring her with her eyes, put it on the side table. Mahi knew it was not possible but that didn't mean she didn't want it. Krish looked away. She felt guilty enough sleeping with Mahi. But now, knowing how much she owed Kabeer, she just couldn't do it to him.

Kabeer got a phone call and Krish excused herself to go to the bathroom. Mahi found herself with Allie alone. *Just don't ask me if we slept together.*

'So Mahi, would you like to move to Hollywood to do American movies?'

Mahi exhaled. This question she could handle. Mahi really appreciated that the conversation with Allie had been interesting. It was not about clothes or fashion or even Krish for that matter. Mahi had asked Allie about her work and her career path. And Allie had done the same. They definitely passed the Bechdel Test. This made Mahi happy. 'Ummm…I guess. I haven't found a meaty enough role to justify it yet. I don't want bit part heroine roles where all I have to do is look pretty. I am finally getting substantive roles here. I definitely don't want to give that up.'

'What are you willing to give up for it, though?' Allie asked softly.

Mahi was taken aback. She replied, 'Something that's not mine.' Then she looked at Allie and asked a question that had been burning her ever since Lauren had brought it up, 'Allie,

Lauren said that Krish is different with me. How is she with you? How is she in America?'

Allie thought about this for a few moments. 'Previously, I would have said that Krish was her own person, she was often in a world of her own, like many writers are, you know? But that she was caring, thoughtful, considerate, kind, and really smart when she joined the world of the living. Now I realized, she wasn't in her own world. She was in your world. Maybe she imagines you with her. It's little things you know, like the look she gets when she smells Opium. That's what you're wearing today, right? It's your signature perfume, I'm guessing?'

Mahi nodded.

'Krish has an incomplete self in the US, the rest of it is with you. She never moved on. I think she's still waiting for you. Question is, is she going to wait forever?' Allie looked at Mahi purposely, hoping the words would sink in.

Allie saw Krish walk back to where they were seated, 'Krish,' Allie exclaimed. Sweetheart, what's that song you sing sometimes. It goes, Kaaga re Kaaga re...

Krish looked at Allie alarmed. 'From Rockstar? Ummm ... why?'

'I was just telling Mahi about it. Will you sing it for us? You have such a nice voice.' Allie turned to Mahi and said, 'Don't you just love it when she sings?'

Krish felt the heat from both sets of eyes on her. She demurred. Just then Kabeer returned, 'Are we singing Hindi songs? Why such a morbid one? I mean, the visual is so horrifying.'

Allie looked puzzled so Kabeer explained the song, 'As this man is dying, the crow has come to eat his flesh. And the man is saying, you can eat any part of my body. But please don't eat my eyes ... I have one last wish to see my beloved.'

Allie knew it was a sad song. She hadn't realized it was so tragic. She looked at Krish astonished. Her eyes looked pained. Allie looked pointedly at Mahi, who had looked away. Tears welling up inside her. Krish shrugged. 'It's just a song. You know, nothing else. You're right. It's pretty morbid. Let's talk about something else,' said Krish. Desperate to change the topic and move away from the pity in Allie's eyes, Krish sat down next to Mahi. 'Mahi, why haven't you eaten your rabri gulab jamun? They are your favourite.'

'Umm...I'm not...' Mahi was making an excuse. Till she realized what Krish was attempting to do.

'What nonsense. I insist,' Krish picked it up and took a spoonful and held it out for Mahi. 'Try it. It's fantastic. You don't believe me? I already had mine, but I'll have another bite to show you.'

'OK. Fine. I'll try a bite,' Mahi said, playing along, a small smile escaping her lips as she took the bite Krish proffered. 'You're right, it is delicious,' Mahi agreed.

'I told you. Now eat it please,' Krish looked at her, widening her eyes and pleading to not make her do any more drama to feed her.

'Alright. If you insist,' Mahi couldn't refuse Krish's big black eyes either. Did they look particularly soulful today?

Mahi had another bite. Umm ... this is good,' she said.

'I told you so!' Krish smiled. For a second, Krish imagined feeding Mahi desserts and then realized she was being crazy. This had to stop! She owed Kabeer that much. She turned away from Mahi.

'So Kabeer, where is your apartment?' Allie asked Kabeer.

'Umm…it's a few streets over. It's not too far,' Kabeer replied, using his hands to show the direction of the apartment.

'And where do you guys spend most of your time?' Allie probed further.

Krish cringed at the idea of Mahi and Kabeer together, spending their time in each other's apartments, in each other's beds. She wished she could shut her ears.

'On the road,' Mahi and Kabeer answered in unison, smiling.

'I see,' Allie smiled.

Krish had to agree, they did make a cute couple. Krish felt small on the inside. She had gone very quiet and was making no effort to make conversation. After a few minutes, Allie said, 'I would love a tour of the house. If you guys give those?' she got up.

'Ummm … yeah. Sure. I can do that,' Mahi said as she finished the last of her rabri-gulab jamun. 'Krish, would you like to join us?'

Krish sat rooted in her chair. 'I'm OK here, I think. Maybe I'll go check out the books.' But Allie swooped in and locked her arms in Krish's and said, 'Come jaan. Let's go.'

Krish couldn't refuse that so she got led into the house tour. Mahi showed them the dining room and kitchen. Her house connected to another apartment she had bought later and now used as a meeting space for producers, directors, journalists – basically all film related stuff. Here Krish saw posters of Mahi's previous movies. Awards from various organizations. Photos of Mahi with Kabeer, with the Prime Minister of India and with various national and international dignitaries and politicians. This was all Mahek Singh. Krish wanted to get back to Mahi's house. Mahi showed them the two guest bedrooms in her house and pointed to an office space. 'Can we?' Allie asked, holding on to Krish a little tighter.

'Yes...ummm...of course. It's not very exciting,' Mahi tried to dissuade them. It was sanctum, her quiet space in her house.

But Krish and Allie independently thought Mahi was wrong. This was the most exciting room. There was another photo of Mahi and Krish as children. This one was more intimate, they were holding hands. And another of Krish and Mahi when they were teenagers on the swing with Krish's back to the photographer. Allie studied the photos. There a photo of Mahi and Sujata, Mahi's mother, when she was very old. There was a couple of photos of Mahi with Karan, Mahi with Kabeer on a holiday and several of Mahi by herself, looking away in a distance, a faint smile, a shadow of hope in her eyes. 'Hmm...' Allie smiled. 'I love this one. She pointed to one with Mahi and Krish as teenagers. One can tell, you're in love with Krish in this one. It's so powerful but so gentle and soft.' Krish looked at the photo, tears brimming to the surface. She looked away, which is when she spotted her book, When Doves Die on the coffee table next to the main armchair. Krish picked it up. 'I see something familiar,' Krish chuckled.

Mahi laughed. 'Of course I have a copy. I was giving away the award for it. Besides, Karan bought everyone a copy for the adaptation.'

'But is it a signed copy?' asked Krish, her eyes twinkling with excitement.

'That it is not,' Mahi admitted, 'Will you sign it for me?' Mahi wondered what Krish would write.

'Of course,' Krish got a pen out of her jacket pocket. A Mont Blanc she had bought from her earnings. She kneeled down to get to the height of the coffee table, opened the book to the first pages, wrote a message, signed her name and then shut it and put it back in its place.

Mahi looked at Krish curiously, picked up the book and read it aloud, 'Shukran, Meher, Karam. Love, Krish Mehra.'

'What does it mean?' Allie asked.

'It means, thank you, love and grace. It's hard to explain. Some of it gets lost in translation,' Krish explained.

'Hmm...' said Allie. And then as they walked past Mahi's bedroom, Allie saw the half open door as an invite and stepped in. 'This is your room, Mahi?' Allie asked innocently. Mahi stopped them from going further. 'Yes. But I am very fussy about it. I don't let anyone in.' Her office space was one thing, but she was going to draw a firm line with her bedroom.

'Not even Krish?' Allie asked.

Mahi couldn't say no to Krish, could she? This time, Mahi knew why Allie had brought Krish along for the tour. She wondered why. Why did Allie want to see her bedroom. Mahi hesitated. That was all the time it took for Allie to find the other photos by her bedside.

'Oh wow! Look at this Krish. It's you again,' Allie said, her eyes looking at Mahi for a reaction. Mahi blushed as Krish looked at the photos. Krish picked up the one of them ready to go to the Imran's party. 'Mahi, you look so different in this picture. What's different?' Krish turned it around and showed it to Mahi as she asked her, staring into the picture to figure it out. 'I had permed my hair,' Mahi replied now uneasy about them being in her very private space, looking at her very personal photos.

'Ahh, yes. I remember. You looked so different. But nice. I mean, you always looked nice,' Krish smiled. She looked at the other photo as she returned this one to its space by the bedside. She had the same photo at her house. The one of her looking at Mahi at the Big Bs Awards night.

'Ummm…are we done here,' asked Mahi looking very bothered.

'Yes. of course,' Allie said, who was now holding the photo that she quietly put away. Then as they were headed out, she said, 'Mahi, do you mind if I use your bathroom for quick minute?'

Unable to say no to the request, Mahi nodded stiffly. Mahi wondered for a second if Allie was taking pictures of her house. Why did want to see every nook and corner. Mahi was fuming at her invasion of privacy. Krish and she waited outside as Allie went to the bathroom.

Krish moved in closer to Mahi and whispered in her ears, 'I'm sorry.'

Mahi relaxed visibly. She held onto Krish's arms and leaned into a hug.

'Why didn't you tell me, huh?' Krish whispered softly. 'Stop it Krish. I did it for Ma.' Mahi sounded serious. 'But Kabeer…'

'I know. But please don't stress about it. This is what we do. Trust me. Now please stop brooding over this. And say something else…quickly!'

'Did you have a good time tonight?' Krish whispered.

'I loved it best when you fed me,' Mahi smiled at Krish affectionately.

'You're such a nautanki. Would you not have eaten it, if I hadn't fed it to you?' Krish wondered.

'I always knew you'd come through,' Mahi said smugly. 'But what if I hadn't...' Krish sounded mildly exasperated by Mahi's smugness.

'I guess we'll never know.' They both chuckled.

Allie came out of the bathroom and they left the room. As they were leaving the house, Krish was thanking Kabeer once again. Kabeer looked embarrassed. Allie took this moment to thank Mahi for dinner. 'You have a beautiful house, Mahek. You are very present in it. As is Krish. You know who seems absent from it? Kabeer. I mean, he's very present in your office. But apart from 2 photos, one in your living room and the other in your office, he's barely there. He doesn't even have a toothbrush around in your bathroom.'

Mahi said nothing. Ahh, that's why the visit around the house and the bathroom.

'When are you planning on telling her?' Allie asked cuttingly.

'I am not sure,' Mahi replied, honestly sounding tentative. 'You were waiting for me to resolved. So you're hoping I leave her because she cheated on me.' Mahi looked shocked. 'Oh gosh, I know. I knew when Krish met me at the airport.

Her face is such a traitor. I came tonight because I wanted to see how you felt. That answer is pretty clear too, right?'

'I'm sorry,' said Mahi. Not sure what to say to Allie.

'I would be too. But I realized, I never really had her. I mean who sings about crows eating their flesh? She would pick a thousand deaths to have one life with you. Just like Rehan does in her book...Anyway, at least my friends will believe me about meeting you guys. Don't worry, I won't out you.'

'I didn't think you would. Allie, but you truly surprised me. And I'm not easily surprised by people,' Mahi said with some admiration in her voice.

Krish and Kabeer joined them. 'What was that about?' Allie asked.

'Nothing just thanking Kabeer. I wish I had known. I feel so inadequate. I don't know how to repay them.' Krish nodded to Kabeer. 'Thanks so much for the dinner Mahi.' Krish hugged Mahi and whispered, 'I owe you so much.' Mahi didn't tell her Allie knew. She figured Allie had a plan to tell Krish. She owed her the right to end it on her terms.

'Thank you Allie,' Mahi kissed Allie.

Allie turned to Mahi and said, 'Meher, right? I remember Krish once explaining that it also means Benevolence, yes? Pretty much sums it up, doesn't it?' Allie smiled, happy with herself. She didn't want to be in a relationship where her lover was in love with someone else. 'Yes, benevolence,' She nodded to herself.

'Yes,' Mahi said surprised. Allie was something else. Mahi understood what Lauren meant when she said they were a powerhouse in their own right.

Mahi closed the door.

26

KRISH GOT INTO THE CAR AND WAS PUTTING ON HER seatbelt when Allie said, 'Krish, Can we please go for a drive?'

'Now? At this hour? I'm tired.' 'I know. But we need to talk.'

'Oh-oh' thought Krish. They went for a drive around Marine Drive. As they drove, Allie turned to Krish and said, 'I love you Krish. I really do. But today, after I met Mahi, I realized that there were always three people in our relationship....You came to the US leaving everything behind but you didn't. Not really. You brought Mahi along with you. Every relationship of yours had Mahi in it.' Krish said nothing. She had tears in her eyes. She stopped the car. 'I know you tried to move on. I know you were faithful to me. At least in the US. And I know you meant it when you said you loved me. But you don't. You don't really love me.'

'Allie, I'm sorry. It was just this one time. I swear I was not expecting it to happen. Please forgive me.'

'I believe you Krish. But that's not the point, right? The point is that even if we got back together, you are still not in love with me. Not like the way you are in love with her. And I deserve that. I want someone to look at me the way you look at Mahi.'

'I…I don't know what to say.' Krish was having a rough night. First Kabeer's declaration and now Allie's avowal. Her whole world was crumbling. She felt small.

'Krish, take some time to figure out what you want. And then go for it. You've spent a lifetime running away. Maybe it's time to come home. And your home is not with me. We're done.'

'Wait, Allie…I…I am sorry. You've been wonderful. And I truly don't deserve you. I am sorry.'

'So am I,' Allie got ready to step out of the car and walk away. Then as if she changed her mind, she turned around and said, 'Did you know there was only one toothbrush in Mahi's bathroom?'

'Huh?' Krish looked up. Confused. 'Nothing. Just think about it.'

Krish drove home, unsure what to do next. Allie was not stupid. Of course, it wasn't fair to her. Krish knew that. It wasn't fair to any of her girlfriends. Why had things gone so wrong? She had lost Allie. She was now indebted to the one man she had loathed. Krish crumbled at the idea of Kabeer dancing at Dr Pandey's wedding to save her mom's life. She hated it all. All she wanted to do was run away. Get away from Kabeer, get away from Mahi. Maybe Lauren is right, Krish thought. They were on a collision course. Krish couldn't get in the way of Mahi's happiness and her relationship. No, she would leave right after Karan's party. She was done with Mumbai.

The next day, Allie's Instagram showed a picture of her alone on the beach. It said, 'In a world of a billion people, when you find yourself all alone. I'm single again and ready to start a new journey.'

Mahi was having breakfast when she saw the post. She messaged Krish, 'Are you OK?'

Krish saw Mahi's text and decided not to reply to it. Then she heard Lauren's FaceTime call and rushed to answer it. Lauren simply said, 'I just spoke to Allie. How are you doing?'

'You're not angry with me?' Krish asked surprised.

'I am. But I'm also your friend. She told me she broke it off with you,' Lauren said gently.

'Yes. I mean, I was the one who cheated.' Krish's shoulder drooped. 'She knew. The whole time!'

'Of course she knew. How else did you think I knew when to call and shout at you the last time. She told me when she saw you. Gosh, Krish, you're so clueless,' Lauren shook her head in disbelief at how daft her friend could be sometimes.

'What!?' Krish looked at Lauren in shock. How was she so clueless! Seriously, if it was up to Lauren, she would be grabbing Krish by her collar and shaking her into her senses. 'Ohhh! You're right. Jeez, I'm such an idiot. How am I such a big idiot?' Krish said in amazement at her own cluelessness. 'Anyway, don't worry about Allie. Wendy has already found a great investment banker for her. I have met this girl, she is hot and sexy and so freaking rich already!' Lauren chuckled. Wendy was in the background laughing, 'Don't be jealous Lauren.'

Krish laughed at them squabbling.

Feeling a bit better she hung up. And got ready for practicing her Taekwondo at Soho Club. She looked forward to her daily routine. She started with her forms, all the way Chon-ji to Choong Jang and Juche. Then she practiced her kicks and her hand movements. By the time she was finished, she was sweating and ready for a break. She finished every session with 100 push-ups and 100 sit ups. Krish liked this routine. She took a balti bath and had lunch with Ma. They'd talk about life and Krish was learning all sorts of stories about Ma's childhood and college years.

Today the conversation with Ma was a heavy one. She told her about the deal Mahi and Kabeer made with Dr Pandey. And about Allie breaking it off with her. Though she didn't explain why. And she said, 'Ma, I want to go back. Will you come with me?' Ma understood why Krish wanted to go back. She didn't say anything.

That evening Krish told Anaya, 'Hey kiddo, I guess I will see you at Columbia soon.'

'Are you heading back?'

'Yes!' Krish didn't look happy as she said this. 'Ohh!' Anaya's face fell.

'What is it?' Krish queried.

'Nothing. I was hoping I'd see your love story get a happy ending here.'

'I'm not writing a love story,' Krish looked confused.

Anaya didn't explain. 'Well, anyway, I am bummed. I liked our writing sessions.'

'Me too! I liked our schedule too.'

≫

Mahi hated her schedule. It was jam-packed and she desperately needed a break. Her action movie was about to be released and she was on all evening, and afternoon shows promoting the heck out of it and doing events all over the country. Contact with Krish had been intermittent and after what Karan had relayed of his conversation to Mahi, Mahi was also closing the door on their relationship. Maybe this was not the right time. Krish wanted all or nothing. Mahi couldn't give her all.

'Seriously? Does that mean you'll both end up with nothing? She's single Mahi. She's single!! What are you doing?' Karan implored.

'I am not sure Karan. But her life is there and my life is here.'

'She's a writer. Her life is anywhere you are. And you can look for jobs there. You can be our next Priyanka Chopra. No one would even bat an eye-lid. What are you both scared of? Anyway, you'll see her tomorrow at our launch party. I think the name you suggested really worked. We discussed it at the screenplay meeting and everyone loved it.'

'I hadn't thought of it. It was Allie,' said Mahi. 'Krish's girlfriend?' Karan asked surprised. 'Her ex-girlfriend,' Mahi corrected.

'Hmmm. Who would have thought. By the way, did you think about playing Rehan?' Karan asked Mahi.

'Yeah, that's such an interesting idea. And you said Krish came up with it?' Mahi had been quite surprised by the idea but she was coming around to it.

'Well, to be fair, Krish said another writer came up with it. But she found it intriguing enough to run it by me. It definitely gives you a much wider berth in terms of proving your acting chops. You'd have to play a butch lesbian. I find the idea intriguing too. To play Krish, that's kinda special, no?'

'Yeah. I am definitely thinking about it. Can we try some looks?'

'Oh fun! Lets!' Karan sounded gleeful.

≋

The launch party was a success. Wine was flowing, appetizers were passing around and people were mingling, networking and doing all things they do at filmi parties. Karan looked happy as he looked around at the who's who, who had attended his little bash. Krish was wearing a new suit. Apparently Italian tailored suits were the way to go and she needed a new look. That's what Mahi had told her when she informed her about the suit. It had started like this,

'Will you be wearing your blue suit at the launch party?' Mahi had texted her.

'Yes'

'No go! You need a new suit. I'll have Ruchi send you the details for your fitting. I have picked out some material for you.' Mahi texted.

'Material?' Krish wasn't exactly sure what Mahi meant by it.

'Italian. Chambray. Just go for the fitting, OK?' Krish could almost sense her annoyance through the phone.

'OK. Also, can we talk soon? I am thinking of leaving early next week.'

'Soon. I promise. I wish I was there at home with you, but I'm stuck on the road promoting this movie. In good news, it releases tonight so I'll be free this weekend. Let's plan on brunch on Saturday?'

Now Krish was standing at Karan's party in her perfectly tailored dark grey Chambray suit and white shirt with a yellow polka dotted tie and yellow and grey polka dotted socks.

Ma was looking excited. The aunties and Ma were sitting in one corner and looking at everyone and chattering about it. Krish smiled at Ma. She looked happy. Krish mingled with some folks from the production house that she'd gotten to know over the past few weeks. She was in mid-conversation when all heads turned towards the entrance. Mahi had come to the party! She was wearing a yellow and purple saree with a very sexy, very slinky blouse. 'It really just needed a tug,' was the first thought that came to Krish's head. Mahi shook her head from side to side, looking scandalized, almost as if she had read Krish's mind. They both slowly smiled at each other. But then Krish's smile disappeared as Kabeer joined Mahi and put his arm around her waist. Her very bare waist.

Ma walked up to Kabeer and Mahi, 'I wanted to thank you both. Krishi told me. That was way above and beyond...' Ma had tears in her eyes.

Krish walked up to the three of them standing there, 'We can't thank you enough.'

Kabeer was quick to interject, 'Please don't worry about it. Mahi's Ma is my Ma. I was happy to do it.'

'Yes, but...' Kabeer put his arm on Krish shoulder. Krish had to fight all her instincts to take that hand off, violently.

'Beta Kabeer, I've heard all good things about you. Now I can see that they are all true. Mahi is very lucky to have such a good life partner.'

Those words stung Krish. The room felt so hot. Her fingers went to her collar button. She loosened her tie. Mahi smiled at Ma but her eyes showed concern for Krish. Krish didn't want her pity. She had to admit, what Kabeer did was magnanimous. She couldn't hate him anymore. Krish felt small and petty. She wanted to disappear. She slunk away to one corner of the bar. Wishing she could disappear from India. From Mahi's life. From this moment. Krish ordered a drink.

'Hey,' said Shreya who was at the bar getting her drink. She looked like she had started early. Like way early.

'Hey,' said Krish. 'How's it going?' Taking a seat next to her.

'Hey Krish, it's so nice to see you. How are you my friend?'

Shreya was already slurring her words a little. Krish winced. 'I'm well. Thanks.' Now looking around, wondering how she could leave this situation.

'Well. I had a great time working on the project. I was really worried about working with the author, because usually those always stink. But you were not so bad.'

'Thanks. I will take that as a compliment,' Krish chuckled. 'It was.'

Krish grinned. As did Shreya. Shreya looked around the room and said, 'Oh, I see the beards are here.'

'Huh?' Krish's eyes went to Shreya's gaze and she looked at Kabeer and Mahi who were kissing Karan on his cheeks.

'What do you mean?' Krish asked Shreya, unsure as to what she was getting at.

'Nothing. Have you never wondered how this ideal couple has never had any rumours or fights? Like they are too perfect?' Shreya looked beady eyed as she talked about them.

Krish stood there at the bar, her drink in hand, taking in what Shreya had just revealed to her. Krish's mind now sifting through all memories of her talks with Mahi, of all her interactions with Kabeer. That night at their house Kabeer didn't seem fazed by her intimacy with Mahi. And after they had slept together, while Krish was wracked with guilt, Mahi didn't seem worried about telling Kabeer. And then Krish remembered the conversation with Allie, when they were breaking up and she was telling her about the toothbrush ... Wait...

Krish gulped the drink down. She needed to talk to Mahi. NOW. Where the heck was Mahi. Krish was feeling hot. She loosed her tie and opened her button. Why couldn't she locate Mahi anywhere? She found Ruchi and motioned to her? Ruchi pointed to the stage. Of course, Mahi was on stage, talking to reporters, answering questions. Karan was calling Krish on stage. Shit. Why did this all have to happen now. They were unveiling the movie title. Krish walked up on stage with Ma, standing there with Karan and Mahi and some other actors, she smiled, Ma smiled. Mahi went and hugged Ma. Flashbulbs went off. Karan revealed the title, 'Maahi Ve' and everyone clapped. The fonts, the colours were all perfect. It had a magical realism feel without it being too fairy tale like or too sinister. It was done just right. It had that Karan Raichand touch. Ma looked so happy.

As they got off the stage, Ma said, 'Beta, I'm tired. I'm going home with Veenu aunty. Theek hai?'

'OK Ma! I'll come home later.'

'Take your time. Veenu aunty is staying over tonight. And the nurse is there too! Stay out late. Enjoy your moment.'

Krish dropped Ma off and then headed back to the party. Her eyes fell back on Mahi and the urgency to talk to her returned.

Suhani was there with Imran Faiz. 'Hey Krishi! Congratulations. Mahek is lucky to have you as a friend.'

'And me, her' Krish smiled.

Photos, so many photos later, Mahi finally came down from the stage. Krish was waiting for her. She reached for Mahi's elbow and pulled her towards her. 'Mahi, I need to talk to you urgently.' Mahi looked at her startled. Reporters were watching. What the heck was Krish trying to do?

'Please. Now,' Krish's voice was desperate.

'OK. Calm down. I'll find us some space. OK? Just a little patience.' Mahi called Ruchi and after a few minutes of mingling she disappeared. Krish was looking for her everywhere. Her face, frantic. Her hands were shaking.

Ruchi approached her. She whispered in her ears and Krish took off. She walked into the hallway of the hotel, looking for the room number Ruchi had told her. Before she could knock, Mahi opened the door and pulled her in.

Krish was caught off guard as she found herself face to face with Mahi. The drapes were shut. 'What's going on Krish? I'm getting tired of this? You don't message for days and then suddenly...' Mahi was irritated. She had been scared when Krish had accosted her near the stage. Not scared for her safety, scared for her cover to be blown.

'Why didn't you tell me,' asked Krish.

'Tell you what?' Mahi asked, adjusting her saree. 'Don't fuck around with me Mahi. I know.'

Mahi looked up and looking serious, she asked slowly, deliberately, 'What do you know?'

'About Kabeer. He's your beard. You're his beard. Amiright?' Krish needed confirmation. She needed it now.

Mahi bit her lip and said nothing.

'That's why there are no real photos of him in your house. There is no real anything. Why didn't you tell me Mahi. Why did you let me believe you loved Kabeer? That you were getting married? I would have left Allie.'

Mahi looked at her, not saying a word.

'All these years? I thought you had chosen him. But you hadn't. Tell me Mahi, tell me you love me. You've always loved me. That you didn't throw me away. That you didn't leave me. That you didn't pick him. Mahi, please!' Krish broke down in front of her. She was sobbing her eyes out. Mahi wasn't sure if it was in pain or in relief. Mahi walked over to Krish and bent down to hold her. She held Krish's face gently, wiped away her tears, caressed her cheeks and said, 'I have only loved you. I will only love you.'

Krish cried for a few minutes and Mahi held her. Finally Krish quieted down. Then she got up and Mahi thought they would probably headed out when Krish pinned her against the wall. Needing her so desperately. There was no guilt, no hiding, no shame. Just her and Mahi. Two people who had only loved each other. Krish kissed her with wild abandon and Mahi responded with equal enthusiasm. No more secrets. No more lies. No more walls. 'I want you, now.' Krish whispered as she kissed Mahi.

'Hush, patience my little grasshopper. If we stay now, we will be noticed and missed. Let's go out to the party. Stay another 20 minutes and then leave. Separately. And then meet at my place? I'll have the car waiting for you downstairs, OK?' 'Fuck no. Mahi. I need you, now!' There was an intense urgency in her voice. It made Mahi tremble. Krish reached behind to pull Mahi's blouse strings.

'No. Krish,' Mahi said firmly, 'Not now.'

Krish stopped. She looked deflated. 'Only 20 more minutes. Then we can be together, all night. Ok?' Mahi said sweetly.

'OK.' Krish smiled at the idea. 'Listen, keep this saree on though. Please.'

Mahi slapped Krish gently on her face and then left the room.

Krish left a few minutes later.

As Mahi reached the party she started mingling with the guests and reporters in a hurried state. Krish just went and sat at the bar and ordered a diet Coke. She didn't want to be drunk for her first night with Mahi. Her eyes never left Mahi. Mahi whispered something to Karan. Karan looked startled but happy. Did Krish see him mouth, 'Finally!' as he waved her off. Mahi headed to the door. She looked at Krish one last time and then left. Krish counted the clock for another 5 minutes. Then she got up. Unlike Mahi no one would miss her absence. She was just one cog in a big wheel of movie-making. No one cared about the author.

Just then she met Anaya and her mother. 'Hello Krish! Nice party. You look nice too!'

'Hey!' Krish said smiling at the kid. 'It's nice to see y'all. Are you having fun so far?'

'Yeah. It's great. I think there are some spectacular displays of propriety and impropriety at these parties. It makes for some very interesting people watching,' Anaya smiled.

Krish wondered what she meant but couldn't stop to ask her. Not today. She was on a mission.

'Alright kiddo. I got to go. Catch you next week at the club. Bye.'

Anaya smiled. She had seen Mahi leave earlier. She knew about Allie and Krish breaking up. 'Finally!' she whispered.

'What finally?' asked her mother innocently.

'Nothing.' Anaya smiled. 'Let's get some food? Look, there is your friend, Suhani!'

Suhani was standing with Imran when she noticed Krish leaving. She had noticed their absence earlier and then seen Mahek leaving. She smiled. Over the years, she had realized the reason Mahek had chosen not to go for Jodhaa Akbar with Imran. Suhani was always glad for that reason. 'Finally!' she said as she squeezed Imran's arm.

'Huh?' Imran asked, completely clueless.

'Nothing. Just happy I found you!' Just then Anaya and her mother walked over to say hello.

Ruchi was waiting downstairs with the car. Krish got into the car with Ruchi.

Ruchi smiled at her. As if she knew what was happening. Or what was about to happen. Krish was all nervousness and excitement and anticipation. Her legs felt like jelly. The ride was taking too long. Krish was getting so impatient, so nervous. Why was she nervous? Krish tried to talk to Ruchi but no words came out. Ruchi had thankfully put on the radio and that was helpful. There was a romantic number streaming. Krish tried to sing but no words came out. So she just listened. Just then the car stopped and before Ruchi could say anything, Krish raced out.

'Finally,' said Ruchi smiling widely. 'What madam?' the driver asked. 'Nothing,' Ruchi smiled. 'Tum chalo.'

The elevator could not take any longer! Thought Krish, frustrated with all the steps necessary to reach the woman she loved. And love her. Finally.

Upstairs, Mahi waited just as impatiently. She had given the servants chutti for the weekend. She had given them each

Rs.10,000 and said come back Monday morning. They didn't ask twice. They just left. Now Mahi was waiting for Krish to come home. Finally come home to her. How long they had waited for this. Mahi had tried telling Krish about her and Kabeer on the night that Krish told her Allie was coming. Mahi had hoped Krish picked up the clues that she had left around, clues that Allie could sniff out in one evening but Krish had been completely oblivious to. How would this work? What would happen to Kabeer? Would Krish agree to an arrangement of sorts? How would their future play out? All kinds of questions popped into Mahi's mind. But right now, she didn't want to think about it. Right now she was glad her movie was releasing and she could pretend to be shuttered in because of anxiety and nerves about the movie's reviews and reactions. Right now all she wanted was the person who was going to walk through the door. She wanted her hands all over her. And she wanted to be taken. Right here. Right now.

Krish came out of the elevator and Mahi was standing there in her house. Still wearing the yellow saree with that slinky blouse. 'All it needed was a little tug,' thought Krish. And she was the person who was going to tug those cords. Not Kabeer. Just her. Krish's smile was so wide, her cheeks hurt. Mahi's smile was full of anticipation. She pulled Krish inside and pinned her to the door. Mahi started removing Krish's jacket, as she kissed Krish. Their lips were seeking fulfilment in a different way this time. A new hope emerged between their lips. The idea of forever, that had first taken root all those years ago when Mahi had promised to love her Ishq forever, was now an actual possibility. Krish kissed her deeply and said, 'I love you Mahi. I've loved only you.'

Mahi finally uttered the words she had been wanting to say for so long, 'There was only you. There will always be only you. I love you Ishq.' Words she had said when she had first told her Ishq I love you. And now she could say them again freely. They were together again, finally.

Mahi was crying, tears of happiness and relief streaming down her face. Krish stopped kissing her, 'What happened?' she asked looking concerned. 'What is it Mahi? Are you worried about something?'

Krish stopped and held her. 'Mahi, babe. Talk to me.' 'Nothing. It's just tears of happiness. After our first meeting

on the plane and everything you said to me, I had felt so lost, so scared. But over the past few months, we've chipped away at all our old resentment. It's been a long road. I had almost given up. I dunno, I'm babbling. I don't make any sense.' Mahi rested her head against Krish's shoulder.

Krish lifted her head and looked at her and smiled gently, 'I know what you mean. I am so excited, so happy, I don't know what to do with myself. I feel l barely make sense right now. All I know is I am your Ishq and you are my Mahi, and I'm in love with you. And we're together. Finally!' Mahi smiled. 'And there is a cord that has my name on it. And I'm going to pull it now.' Krish looked at Mahi for confirmation. Mahi nodded. And Krish pulled it. Krish looked at Mahi in wonder and joy and lust and longing as her blouse fell off. Mahi opened her saree and let it fall and she stood there, pulling Krish to her bosom. Krish didn't waste any time. Quickly removing her pants and shirt, she and Mahi made each other whole. Finally, lovingly, forever started now.

27

—›‹—

MAHI WOKE UP WITH A START. IT WAS HOT. SHE WAS ON her own bed. And there was a hand on her. It stirred when she stirred. 'Mahi, are you OK?' Krish sat up in bed, her eyes drowsy but concerned.

Mahi exhaled. It was a new feeling. 'Yes,' she smiled. 'Everything is perfect.' Krish was naked in bed with her. Mahi had forgotten how hot Krish got at night. Mahi used to call her, her toaster oven. 'I guess I'm just not used to sleeping with someone in my bed.'

'Get used to it. I don't want to live without you.' Krish smiled as she pulled her back to bed. Mahi smiled and looked for the clock by her bedside trying to figure out what time it was. Mahi rubbed her eyes and looked at the clock. 'It's 2:30 am.'

Krish's stomach growled. 'I'm kind of hungry.'

Mahi smiled at Krish, her eyes roaming over Krish's naked body, 'Me too.'

'Not that way, Mahi. Geez, you're still the same,' Krish grumbled.

Mahi gave an exaggerated sigh and got up, 'Chalo, I'll feed you. And then…' Mahi's grabbed Krish's butt. 'Then you need to work it off.'

'Hey Ram!!!' Krish groaned. But she was still smiling so widely, her cheeks hurt. Mahi put on a long t-shirt and threw a t-shirt and pair of shorts towards Krish. 'Where did you get these?' asked Krish as she quickly put them on.

'I had bought them. Just in case,' Mahi smiled.

She caught up to Mahi and held her hand and turned her, so that she was facing her. 'Wait, you bought night clothes for me? Just in case.' Krish looked surprised.

Mahi giggled, smiling so seductively. It made Krish melt. 'Fuck Mahi, you're so cute. How are you so cute? I am so madly in love with you. I could eat you right now.'

'Really?' Mahi asked, her eyes wide and hopeful.

'No. Not really. Not till I eat food,' said Krish as she ran into the kitchen. Mahi giggled as she followed.

There in the kitchen, Mahi opened the fridge. It was full of cut up fruits and yogurt. 'Ummm…I am not sure what you'd want here. Wait, I'll cook something for you!'

'Mahek Singh and cook? Rehne do. Let it be. Do you have any eggs? I'll eat an egg.'

Mahi started opening her fridge but it was clear she was not sure where things where. Krish took over and asked her how she wanted her egg cooked. She got into action opening drawers, finding knives and getting the onions, cilantro and green chilies from the refrigerator. Mahi sat on the counter and added, 'Don't forget tomatoes. I like mine cut up fine.'

'Hey bhagwan. Now madam is thokoing orders,' Krish grinned.

'That is what happens when you date Mahek Singh.'

'I'm not dating Mahek Singh. I'm dating my Mahi,' Krish reached up to kiss Mahi. Mahi pulled her in for a deeper kiss. 'Ummm…I want you again.'

'First eggs. OK?'

Krish cut up onions and started sautéing them and while they were cooking she cut up the tomatoes and the green chilies. All very finely. And then she added them at the right time and stirred. Then she tapped open three eggs and whisked them in a bowl. 'Do you have any milk?' Krish asked as she opened the refrigerator again. 'Ah, here it is.' She opened the milk and added a splash to the eggs. She turned around and Mahi was standing right in front of her. 'I can't wait. Watching you cook is making me hot.' She took Krish's hands in her hands but Krish knew this paitra well. 'Nooooo. First food. You're going to put my hand on some part of your body and I won't be able to say no to you. But I want to eat first.'

'Come, look. One more minute,' Krish poured the eggs mixture into the pan and let it cook. Krish was cooking the eggs when she felt Mahi's hands against her back. Mahi was hugging her, 'Umm...I love you Ishq, you're so sexy,' Her hands traveling to Krish's butt. She rubbed her whole body against Krish's back.

'Stop. You're killing me,' Krish pleaded.

'You've been killing me for the past 20 minutes.' 'Shhh.... here. Food is ready. Come. Let's eat,' Krish smiled. 'You feed me,' Mahi said, petulantly.

'My nautanki, come here.' Mahi sat in Krish's lap and Krish fed her. 'Umm...this is yummy, Mahi said in between mouthfuls, 'First poha, now eggs. When did you become such a good cook?'

'Someday when we're back in the US, who will cook for you? Me, no?' Krish smiled as she ate a bite in between feeding Mahi.

Mahi got silent. 'Hmm...' she said distractedly. Krish looked so happy feeding Mahi. And their lovemaking went on till morning. Mahi didn't bring up the future. There was ample time for the future.

The next morning, Krish slept in. Mahi was on the phone with Karan.

'First give me the dirty details,' Karan was practically drooling on the phone.

'Oh Karan, it was so dirty, I don't want to fill your head with such filthy details,' Mahi giggled. 'We were at it all night. And then she cooked for me. And then I made her work it off. Oh, in so many different ways.'

'Haha,' Karan laughed. 'So have you spoken to her? Should we set up Twitter about your break up with Kabeer?'

'She's sleeping,' Mahi said as she looked in the direction of her bedroom. She had left Krish sleeping, naked on her bed when she sneaked out this morning for her coffee and toast.

'You've exhausted her out? Tch tch.'

'Yes, Karan. And she enjoyed every bit of it,' Mahi smirked.

'Fine. Talk to her soon. I'll get our team started getting stuff ready to announce your and Kabeer's break up on Twitter,' Karan said as he hung up.

When Krish woke up, Mahi had made breakfast for her. 'Aww. Thanks so much. I am starving.'

'I wonder why?' Mahi giggled.

'Stop it! My god, you were always so insatiable!'

'Shut up. I haven't been muh maroing everywhere like you. I was waiting for you. 10 years is a long time to wait,' Mahi thwacked Krish.

'Why did you wait, Mahi?' Krish asked in all earnestness.

'What do you mean?' Mahi looked at her in surprise.

'I mean, why didn't you just come and find me. You knew where we lived. You just had to leave a note. I would have been on your doorstep the next day.'

'It wasn't so easy. By the time I got to the point that I could leave my family behind, it had been a while Ishq. You were with someone. Noelle, was it?'

Krish nodded.

'I used to stalk you on Facebook. I figured you had probably moved on. I had imagined someday leaving it behind, finding you at a café in New York. Only I hadn't realized you were so angry with me. Honestly, I don't know what I would have done if it hadn't been for Kabeer and Karan conspiring to put us on that plane together.'

'So how did that come about?' Krish asked.

'You knew Karan had paid for your flight. Kabeer and he had talked about it. They got us together. Karan thought it was a win-win – acquiring your book was a good deal and a chance for us to interact again. I guess he figured it was time we got together too.'

'And then Ma's illness.' 'And then Allie,' said Mahi.

'So many people have conspired to get us together. Why does our love seem so impossible?' Krish mused.

'I don't know. Anyway, listen. Let's get ready and head home. Ma must be worried.'

When they headed home, Ma opened the door and took one look at Krish and Mahi and said, 'Finally!'

'What? We haven't even said anything. How did you know?' Krish asked as they came inside the hallway.

'You both look so happy. So radiant. Yet so calm and contented from inside. Anyone who knows you can tell.' Ma kissed Mahi's forehead as they hugged. 'I'm so happy. My daughter-in-law is finally home.' Krish's heart burst open with love. She had no idea she could be this happy. What a tumultuous road it had been.

Later that morning Krish and Mahi and Ma sat and chatted about next steps.

'Obviously we can't out Kabeer. So we're going to say Kabeer proposed to me and I said no. OK? That leaves the door open for him for another beard. Karan is working on it, as we speak.'

'And you? What about you?'

'We have to come up with a plan. My agents are looking at roles in Hollywood,' Mahi shrugged. She didn't seem excited by her prospects.

'You'll leave India for me?'

'Well, we can't live in India, no? Not with you wanting us to be out,' Mahi smiled. Why did these choices have to be so hard. When she had all the fame, she was lonely and pining for love. Now that she had love, her fame was would evaporate like an ephemeral dream.

Krish said nothing. She ate in silence. Ma looked at them both.

Mahi continued, 'And you're very clearly out. So once people see us together, they'll put two and two together. Plus, your eyes, Ishq. They are traitors, your eyes. They give you away every time. You look at me with so much love,' Mahi smiled. She was proud of Krish and happy about the way she looked at her. But realistically, they wouldn't last 10 minutes without being outed.

Ma looked at Mahi and asked, 'So you two won't live here?'

And Krish added, 'And you have to give up everything you've built over the past 10 years here?'

Mahi said nothing.

'That's unfair Mahi. I can't live with an asterisk next to your name. With all your work down the drain.'

Ma got up to go to her room. She was tired and needed a nap. Besides, she figured the best solution would be for the kids to figure out for themselves.

'Ishq, I've waited for 10 years to be with you. We're finally together. I never wanted any of this, remember? I always wanted to be with you.'

'Yes, I know. But then after a few months, when I've whetted your appetite...' Krish said the last past softly, in a whisper.

Mahi raised her eyebrow at the pun. Krish smirked. 'Yup, that was an intended pun.'

'Anyway, after a few months, my dearest Mahi, when you are completely satiated with my body, you're going to miss it all. You're going to miss the servants and the fans and the limelight.'

'We can't have servants in USA? What? I mean, I've made enough money for such stuff, nah? I'm not flying economy and all, now. I've invested wisely. I have enough money for us.' 'I'm not talking about flying economy. I'm just saying, life in USA is different no. You're a nobody there. You're Mahek Singh here. The prime minister's favourite female protagonist.'

'Yes. But I can't have you here, no?'

'Right now? Like today? Yes, you can. You can have me right here, right now,' said Krish as she reached for Mahi's t-shirt. 'We just have to be quiet. Can you handle that?'

Mahi bit Krish's ears. 'We were always quiet here.'

At that moment, Twitter and Facebook and Instagram were all blowing up with the news of Kabeer and Mahek breaking up while Krish and Mahi were having some mind-blowing sex.

By late afternoon, India was ablaze with the news of Kabeer and Mahek's break up. People from all over were calling her and texting her offering their two cents on the news. Mahi was in Krish's bedroom. Their bedroom. Krish was nibbling on her toes and working her way to her knees. 'You should have told them, I've found the love of my life,' said Krish after Mahi had hung up with the last caller. 'And they would have invited you for dinner at their residence. And then kicked us both out after seeing you and me together,' Mahi giggled as Krish kissed her ears. 'Umm…there.'

On Sunday evening, Mahi had finally gone home. 'Mahi, I miss you already. Come here nah?' Krish was on the phone with Mahi.

'I wish. But I have to go to Hyderabad for shooting tomorrow. It's that big budget epic film based on the Mahabharat that we're shooting.'

'Oh, where you're playing Draupadi?' Krish asked.

'Yes. Thankfully the writers have read Palace of Illusion so it's not too terrible,' Mahi liked the idea of playing this powerful queen from the great Indian epic.

'How many films do you do Mahi?'

'Achha, abhi se khit-pit. Soon, you'll be saying don't do on screen kisses and don't act with this actor and that director. And why did he touch you in this scene and all that,' Mahi laughed.

'Yuck. That's not how I am. But now that you bring it up….' Krish was laughing too.

'Relax. I know what I'm doing. Ishq, you have to trust me on this. Alright?' Mahi got serious.

'Alright. I know you've been doing these things for the past 10 years. And I've seen you do all these things. And yet now, it suddenly seems weird. It's not easy, dating an actress. I mean, I trust you. That's never a question. But it's just so much to deal with suddenly,' said Krish. The reality was finally sinking in. She was dating Mahek Singh.

'Yeah, it never gets easy. In some ways it was a lot easier with Kabeer because we didn't care what the other person was doing.'

'True.'

≈

Monday morning there was a theory brewing on the internet fuelled by pictures from the Big B Award and Allie's Instagram picture with the four of them. Someone had pointed out that after that night Allie had broken up with Krish. And that Kabeer and Mahek were now broken up. And was Krish responsible for this? Then there were pictures of Mahi and Krish hugging at the Big Bs book awards with the hashtag #HappyEndings that were submitted as proof of this intimacy. This conspiracy theory, which of course was true was further fuelled by someone sharing a photo from the more recent Karan Raichand's launch party when Krish had accosted Mahi. Mahi looked a little surprised and scared in the photo. Which then added speculation that Krish was blackmailing Mahek into a lesbian relationship.

'Shit,' said Mahi as she saw these reports in Hyderabad.

'Shit,' said Karan as he saw these reports on his way back from London.

'Shit,' said Krish, as she saw the picture. 'Mahi, I'm so sorry. You really do look scared. I didn't mean to scare you.'

'Stop it Krish, you had just surprised me. I wasn't scared of you. You big baby. I have never been scared of you. I was worried about reporters catching the moment. And clearly someone did.'

'OK. I'm sorry nonetheless,' Krish apologized.

'Just stay safe Ishq. People are crazy,' Mahi said soberly.

Her fans were crazy. Indian mobs were crazy.

'Don't worry. I'll be safe,' Krish said rather flippantly. 'Besides, it will probably die down soon.'

But the reports just gathered steam and India became obsessed with this idea of Mahek Singh being ensnared in a trap by a lesbian from America. Think pieces started coming up on the issue. 'News' shows gave it air-time.

'Who has a name like Krish Mehra,' said one news reporter. 'This is very unnatural,' said some aunty interviewed on TV.

'No, it's not. It's how people are born. India has decriminalized homosexuality,' screamed the gay coalition. Who, of course, were thrilled at the idea of claiming Mahek Singh.

'Yes, But clearly Mahek was not a lesbian. She's being blackmailed,' shouted the other group.

'She's too beautiful to be a lesbian,' claimed another set of people.

'Maybe that lesbian is giving her some potion or doing some jaadu tona, which is how she's managed to get Mahek,' someone claimed on TV. Trolls were having a field day on Twitter. Mahek was flooded with interview requests and questions from reporters. Mahek had promised her story to one reporter. And she just told the other reporters they'd have to wait for that interview.

'You need to do it sooner than later,' advised Karan.

'Yes, I know. But I have an idea I want to run by you and Kabeer. Now that you're back from London, we can chat soon. I'm coming back to Mumbai tomorrow.'

Krish was laying low and staying home. Anaya texted her and said she was happy if the rumours were true. 'Thanks,' was all Krish replied. The big smiley face attached to it though said it all.

'Why don't you go out of the house? It will be good for you' Ma suggested. 'Go write with Anaya.'

'Ma, are you OK with all this? The aunties? Are they whispering again?'

'People have evolved Krishi. India has changed in the last 10 years. Maybe not as much as the US. I know you both can get married there. But India is changing too. We need more people to come out. We need more visibility. If people see that their normal, everyday friends and family are gay, it won't be such a weird thing anymore.'

'I know Ma. But it's hard. I wish Mahi and Kabeer would come out. But if she did, her career would be ruined. I am so confused. I don't know what to do!'

'Change will happen Krishi beta. Just give it time. In the meanwhile, all the aunties are super jealous I have a daughter-in-law like Mahi!'

'Haha!' Krish laughed heartily. Maybe India had changed after all.

The next day Krish decided to leave the house and go to Soho Club. People were staring at her. Krish wasn't sure what they were thinking.

'They're probably wondering if it is true,' Anaya responded to Krish's thoughts.

'Hmm...' Krish smiled. 'You are getting wiser beyond your years. Watch out world. A new writer is on the horizon.' They walked together to the writing booths and started chatting about work.

At lunch over milk-shakes and French fries and veggie burgers they chatted more about the novel they had both read. I have a friend, Parthiv. He wants to join our book club.'

'We have a book club?!' Krish wondered aloud. 'Well, we read a novel every week and discuss it.'

'Yes, but we discuss the craft of it. Not necessarily it, it. Though we eventually get to that too. Would he still be interested? Is he a writer?'

'No. His family is into tech products. But...'

Krish didn't need to hear the rest. It was obvious from Anaya's blush. 'Of course. I am happy to meet Parthiv and have him join our 'book club,' said Krish happily.

Anaya texted Parthiv and he joined them shortly. They chatted for a while. Krish liked him right away. He was polite and sweet and clearly respected Anaya. And their puppy love was just adorable.

Eventually it was time to go home. 'Alright, I'll see you both tomorrow,' said Krish as they walked out and parted ways.

She didn't see it coming...Bam!! Someone had hit her hard!

Krish stumbled to the ground. She felt another kick to her stomach and fell. But years of Taekwondo kicked in and she could break-fall and get right back up. There was a splitting sound in her ears and she was sure she was bleeding. She could feel wetness near her ears. She didn't bother touching it. Instead she looked around to find her assailant. Her vision was a little blurry. A crowd was gathering.

Anaya and Parthiv ran over. Krish stopped them. 'Parthiv, Anaya go inside. Go now! I got this.' Krish was in fighter position, her hands ready to hit, scanning for the next attack. Instead of helping, people had removed their phones and were taking videos. Anaya ran in to call the police. Parthiv stayed outside and he too started taking a video. Three men were circling Krish. They were wearing bright orange and yellow clothes. Krish looked at them and smiled. She motioned them with her fingers to come get her. Taunting them. All three ran forward. Before they could even touch her, Krish used all her strength and years of practice to kick the crap out of her assailants. Thwack, crack, and piercing screams came out of the screen of Parthiv's phone. The first guy who had run towards Krish, now lay on the ground, his hand was broken. The second one's right leg was broken.

Some people that had gathered in the mob ran towards their hurt community members.

Two more men wearing bright colours ran towards Krish. Krish kicked one in the head and kicked the other on the back of his legs. Hard enough that he fell to the crowd screaming in pain. The one kicked in the head was going to get a concussion. He looked like he was dizzy. Krish was standing in her spot, shifting her weight on the balls of her feet from side to side, looking agile and strong, ready for action. Her hands in a warrior pose – ready to hit. And she was not taking any prisoners. Not today. Not ever again.

The people in the crowds were oohing and aahhing every time Krish hit someone. 'This is crazy,' said one as they live streamed it for the world to see. Parthiv looked at Anaya who had come out with the security. Her eyes were wide open in horror. 'This feels like its straight out of a movie,' said the security manager super impressed by Krish. He would have never guessed this outcome. They watched in awe as the scene was playing out in front of them.

Krish was standing there, she saw the four people injured on the ground, their friends helping them and taking them away. Some of the other people who had gathered were now just looking at her, in shock and amazement. No one was willing to approach her but they couldn't just slink away. Just then the police siren was heard. The men scattered, the siren allowing them an opportunity to save face.

When the police reached the crowd had largely dispersed but some shared their videos. The security manager said, 'I've got this. You take her.' The injured lay on the road. Parthiv and Anaya got Krish into a car and drove her to the nearest hospital. Anaya took Krish's phone and dialled Mahi. Karan and Mahi rushed over to the hospital.

Krish looked up when Mahi walked in. The ear was bleeding through the white bandages. There was dried blood on her face, neck and t-shirt. Mahi gasped in horror when she saw Krish. 'It looks worse than it is,' Krish tried to placate her. The doctor came in. 'She will need a few stitches and we're assessing her ear damage. She may also have a mild concussion so she needs complete bed rest for the next 24 hours.'

'Who is doing the stitches? Can we get Dr Negandhi,' Mahi asked taking charge. Ruchi started calling Dr Negandhi right away.

Mahi lunged onto Krish after the doctor left and started crying. 'What was that? I told you to lay low, right? Why were you out? Why were you doing all this herogiri? You've got the girl. Now stop it. Stop it. What if something had happened to you? I just got you back. Didn't you think of me for one second?'

Krish just held Mahi, 'Shh, shh…it's OK babe. I've been training for the past 10 years for this day. I was ready. I was ready this time. I was not hiding inside like when your brothers were beating down our door.'

'No more of this nonsense. You've proved whatever you needed to prove. No more. You hear me Ishq? Swear on me? Please promise me you won't do this again.' Mahi was crying. Krish just smiled. 'Don't worry Mahi. I got this. I won't let you down, OK? I want to be around forever. I want to be with you. I want to marry you. Have kids with you. Have grand kids with you. Right? Just relax.'

Anaya and Parthiv had gone to get Ma. Ma's face shuddered involuntarily when she saw Krish. But she kept a brave face on. 'Mera sher bachcha! I saw the video Krishi. Well done beta.'

Mahi was not expecting this, 'Ma. Please tell her to stop this nonsense. They could be carrying lathi's next time. Or knives. Or god forbid a gun.'

Within the hour, Mahi had set up two very big, thug looking men as Krish's security. They stood outside her door now in their grey safari suit.

Karan laughed, 'After that fantastic show your girlfriend put on this morning, I doubt these men can do better. Krish might end up saving their asses.'

Krish smiled at the compliment.

'Karan don't encourage her. Have you all gone crazy? What if they had cut her with a knife? Or thrown acid on her? Krish, You have to get out of here. You're in danger now,' Mahi was getting agitated.

Lauren and Chelsea called on FaceTime. 'Duuuude. Are you OK? We saw the video.'

'Of course she's OK,' said Wendy. 'Didn't you see her beat their asses. Good for you Krish!'

Krish smiled. Mahi just rolled her eyes in the background. 'Oh hey Mahi,' Lauren and Chelsea said Hello!

Wendy came over to the screen, 'Is Mahi there? I want to see her too.' Mahi came to the screen to say Hello to Wendy. 'We're looking forward to coming to the wedding,' she said. 'Krish said I could be her plus one. I hope that's OK.'

'Yes. We had to make adjustments because Allie will be there too,' said Lauren.

'Of course, we'd love to have you,' said Wendy a lot more amiably, giving Lauren the don't be mean look.

'Were those your fans?' Lauren asked Mahi rather pointedly. But before Mahi could answer, Krish came up to the screen, 'No, they were just some homophobic assholes.' Mahi gave Krish a look of gratitude. She knew Krish would always stand by her side, no matter what. But she needed Krish to stay alive to do that. A thought occurred to Mahi.

'Lauren, you know I was just telling Krish that she should return to New York right away. That her life is in danger here. Surely you both agree too, right?'

Lauren and Chelsea both were on board with that idea. 'Yes, Krish, dude. You can't stay back there. Go to the embassy, they'll work on getting you out,' Lauren suggested. 'Just catch the first flight out. This is not worth it. You can be with Mahi soon. You're together now. She can come visit and stay together for as long as you want. In the land of the free,' said Chelsea. 'And the home of the brave,' said Lauren. 'Ohh, she can star on TV here like Priyanka Chopra. And they recognize gay marriage so she can get her US citizenship too,' said Lauren adding, 'Eventually.'

'Wait, wait,' cried Krish. 'Stop. Don't go down this future train.'

Krish hung up with them and focused her energy on a rather freaked out Mahi and Karan.

Karan was monitoring her social media and he exclaimed, 'Krish, you're like a hero around the world and especially in India. Have you seen your Facebook page or your Insta? You suddenly have like millions of followers. And people are totes in love with you. Teri toh nikal padi!'

'What? Why?' Krish who was still confused. She wasn't sure she could still understand why everyone was so freaked out.

'People love a woman defending herself. And you were merciless with those men. Not that they didn't deserve it. It was totally straight out a movie,' Karan grinned.

Karan looked at Mahi and said, 'Your love story has all the masala, no? Mother's illness, love triangles, fight scene, now all you need is an airport scene.'

'Don't give her ideas. Mahi is totally working out an airport scene with me. Mahi, I don't want to go,' said Krish.

'Why not? What's here? A few weeks ago, you were dying to go. Now I'm begging you to go. Why do you want to stay? Do you not understand, you're not safe here?' Mahi asked, tired, angry and scared.

'A few weeks ago, you were not my girlfriend.'

'I'll still be your girlfriend when you go to USA, nah? I'll come visit very soon,' Mahi implored. 'Ma please tell her! Only you can convince her.'

Krish looked sober, 'Mahi, you remember this is what happened last time? Last time, you had to choose your career or me. You sent me off to the US and you never came. Mahi, I waited for years for you. And you never came. This time, I'm not leaving. I am here. Aar ya paar (now or never). I'm not leaving.' Krish dug deep.

Krish looked at Ma. She nodded her approval.

'Krish, you duffer. You could die. Stupid, aar ya paar. This is different no? Last time around, my mother, my brothers wouldn't leave me. This time I'm an adult with means, no?'

Karan stepped in, 'Krish, last time around, the day you left, this idiot was going to kill herself. This time around, she's looking forward to a whole new life with you.'

'You were going to kill yourself?' Krish looked horrified as Karan's words were reverberating in her ears. 'What the heck, Mahi? Why didn't you tell me any of this? You just took all my nonsense. And you never explained your side. Why Mahi?'

'I was wrong. You were right. I should have found you. I should have had the courage to run away. I didn't then, Krish. I was a coward' Mahi was crying, 'But I do now. I won't leave you this time. I promise. Please, just go. I can't live in the constant fear that someone will kill you,' Mahi looked firm in her resolve. And then she used her Bramhastra, her ultimate weapon, the one that had never failed yet. 'Ishq, if you love me. You will listen to me.'

Krish's shoulders drooped. 'Fine. I'll go... But if you don't come within the month, I'm going to come back here and stand outside your apartment with a Boombox.'

'I promise baba. I'll be there. Now start packing. Ma can come with me at my house. Once I've settled things here, the two of us will join you. OK?'

Just then the doctor called. 'Shit. I need to take this call.' Then, as if struck by a bolt of lightning, Karan said, 'Mahi, you go take the call. I'll handle Krish's flight and all.'

Karan went into Krish's room and told her and Ma his idea.

Krish smiled. 'Yes, of course,' she jumped on it right away.

Karan was now in director mode. He needed a few people to come through. He called Kabeer. 'This is it, Kabeer. This could be that moment we've been talking about.'

'Are you sure about this? I mean, I saw the mob attacking Krish and dude, I don't know any Karate or Taekwondo or whatever it is.'

'Hopefully we may not need it. I mean, they've decriminalized it, right?'

'It means my acting career may be over,' Kabeer sounded reluctant.

'But we can finally live openly!' Karan beseeched him. 'That's a very big price to pay. I'm not sure Karan,' Kabeer was still hemming and hawing when Karan said, 'I'm sure. I'm tired Kabeer. Aar ya paar.'

Krish's eyes went wide when suddenly she said, 'Wait, you and Kabeer? For how long?'

'Shh ... Krish. Finish packing,' Karan smiled.

'Mahi, we need a big reveal. Your interview won't do the trick anymore. I have an idea,' said Karan. Mahi was finally able to breathe having sent off Krish packing to the US. She couldn't go to the airport and they had arranged for heavy security but Mahi had been Whatsapping and calling Krish till she boarded her flight.

'Karan, are you sure the country is ready for this? Nobody knows. We've managed to keep it a secret so long.'

'I was the one who told you to get a boyfriend to keep it a secret. And now I am the one telling you to come out. It's time Mahi. Besides, do you have another choice?'

Mahi said nothing.

Karan tried to soothe her, 'I know it's a gamble. But if it pays off, you'll be able to live freely, love honestly.'

Mahi was crying.

Karan continued, 'Isn't that all we want. Just to breathe. To live. To be ourselves.'

'It's not going to be easy, Karan.'

'It's not easy for anyone…anywhere in the country. You think it's easy for some Mahi in Assam or Kerala or Punjab? Forget any of these states, you think it's easy for some Mahi or some Krish in Bombay or Delhi?'

Mahi imagined for a moment, a young Krish and Mahi somewhere in this country. She imagined Krish being called names. The whispers. Not all Krish had someone as loving as Ma. Karan was right. She had to do this. Not just for her Krish but for all the Krish and Mahi's out there.

She nodded, quietly but firmly.

The next few days Mahi and Kabeer, separately were talking to producers and directors. Changes were made and deals were drawn. Karan spoke to Shalini Baweja and other major players in the media industry, and members of the film fraternity, especially the big names. Mahi spoke to industrialists and some key politicians. They needed all the support they could get. It was not a fun conversation but it had to happen.

Kabeer and Karan spoke to each other that evening. 'Are you sure about this?' Kabeer asked.

'It's too late now. We've already opened the dams. It's all going to come rushing out. It's a matter of time.'

'The impact…it will decimate our careers.' Karan chewed on that thought for a bit.

'You're a producer and director. You're behind the scenes. But no one wants a gay guy romancing girls. My career is over.' 'Look, that's the fear everyone has, right? But look at Ellen DeGeneres? She came out and it was hard for several years

but now she's stronger than ever, married and successful.' 'Ellen is a stand-up comic. I am an action hero. And you saw what happened to Rupert Everett.'

'That was over 10 billion years ago! Even Hollywood has evolved. Look at Neil Patrick Harris!'

'In television. All gay actors are on TV. Neil Patrick Harris, Jim Parsons. I read trade magazines too! Hollywood hasn't evolved that much,' Kabeer was tapping his feet. He was agitated and nervous. He got up and started pacing.

Karan got up and put his palm on Kabeer's cheeks, gently. 'It will be OK. And more importantly, we will be able to love honestly. Imagine for a moment, you're free to be you. Like you can breathe, finally.'

Kabeer let out a deep sigh.

'I've got you Kabeer. We're in this together.' Karan promised.

Kabeer leaned in for a kiss. Karan closed his and eyes and kissed him deeply.

All over the country in the media and press there was anticipation of a big announcement. Was Mahek Singh really a lesbian? The people wanted to know. The rumour mills were going crazy. Karan capitalized on the gossip. He was planning a big reveal. He would play host and interview Mahi. A huge tell-all. Karan hadn't told her about Kabeer though he had hinted on it. The channel had been advertising it non-stop. It was going to be a HUGE draw. The channel bosses were excited about the potential millions and were scared of the potential loss of millions if things went south.

On the day of, millions of people tuned in from around the country. After Krish's video, her image had gone from blackmailing, potion-making lesbian to who's that awesome woman and can I have what she's having.

Karan looked happy that morning over breakfast. The phone had been ringing non-stop. Everyone was panicking or sending good wishes.

The bell rang. It was Ma. 'Are you sure about this Karan? I am worried about Mahi. Her life, her career. And Krish...'

'I am not going to promise you rainbows. It will be hard, especially for Mahi. But it's the only way to do it right. We owe that much to Krish!'

Ma sighed. 'I know you've managed to convince Krish...' 'Trust me! Please. I'm doing this for everyone's best.'

Ma was sceptical. But she decided to trust Karan.

Karan was directing the show of his life. He looked at himself in the mirror in a glossy black suit. He looked good.

'This is it,' he thought to himself. 'Life will never be the same again.' For some reasons Krish's words, aar ya paar stuck to his head. He sighed as he started walking into the main set.

Lights, camera, action.

'We're live from the studio and I'm Karan Raichand, director, producer and your host for tonight. We're in an exclusive interview with Mahek Singh. Mahek's life has been turned upside down these past few days. And today we are going to find out why.

Mahek Singh needs no introduction, she's an award winning, talented and beautiful actor. Someone who has it all. And our question tonight, is has she lost it all. Let's find out.'

And with that Mahek walked out on the set.

'Hello Mahek. Welcome to our show,' Karan smiled as Mahi walked down the steps to his set. Mahek was wearing a beautiful red and green saree. She was dressed traditional and conservative, while still fashionable. But no slinky blouses tonight. Krish thought as she saw her on the screen. Krish was nervous. This was it.

'Thank you Karan.' They air-kissed and then Mahi took her spot on the black couch.

'Are you nervous?' Karan asked.

'I am. I feel like there has been a lot of speculation. A lot of name calling. A lot of conjecture and absurd theories out there. I figured it was time to put it all to rest. So I'm here.'

'So let's start with that. Mahek, you started your career in film 10 years ago with a Raichand house film, 'Kya hua tera vaada?"

'That's right and it was a big hit,' said Mahi, smiling.

'The people really loved your performance and you won your first Filmfare award.'

'Actually, I won two Filmfare awards, for best debut and best actress that year,' Mahi smiled sweetly.

'That's right,' laughed Karan.

They had rehearsed this piece. It was going smoothly. Karan wanted to set the pace and start easy before he went to the juicy parts.

'And the rest is history,' said Karan.

'I've been fortunate to get good roles and people have appreciated my work,' Mahi said modestly.

'And then Kabeer came into your life,' Karan ventured into the scary territories.

'That's right,' Mahi said.

'And is it true you recently broke up with Kabeer?' Karan asked directly.

'Yes, that's true,' Mahi answered honestly.

'Why is that? Can you talk about it?' Karan opened up the stage for her to take it away.

'Yes, sure. Karan, I came into the film industry 10 years ago. But I didn't want to come into the industry. I was forced to come into it by my family. I was actually in love with someone. Her name was Krish. She was my neighbour. We grew up together. We had been inseparable since we were 6 years old. But when I got older, I realized that I loved Krish more than just my best friend. I was in love with her. One night, I told her my deepest feelings and I kissed her. And she...she kissed me back. Here was the smartest girl in her school, my best friend and the one I was madly in love with. And she was in love with me too. It was heaven. She was my everything.

But my mom found out. She separated us. And cut all contact between us. I was not allowed a phone. I was not allowed to talk to her.' Mahi cried here. Tears were streaming down her cheeks. She had to pause for a few seconds before she continued with her story.

'I pushed Krish away. She had gotten a full scholarship to NYU. I figured she'd be safe there. She could be free,' Mahi said sadly.

'When you were clearly not. I remember the night we met, you were going to commit suicide,' Karan said gently.

'Yes, that's true. I didn't want to live without Krish. She was my life. But I had no way of going to the US and like I said, my family was pushing me into the industry. And thankfully I met you that night. And then Kya Hua happened.' Karan was amazed at how well it was going. Mahi was a fantastic actress, but she didn't even need to act today. She was genuinely emoting.

'So what happened after all these years? How did you suddenly meet?' Karan asked, moving the story to present day.

'Kismet. See, Krish had become a famous writer and her first novel was a huge hit, winning a Booker nomination and the Big B Book award. As fate would have it, she won the award and I was the one giving away the prize. We met. And things just progressed from there. We both had our relationships. But you know first love is…first love. So we broke off our relationships and got together. Finally.'

'So how does it feel?'

'It feels like I am complete again. All these years, I felt incomplete without her. I feel like I can finally breathe. That oxygen is back in the air. That I'm no longer existing. But I am finally living. I am so happy Karan.'

'So does this mean you're gay?'

'Yes, I am. 100% gay. And madly in love with my childhood sweetheart.' Gay Indians all over the country were going to love this answer. Someone somewhere was already making it into a video on a loop.

'And what about Kabeer? What did you have with him?' Karan asked the question that he knew would be asked of Mahi very soon. The question that had stopped her from coming out to Krish for so long.

Kabeer entered the set stage at this point, with the statement, 'We were friends. Always were. Always will be.'

Mahi stood up, her face in shock. Karan's face a happy director who has managed a big bombshell.

'Kabeer Agarwal, welcome to our show,' Karan got up and greeted Kabeer. Mahi now made room for Kabeer on the couch. If she were being honest, she felt a little relieved to have some company in the hot seat. She wondered if Kabeer was going to do it too? Could the industry handle it? Could India handle it?

'So Kabeer, you and Mahi were together for 5 years. Rumours are you proposed to her and she said no. Is that true?'

'No. Truth is Karan, that Mahi and I are like brother, sister. We're not attracted to each other at all. She's in love with Krish. Always has been. And I knew that going into 'our relationship'' Kabeer said with air-quotes. 'And I have been for the past 3 years in a serious, committed relationship with someone else.'

'Wait, are you telling us…'

'Yes, I am gay too,' Kabeer smiled. His nervousness was showing on set but he tried his best to hide it.

'This is big news. I am certain the country has just taken one collective gasp. Why all these lies?' Karan asked.

'For one, homosexuality was criminalized in our country by the British and then the laws were never changed till a few years ago. Even though our temple walls across the country depict men having sex with men.'

'Or women with women. Heck, even our Kama Sutra has stuff about women sleeping with women,' added Mahi.

'And our Puranas. I mean, our mythology, our epics, our history is full of them,' explained Kabeer.

'So, how do you think the industry is going to react to this news?' Karan asked.

'I am still Mahek Singh. I am hoping that people will still see my work as my work and appreciate the effort. That they'd rather I live the truth than die on the inside everyday living a lie.'

'Are you worried about your safety?'

'We are.' Kabeer and Mahi said in unison.

Mahi continued, 'I am sure many of you have seen, the mob that attacked Krish. It has got millions of views on YouTube. That mob could have seriously injured her, killed her. I mean, I was lucky she is a black belt in Taekwondo but I was so scared after that. I can't live without her Karan. I will die if something happens to her.'

'And she's back in the US now?' Karan asked Mahi.

'Yes. I sent her back there,' Mahi looked apologetic and scared.

'Would you prefer she was here?'

'Yes. I absolutely want her here. With me. We want to get married. We want to live a normal life. Come home, make dinner, fight about who gets the TV remote. She wants to continue writing novels, I want to continue making movies. We just want to do it together.'

'And are you in touch with her?'

'Of course. We talk every day. Several times a day. She sings to me every night. I love her voice,' Mahi smiled.

'Really. Can we call her right now? Can she be on air?' Karan asked.

'Ummm…sure.' Mahi was not sure where this was going.

Her face looked sceptical.

Karan asked Mahi to call Krish on her phone. It rang but no one answered. Mahi was unsure what Karan was up to. 'Maybe she's sleeping?' she suggested and was about to put her phone away when Karan said, 'Try again.' Mahi tried again and this time the phone rang in the studio. Mahi looked up and saw Krish, standing in the doorway, wearing a cream and red churidar-kurta. Mahi got up and ran to Krish. 'Oh my god, what are you doing here? I thought you were in New York.' Mahi hugged Krish as if she was clinging on to dear life. No amount of acting could have prepared her for how she felt in that moment.

'I was, Mahi. I was heading back. But then I remembered I had forgotten something,' Krish said.

Krish got down on one knee and removed a ring from her pocket. Mahi's hands covered her mouth. Oh my god, was this really happening?

'Mahi. You are my moon and my sun. You are all the stars in my sky. Will you marry me?'

Mahi who was still in shock looked at Krish with so much love. She picked up Krish off the floor and hugged her and said, 'Of course, I'll marry you. You're my forever.'

'India, now you have to decide, will this couple get a chance at true love. Do they deserve their own happy ending or not? You get to decide.'

As Karan finished his little speech, Krish cleared her throat. There was one last surprise for the evening. Krish got up and smiled and said, 'Karan, I think there might be another proposal today?'

Karan, who had been so focused on Krish and Mahi's proposal turned around and saw Kabeer on the floor on one knee with a ring in hand.

Mahi and Krish looked on as Kabeer gave his little speech, 'Karan, you've been my dearest friend and so much more. These past 3 years have been the best years of my life. And I am certain I want to spend the rest of my life with you. Will you marry me?'

'Oh my god. What a crazy surprise. You guys!!!' Karan squealed in delight. 'Yes, Yes, of course. I will marry you.' Karan and Kabeer hugged. And Karan wrapped up his show. 'Krish, in your speech at the Big B book award you said the award gave you hope for a newer, better tomorrow that is more loving, and more tolerant. One where even people like you and me can hope for a happy ending. So here is our #HappyEnding.'

Ma now came in front of the camera and said, 'Please, let them live honestly. Let them love and be loved. And let them get married.'

As the show ended, the hashtag, #InkoShaadiKarneDo (Let them marry) was trending all over the country. From major film stars to big names in art, science, business all had tweeted or showed support on social media. Anaya had convinced her father, the minister to call Mahek Singh and tell her how inspired their family was about her life story and that they would definitely support any step she took. Mahi looked at Krish and smiled.

Now when she went out, people came forward to give Mahek their aashirwad. And public support grew stronger as they saw Krish and Mahi do every day things together. Mahi posted pictures of Krish cooking Baingan ka Bharta with Ma instructing her in Mahi's kitchen on her Instagram and got millions of likes and thousands of comments, most of which were overwhelmingly positive. The interview had changed the course of their lives.

Karan had directed his greatest movie never made.

Epilogue

-*/|*-

2 years later.

'WHY DO WE HAVE TO DO THIS AGAIN?' KRISH ASKED AS Mahi put the Sherwaani, shoes and jewellery in the closet in the hotel room. It was a cream coloured Sherwaani with a floral embroidery in green, purple and red, with a ruby and emerald bracelet and buttons.

'I have the person coming for yours and Ma's very-light make up. You will take care of everything, right?' Mahi rolled her eyes at Krish and smiled.

'You didn't answer the question,' Krish said crossly as she reached for Mahi's arm.

Mahi held Krish in her arms and touched her face and gently said, 'I explained it, right? We were the ones who opened the door to the legislation so it would be best if we got married first, now that gay marriage is legal in India.'

'But my darling, we're already married. Remember, when we went to Lauren and Wendy's wedding. We got married in USA at that rooftop hotel in New York. Ma was there. Our friends were there. Our marriage has been legal for a long time,' Krish said exasperated at this fake wedding they were doing.

'Yes, my dear, I know you're my wife legally. And I still love saying it. But here in India, we're not legally married nah?' Mahi explained for the hundredth time. 'Look, millions of people are supporting it. Would you have imagined this Krish, 2 years ago when we came out on national TV, would you have imagined that we'd be able to get married in India so soon? That too with the full blessing our nation's legislature and politicians and ministers attending our wedding. This is monumental Ishq, come on, even you get that!'

Krish said nothing. Mahi said finally, 'Look, you're marrying me again. What is your issue? Think about it, you get the whole package, including a suhaag-raat and a honeymoon in Virgin Islands.' Mahi gave her come hither eyes to Krish. Krish giggled every single time about her honeymoon in the US Virgin islands.

Mahi rolled her eyes again. Krish stopped laughing. 'Hmm…you in a bikini for a whole week does make all this so much more bearable!' Krish grinned as she reached for Mahi's waist pulling her closer. 'Wait, I knew about our honeymoon. What is this suhaag-raat business now, not that I'm complaining too much' Krish inquired looking suspicious. 'It's all Karan's doing. Anyway, I'm going to get ready. Ma

is next door with all your friends. Go hang out with them. And then the cars will be here to pick you up in 4 hours,' said Mahi as she started getting ready to go.

'I love you my dear wife. You make me the happiest wife in the world!' Krish smiled.

'Me too!'

As Mahi left for her house, Krish opened the connecting door to her Ma's suite and all gathered in her room. There were Anaya and Parthiv, Lauren was with Wendy, Chelsea was with Sophia (and they had been dating for the past year), and Allie was with Mariella, the investment banker Lauren had set her up with. Everyone was having drinks and appetizers. Krish joined the revelry.

'So, I heard you're blowing people's mind with the changes in the ceremony,' said Anaya as she intertwined her hands with Parthiv. 'I've been reading the thought pieces from around the country. Heck, around the world.

'Well, if we are doing it, we're doing it right. And I'm not taking saat pheras with stuff like, if death comes, let it come to me first. So I changed it to 'When death comes, let us be together,' Krish explained, a tad defensively.

'But it's not just that one, you've changed the others too, right?' asked Wendy. 'I have been hearing about it non-stop in the news.'

'Yeah. We're promising to be faithful to each other, to love and cherish each other. I did away with the I'll offer you food and take charge of the household responsibilities. Instead, we've got, we will grow under the vine of our effort, reap what we've sewed together, and be happy in the fruits of our labour.' 'Sounds poetic,' said Anaya. Krish smiled. Anaya was at university already and blooming into a wonderful writer and poet in her own right. They still worked together though Krish had gotten her own office space now. When her second book had won her the National Book Award in the United States. Anaya was present for the ceremony along with Ma and Mahi, of course.

'I hope so. I figured if so many millions are watching it…I might as well work on it,' Krish grinned. It wasn't easy being the poster child for marriage equality in India. But Krish understood the huge privilege and responsibility it bestowed on her. She wasn't going to let her community down.

'You know, you're being called one of the hottest couple in the world right now! Can you imagine, a lesbian couple is the hottest couple not just in Bollywood, or India but globally! I mean, you guys are on *Colbert* and on the cover of *Time* magazine. You're just all over the place,' said Allie.

'I think whomever is with Mahi, gets to become the hottest couple. I mean, she's the big draw,' Krish shrugged.

'I think you undersell yourself Krish,' Allie said. 'Her success in the US comes from your fame and success.'

'Anyway, I don't know what fuels what, I know I'm nothing without her,' Krish smiled.

Krish was grateful for her friendship with Allie and the role she played in getting her together with Mahi. Allie had started dating Mariella soon after returning to the US and they were both happy. Krish and Allie had reconnected as friends at Lauren's wedding. Mahi liked Allie a lot and vice versa. Allie and Mariella had visited them a few times in India and they had even vacationed together in Fiji recently.

Soon it was time to leave for the wedding. Krish put on the Sherwaani and Lauren and Chelsea helped her with the buttons. 'Wow, you look nice!' said Wendy. Anaya and Mariella nodded in agreement and Allie gave a low whistle when Krish came out. Ma came forward and did the puja and the Hindu rituals. She looked at Krish. Her eyes were brimming with love and gratitude. In a way, Ma felt she was getting her own happy ending. Her own little family.

Krish rolled her eyes when Ma started the puja, but then saw the happiness on Ma's face and stood there seriously. Ma and Krish had moved into Mahi's house soon after Krish had proposed. They had still kept their old house which was currently occupied by their relatives from Meerut and elsewhere who had come down for the festivities. No one wanted to miss the wedding of the year.

≫

There was loud music and dancing at the wedding venue. Lots of people dancing, lots of people gathered to look at the stars dancing. Karan and Kabeer were leading the pack along with several of Mahi's co-stars and friends including Suhani and Imran. There were reporters from all over the world filming, doing interviews and taking pictures. Kabeer's career had faltered for the first year and a half, but being married to Karan had its own perks. Last year, Karan launched Kabeer in an action packed web series that went on to win awards internationally and in India. Kabeer's career was picking back up slowly.

Mahi's career had faltered too. She had been replaced in a few films. Mahi had suggested the producers take Nirali for Draupadi's role. And Nirali had been grateful for the chance. She was no longer friends with Mia, who had faded into obscurity. Mahi had hated losing the project but it was a small price to pay for the love of her life. In the end, Maahi Ve, had saved the day winning her several awards. The film had gone on to do Rs, 500 crores of business and had been recognized internationally too. She had received offers for meatier roles in American films and was filming for one.

Krish and Mahi's careers had gone from strength to strength, as had their relationship. The two halves were finally whole and still able to create magic in their work and at home. Life had been hectic but having each other to come home to was definitely worth it.

Krish's eyes searched for Mahi and she came out with the garland. Mahi was wearing a red and green outfit with beautiful, traditional jadao jewelry. She looked like a princess from a Raj-Gharana in one of those epic films. Mahi looked so gorgeous, so poised as she walked out with the garland, her eyes on Krish. Krish remembered thinking how could someone she'd seen every day look so beautiful in this moment? Someone handed Krish a garland and then there were flashbulbs and people. Krish went to garland Mahi and Kabeer, Karan and her friends lifted her up, making it difficult for Krish to reach her.

Everyone laughed.

'You're not going to get her so easily!' Karan laughed as Kabeer lowered Mahi back to the floor. Krish tried to get to her quickly. But Kabeer was faster than her. He lifted Mahi up again.

Now as Mahi sat on the shoulders of Kabeer and her friends, she teased Krish. 'Come get me Krish.' The film folks from Hollywood were thoroughly enjoying these fun and games.

Krish turned around to find Parthiv and whispered something in his ear. She removed her mojdi's and gave it to Anaya. Mahi was down again and Krish tried to jump to get to Mahi. But again her friends had lifted her up. Again, everyone was laughing.

'Tch tch,' Karan smirked.

At that moment, Krish nodded at Parthiv who kneeled down with his one leg at a ninety degree angle.

Krish's black belt training came in handy as she quickly put one leg up on his knee, to climb on to his shoulders to garland Mahi before anyone even realized what was happening and jumped down, as gracefully as she could manage in her sherwani.

'Whoa!' Everyone applauded in amazement.

Mahi smiled. She went to garland Krish. Krish bowed her head low.

There were lot of 'awwws' in the audience. Then the bride and bride headed to the mandap. Mahi and Krish had decided that Ma would do both their Kanyadaans together. Though many people had volunteered for the privilege of doing Mahi's Kanyadaan, Mahi's brothers, Karan, Kabeer. In the end, Mahi was sure there was only one person she wanted as a part of the ritual. 'Are you OK with this?' Mahi had asked Ma and Krish. Ma had looked delighted at the idea. 'My two girls, my family!'

The saat pheras were a blur. The reception was a blur. Several important politicians were there. As were Bollywood and Hollywood celebrities, some important literary figures from both countries, Indian businessmen and women. But they too all blurred together.

When they finally got into the car on their way to their hotel, Krish was bone tired. 'That was ridiculous, right? I honestly don't remember anything. And it just happened.'

Mahi laughed, 'I was wondering about the deer in the headlights look you gave from time to time.'

It was a short drive and Ruchi was with them. She had several assistants now as she handled US and India business for Krish and Mahi. Mahi and Krish gave all their jewellery and heavy clothes to Ruchi to take home. She'd put them in the safe and keep the key.

Finally, said Krish, as they walked into their hotel suite, that Karan had booked for them. It included a private hot tub on the 65th floor.

'Oh my god, did you see this?' Krish exclaimed as she walked into the bedroom. It was full of flowers. The four poster bed had garlands hanging down and the bed was full of roses. Not petals. Actual roses.

Mahi walked into the room and just shook her head. She wasn't as surprised as Krish clearly was. She had expected no less from Karan.

'It's a pity you got rid of all your saree and jewellery. We could have re-enacted the suhaag raat song from Kabhi Kabhi, right here,' Krish smiled.

'And every other 80s Hindi movie suhaag raat,' Mahi grinned.

They called the hotel staff who removed the flowers after Mahi took a few photos.

Krish and Mahi stepped outside on the balcony. Krish holding Mahi in a tight embrace. 'I can't believe we can get legally married in India,' said Mahi.

'I can't believe I had to climb Parthiv's shoulders to legally marry you in India,' Krish laughed.

Mahi hugged her closer.

Krish turned Mahi to look in her eyes as she said, 'Mahi, I know I haven't said this yet. But you looked so gorgeous tonight. In fact, perhaps I should not attempt to tell you how beautiful you looked because words honestly seem so ineffective in expressing how you looked.'

'Aren't you a writer?'

'But you, my dear, are a goddess. And we mere mortals just don't have the vocabulary to describe celestial beings.'

'Are you buttering me up to get lucky tonight? Because newsflash, you are going to.'

'I never doubted that. I was wrong when I thought you'd get satiated with my body. You, my dear wife, are truly insatiable.'

'You are so lucky. Millions of people around the world would die to be in your spot.'

Krish took her hand and kissed it. 'I know. And I thank the universe every day. I love you Mahi. I'm so in love with you.'

'Ishq, I wanted to talk about something,' Mahi said getting serious.

Krish looked at her curiously. 'What is it Mahi?'

'I'm thinking of children. I know we haven't really talked about it. But now that we're married in US and in India, I think we can start planning nah?'

'I thought we had always planned for children. Do we want one or two?' Krish asked jokingly.

'That's what I wanted to talk to you about. I know we had said we'd each carry one. Are we still on board with that?'

Krish nodded.

'Alright. Because we should start trying soon and think about where we'd live and pre-schools and maids and all.'

'Mahi, we have a whole lifetime for all this. What's the hurry? We're not getting pregnant tonight, right? Let's enjoy right now. We'll figure out the logistics later.'

'But…'

'Gosh, you're such a typical Indian wife. Shaadi hui nahi, bache ki ratt chalu ho gayi!

Krish got a thwack for this one. Krish grinned. She pulled Mahi closer and kissed her deeply. Mahi responded with a deep moan, her hands reached into Krish's hair, pulling her closer. No matter how many times she kissed Krish, her lips always craved more. Mahi opened Krish's Sherwaani, and within seconds had Krish completely naked in front of her. She pushed Krish on the bed and straddled her, quickly removing her own clothes. As she bent down to kiss her, she smiled and said 'Tonight and every night, you are mine, Ishq. Forever.'

Author's Note

—꜔꜔—

To my LGBTQ+ family in India and everywhere else. You are beautiful. Your voice is important. I celebrate you and wish you all your own .

Acknowledgement

—✦—

I am truly thankful for all the people who made this book a reality. My incredible beta readers, Shilpa, Roshni, Abha, Antje, Ferzeen, Preetha, Unnati, Aarathi, Smriti - who deal so patiently with all my ideas and drafts – thank you so much. Your feedback helped me stay on the right track.

I'm thankful for my literary agents at Red Ink, Sarah Zia and Anuj Bahri and my Red Ink editor Sharvani Pandit, who believed in this book from the get-go and whose remarks made it better. My commissioning editor Swati Daftuar at HarperCollins India - your notes and your leadership in shepherding this book through in these unprecedented times was much appreciated.

I'm indebted to my teachers for inculcating a love of reading, and learning.

I've been very lucky to have an incredible set of friends, who have been with me through thick and thin, sick and sin. You know who you are!

My extended family – thank you for all the love.

My grand-father, Mr. Dwarkadas J. Sanghvi, who is forever my inspiration and my aspiration.

I always knew I was gay, but I was worried about coming out – India was very different in 90s and 2000s. I was incredibly lucky and am forever grateful for my parents, Nita and Jayant Sanghvi who accepted me and loved me, no matter what. Thank you for everything.

I am thankful for my in-laws, Robin and Joe Di Maio who love books as much as I do.

When it comes to sisters – I've been super lucky.

My older sister, Nikita Mehta, who never once doubted me – even when I doubted myself. You're the big sister I'd choose every time.

My younger sister, Soneera Sanghvi, who has helped me become a better writer, and a better person. I won the sibling lottery!

I never imagined I'd get to get married and become a parent – I am forever grateful for that joy; My son's birth rendered my heart open to a new love. I love you, to Proxima Centauri and back.

My wife, Megan Di Maio, who encouraged me to write, and whose kindness, warmth, insight and love have filled my life with happiness and cheer. Thank you for our son and our life together. Thank you for my happy ending.

About the Author

―〃〝―

Minita Sanghvi loves reading, writing and learning. She was a curious child and continues to seek answers to her 'but why?' questions even today. She was born in Bombay and loves Bollywood movies and street foods.

She has a B.Com from Narsee Monjee College, an MBA from NMIMS India, an MS from University of Arizona, a PhD from University of North Carolina Greensboro and a Graduate Certificate in Feminist Studies from Duke. She's a professor at a college in Upstate NY where she lives with her wife, son and cat. A hopeless romantic, Minita prefers her drama in fiction and not in real life. You can follow her @ minitawrites on Facebook, and Twitter or visit her website at minitawrites.com

30 Years *of*

 HarperCollins *Publishers* India

At HarperCollins, we believe in telling the best stories and finding the widest possible readership for our books in every format possible. We started publishing 30 years ago; a great deal has changed since then, but what has remained constant is the passion with which our authors write their books, the love with which readers receive them, and the sheer joy and excitement that we as publishers feel in being a part of the publishing process.

Over the years, we've had the pleasure of publishing some of the finest writing from the subcontinent and around the world, and some of the biggest bestsellers in India's publishing history. Our books and authors have won a phenomenal range of awards, and we ourselves have been named Publisher of the Year the greatest number of times. But nothing has meant more to us than the fact that millions of people have read the books we published, and somewhere, a book of ours might have made a difference.

As we step into our fourth decade, we go back to that one word – a word which has been a driving force for us all these years.

Read.

Harper
Collins

HARPER
PERENNIAL

HARPER
BUSINESS

HARPER
BLACK

हार्पर
हिन्दी

HarperCollins
Children's Books

HARPER
DESIGN

HARPER
VANTAGE

Harper
Sport